Praise for Gong Ji-young

"With its exploration of the social origins of crime and its philosophical and religious investigation of sin and salvation, this novel reverberates heavily. But the writer's sensitive touch, particularly in the climactic scenes, will move readers to tears."

– Choi Jae-bong, *The Hankyoreh* (newspaper)

"When it comes down to it, we might all be prisoners on death row, and our lives a farce in which those of us on death row sentence others to their deaths first. [...] By exposing our pretenses, falsehoods, and ignorance as we stand before death, this novel wields the power to wrest tears of compassion from our eyes."

– Jo Yong-ho, *Segye Ilbo* (newspaper)

"A superbly emotional and entertaining read. A fast-paced novel that focuses our attention on issues worth exploring, *Our Happy Time* melds the themes of victim and victimizer, crime and punishment, love and forgiveness, capital punishment and justice."

– Jang Seok-su, *The Flâneur Takes a Stroll Through Books*, Yedam Publishing: 2007

"Knowing how to tease out what readers want and fusing those desires with the concerns that are universal to a generation — that is the strength one wants to have as a writer. Gong Ji-young catches two rabbits at the same time—emotional appeal and entertainment. Perhaps that is why she is so loved by her readers. She excels at fusing the symbols of our era into her stories. [...] The publishing world is in a slump and Korean novels are being pushed out by Japanese novels, and yet her books — *Field of Stars, Our Happy Time, Things That Come After Love* — continue to top the bestseller lists. She astonishes!"

"Gong's intense gaze is both delicate and tenacious— she captures every detail of her characters, right down to the stains on their clothes and the drops of water clinging to their heels. [...] Her love for her subjects is like a warm breath blowing life into her stories. [...] That deep affection takes us to an even deeper place, where the essence of the story is hidden. I've said it before and I'll say it again: Gong Ji-young is a magnificent storyteller."

— Son Jong-eop, *Literary Resistance*, Bogosa Books: 2001

OUR HAPPY TIME

GONG JI-YOUNG

translated by Sora Kim-Russell

MARBLE ARCH
PRESS

**MARBLE ARCH
PRESS**

Marble Arch Press
1230 Avenue of the Americas
New York, NY 10020

First Marble Arch Press trade paperback edition July 2014

Marble Arch Press is a publishing collaboration between
Short Books, UK, and Atria Books, US.

Marble Arch Press and colophon are trademarks of Short Books.

For information about special discounts for bulk purchases, please contact Simon & Schuster Special Sales at 1-866-506-1949 or business@simonandschuster.com

Manufactured in the United States of America

10 9 8 7 6 5 4 3 2 1

ISBN: 978-1-4767-3045-5

ISBN: 978-1-4767-3047-9 (ebook)

Father, forgive them, for they know not what they do.

— Jesus, a condemned criminal
facing execution at the age of 33

Harlem is there by way of a divine indictment against New York City and the people who live downtown and make their money downtown. The brothels of Harlem, and all its prostitution, and its dope rings, and all the rest are the mirror of the polite divorces and the manifold cultured adulteries of Park Avenue: they are God's commentary on the whole of our society.

– Thomas Merton

BLUE NOTE 1

I am going to tell you a story. It is a story of murder. It is a story of a family that was only capable of destruction, where screaming and yelling and whippings and chaos and curses were their daily bread. And it is a story of a miserable being who used to believe he couldn't possibly be miserable—this is my story. The day it all began, two women and a teenager died. I was convinced that one of those women had no right to live, that she deserved to die. I thought that for her to have so much money all to herself was like dressing vermin in fine silk. I thought that if I, in this unfair and unjust world, could use that money for something good instead, I would be doing the right thing.

And there was another woman. She was a woman who had never had anything of her own in her whole life. A woman who had everything taken away from her by others—that woman was dying. If only I'd had three million won, I could have saved her. But at the time, I had no way of getting that much money. With each day that passed, she was closer to death, and though I did not know if there really was a heaven or how long it had been since I last looked to it, I assumed heaven would understand me, and that this was justice. Justice.

Chapter 1

The fine flurries of snow that started in the afternoon were turning to rain. A hazy bluish light flooded the streets, and the damp sky hung low, blurring the line between it and the earth. The clock ticked past five. I put on my coat and left my apartment. In the parking lot, the cars were as silent as graves, and the yellow lights flickering on one by one in the windows across the street began to glimmer like unreachable stars. The trees that lined the road, having long since dropped their leaves, looked like a barbed wire fence dividing the poor people's apartments across the street from the wealthy apartments on this side. I paused before getting into my car and glanced up. The apartment buildings stood with their backs to the sky, their ponderous bodies blocking the clouds from view. Standing there in the fading light of dusk, the buildings resembled a straight, unmarred fortress wall. A thin winter rain fell on the frozen street. I got in my car. As soon as I turned on the headlights, shards of rain like finely shaved ice appeared in the cylindrical light. The dark evening was broken only by the cheerful, colorful rays spilling from the streetlights and store signs—for all

I knew, the rain fell only inside that light. In the darkness, after all, we had no idea what was really falling upon us.

Dr. Noh had called to tell me that Aunt Monica had collapsed and was back in the hospital, that the prognosis didn't look good this time, and that I'd better prepare myself. That probably meant I had to get ready to let go of yet another person. I pictured Yunsu's face as the engine turned over: black horn-rimmed glasses, pale faded-looking skin, lips still red with youth, shallow dimple that appeared in only one cheek when he smiled shyly. I didn't want to remember him. I had spent many sleepless nights trying to put him out of my mind. Nights when I could not fall asleep without hard liquor, blue dawns when I awoke to a strangling phantom.

I used to bury my face in my pillow and wait for tears, but all that would come out of me was a strange moan. There were some days when I thought, *Fine, better to remember, remember it all, remember every last bit of it,* but I would wind up drunk and passed out on the sofa.

After Yunsu was gone, I woke up every morning knowing that I could never return to my old ways. Everything had been turned upside down again; like it was in the beginning. But after getting to know him, I became sure of two things: that I could never again try to take my own life, and that this was both his last gift and the final sentence that he gave to me.

Just like the winter rain that was only visible in the glow of the headlights, there were many things in this world that were invisible in the dark. I learned this after meeting him: just because something was invisible didn't mean it did not exist. After meeting him, I pushed through my own darkness and figured out what that darkness was that breathed inside of me like death. There were things I would never have noticed if not for him, and I would have never realized that what I thought was darkness was actually a dazzling brightness. A light so bright that my eyes were blinded by it. I would have continued thinking I knew everything. Because I realized through Yunsu that if we can love truly, then it is in that instant that we are already sharing the glory of God.

He's gone now, but I still thank God for giving me the chance to meet him.

I drove down the dark street in the rain. Seven years ago, there had been almost no traffic on this road where even the neon signs had held their breath, but now the lanes were packed with cars pouring in from all directions. There was no hurry. Everyone was going somewhere. No matter the destination, they all had to get somewhere. But did any of them really know where they were going? The same question I'd asked myself all those years ago returned to me like an ancient memory. Up ahead, a stop light lit up as red as the sun over the cars racing through the murky, fog-like rain. The cars all stopped at once. I stopped, too.

Poor little legless bird
who lost its mother,

where will you go
when rough winds blow?

Dear wind, do you know?
Dear rain, do you know?

What will carry them
from these woods?.

– Bang Eui-kyung, "Beautiful Things"

BLUE NOTE 2

My hometown... You asked me about my hometown. But did I ever really have a home? I said that if by hometown you meant where I was born, then the answer would be Yangpyeong in Gyeonggi Province outside of Seoul, and I waited for your next question. But you didn't ask me anything else. *It was a poor village*, I said. *There was a reservoir just past a small grassy knoll and our house was always cold*. I stopped there. *It's okay*, you said, *you don't have to talk about it if you don't want to*. But it's not that I didn't want to—I couldn't. When I dig up those memories, it feels like a black clot of blood fills my mouth.

My little brother Eunsu and I used to play in the sun at the edge of the reservoir. One day, Eunsu was spanked by the woman next door. He had gone over there to beg for some rice, but she said he spilled it. So while she and her husband were out working, I took a long wooden stick from an A-frame carrier and used it to beat their kids until their noses bled. After that, none of the other kids would play with us. So it was always just the two of us. Sometimes, if a kind-hearted person gave us a lump of cold leftover rice, we would sneak into a neighbor's barn so as not to wake up our father who was passed out from drinking, and we would take turns taking bites of the frozen ball of rice. The reservoir was always sunny, and when luck was with us, we even got instant ramen from the fishermen who came there from Seoul. On even luckier days, we would go to a store about five miles away and bring back cigarettes for them in exchange for a few coins.

It took me a long time to realize that we were waiting for our mother, who had run away from home. It was only after a very, very long time that I realized that, even though all I remembered of her was her swollen face and the bruises that covered her body from our father's beatings, I was waiting for her to come home, bruises and all, and kill our father who would start beating us again the moment he woke from his drunken slumber in that unheated room. I was waiting for her to rescue us. My very first memory in life is of wanting to kill. But since my mother was out there somewhere, in some faraway place, that feeling of waiting—even when I didn't know what I was waiting for—never went away entirely. I think that was when I was around seven years old.

CHAPTER 2

Aunt Monica and I were the black sheep in our family. Or should I say heretics? Or maybe bastards is more accurate? There was a nearly forty-year age difference between us, but we were as identical as twins. When I was a child, my mother used to tell me, *You act just like your aunt*. I knew she didn't mean it in a good way. No matter how young you are, you can always tell from the way someone says a person's name whether they like or hate that person. Why did she hate my aunt, whom she used to be friends with? Did I hate my mother because she hated the aunt that I took after, or had I decided to take after my aunt on purpose because my mother hated her? I was stubborn and enjoyed making other people uncomfortable. I would cuss in the peaceful faces of those who sickened me, and cackle with laughter and pity as the looks on their faces turned to shock. But what I felt was not victory, like occupying forces singing as they enter a savage land. It was more like an old, secret wound ready to spill blood at the slightest touch, the kind of hurt that would bleed at a moment's notice even when there was no pain. In other words, it was closer to desperation, a parody sung by the surviving soldiers of a failed mutiny. But Aunt Monica and I were also different in many ways. She prayed far more for our family than I did, and she never used them for material gain.

As for me, if I'm going to be really honest, I was a mess. I lived for myself, dragged other people into my life in the name of love or friendship, not for their sake but for my own, existed only for myself and even wanted to die for myself. I was a hedonist. Oblivious to the fact that I had lost myself and become a slave to the senses, I lashed out at the fortress of my strong family. I stayed out all night drinking and singing and dancing. I didn't know that this trivial life-style of mine was systematically destroying me, and even if I had known, I wouldn't have stopped. I wanted to destroy myself. I was only satisfied if the entire galaxy revolved around me. I got drunk and kicked at closed doors, not knowing who I was or what I wanted. I had never said the words out loud, but if someone had held a stethoscope to my heart back then, they probably would have heard: Why can't the sun revolve around me? Why aren't you there for me when I'm lonely? Why do good things keep happening to the people I hate? Why does the world keep angering me and refusing me even the tiniest sliver of happiness?

The only thing more evil than feeling nothing is not knowing that you feel nothing.

– Charles Fred Alford, *What Evil Means To Us*

BLUE NOTE 3

After I started going to school, my little brother Eunsu followed me there every morning. Since he wasn't allowed inside, he used to squat at the corner of the schoolyard wall to wait for me until school was over. Eunsu was different from me. When the other kids hit him, he never grabbed a stick and hit them back. If a stronger kid picked on me, I would fight him to the bitter end, sinking my teeth into his forearm if I had to, but not Eunsu. His fate, like our mother's, was to submit to the lash of destiny and do nothing but cry. School would end and I would rush out to find Eunsu trembling and shivering against the wall, his lips blue from the cold. Our daily meal was the cornbread that was rationed out to the students at school. I used to save my piece and not take a single bite even while the other kids were eating theirs and my mouth was watering for a taste. On some days, I would find Eunsu sitting there with a bloody nose; on other days, I would find him crying with his pepper hanging out because his clothes had been stolen by the other kids.

For a long time after, I used to wonder whether I had really loved my little brother. I don't know. All I do know is that I wanted him to be happy. I think maybe those times we spent together, walking home and sharing the cornbread that I had managed not to eat, might have been the happiest times of both of our lives.

One day, it rained. It was spring, but the weather was cold, and the sky that started off clear in the morning grew dark, and suddenly the rain was like poles of water coming down. I didn't hear a word the teacher said and just stared out the window. There was nowhere outside of the school where Eunsu could stay dry. An image of him in the rain passed before my eyes: like a young pigeon left behind in an empty nest, he was crying so hard that his eyes were swelling up. As soon as the first period ended, I ran out the gate.

Standing there in the rain, Eunsu was so surprised to see me come out earlier than expected that he smiled from ear to ear. The rain beat down mercilessly on his face, but he was beside himself with happiness. I lost my temper. Since I had no umbrella either, I was no better off than he was, and my clothes were getting as drenched as his.

"Go home," I told him.

"Don't want to."

"Go home!"

"No."

It hurt to have to send him back to our house where our drunk father would grab the first thing he saw when he awoke, whether a stick or a broom handle, and beat my little brother with it. But the rain was coming down hard, so I grabbed Eunsu by the collar and dragged him toward home. I left him in the alleyway that led to our house and turned to leave, but he followed me out. I turned around, grabbed him by the collar again, and dragged him back.

I turned and ran, but he kept following me. I ran back to him again and started punching him. And like a fool from the planet of submission who doesn't know the meaning of the word disobedience, Eunsu took the blows while clinging to the hem of my shirt. I wailed away at him like a crazy person. Blood spurted from his nose and soaked into my clothes along with the rain.

"Listen to me," I said. "If you don't go home right now, I'll run away, too. I will leave you and run away. Now go home and don't come out again!"

Eunsu stopped crying at once. He let go of my shirt. My running away would have been worse than a death sentence to him. He gave me a resentful look and turned to go. That was the last time we looked each other in the eyes. And it would be the last clear image of me that Eunsu ever saw.

CHAPTER 3

I'll start with the early winter of 1996. I was lying in a hospital bed. I had been found after trying to kill myself by swallowing a lethal dose of sleeping pills with whiskey—an *attempted suicide patient*, they called me. When I opened my eyes, rain was falling outside the window. A few stray leaves were dropping off of the sycamores. The sky was so overcast that I couldn't tell what time it was.

I thought about how my uncle—my mother's brother who was a psychiatrist—had told me he wished I would cry. He looked old for his age, and if it weren't for the situation, I would have teased him by saying, *You've lost more hair, haven't you? You look like a grandfather. Now that I've survived, can I get a smoke?* Then I would have laughed at the shock on his face. But instead, I had refused to answer his questions, and because he was such a goody-goody, he added, *How could you do this when your mother is still recovering from her operation?* I retorted, *Are you really that worried about my mom? Do you really like her that much?* But he just smiled and said, *I wish you would cry.* It was a sad smile, though, filled with compassion for me. I hated that.

There was a knock at my hospital room door. I didn't

respond. When my mother, whose cancer had been
removed over a month ago, had tried to visit me recently,
I screamed at her and smashed my IV bottle. None of the
other family members had come to see me since then. It
was clear from their faces that they considered me an even
bigger headache than the centimeter-long tumor that had
grown inside my mother's breast. This life that my mother
wanted so badly to live was boring to me. Neither of us had
ever considered whether she—this person I called mom—
had a life worth living. But I shouted at her that since she
didn't want to die, I would die in her place. I would never
have made such an awful scene if she had not come into
the hospital room where I had been brought back to life
and told me she didn't know why she gave birth to me—
the same thing she had been telling me my whole life. But
what made me even angrier was the realization that I take
after her. I thought the knock on the door was my youngest
sister-in-law Seo Yeongja, the pushover who only knew
how to say yes to everyone, bringing me a bowl of abalone
porridge, and I closed my eyes.

The door opened and someone stepped into the room.
It wasn't my sister-in-law after all. If it were, she would
have called out in that nasal voice of hers, *Miss, are you
sleeping?* She used to be an actress, but now she acted like
she owed some kind of debt to the Mun family, as if her
life's goal was to do all our dirty work for us. Whenever
she came to my room, she silently emptied the trashcan
and rattled the vase on the windowsill as she refilled it with
fresh flowers. But to my surprise, I didn't hear her this time.
I knew as soon as the door opened that it was Aunt Monica.
I could tell by her scent. Where did that scent come from?
Back when I was a kid, whenever she came to the house, I
would press my face against her habit and sniff.

What is it? Do I smell like disinfectant?

No, not disinfectant. You smell like church, Aunt Monica. Like candles and things.

Aunt Monica told me that she had graduated from nursing school and worked at a university hospital before suddenly deciding to join a convent.

I cracked my eyes open, as if I were just waking up. Aunt Monica was sitting in the chair beside my bed and quietly watching me. The last time I had seen her was right before I left to study abroad in France, back when I was a pop singer who wore a miniskirt and sang and shook my ass on stage like—as my mother put it—I knew no shame. She had come to see me briefly in my dressing room backstage, so that meant almost ten years had passed. Her age was already showing back then: the hair that peeked out from beneath her black veil had turned gray, and though her shoulders were still square, her back was stooped. Even allowing for the fact that it's hard to tell how old nuns are, her age showed. For a moment, I almost thought about the sad fate of human beings who must live, grow old and die. Aunt Monica's eyes were fixed on me, and I could see that they were filled with a strange fatigue. Her small wrinkled eyes seemed to hold both a slight annoyance and a certain warm maternal love—something my mother had never showed me. There was something else in her eyes, as well, that had always been there for as long as I knew her. It was the kind of look a new mother gives to small living things—a combination of boundless compassion mixed with the curiosity of a mischievous child looking at a newborn puppy.

Since she was being quiet, I smiled and said, "I've gotten old, haven't I?"

"Not old enough to die," she said.

"I wasn't trying to kill myself," I told her. "I wasn't trying to die. I just had trouble sleeping. Drinking alcohol didn't help, so I took a few sleeping pills... I guess I was too drunk to count the pills. I just took whatever was there, and the next thing I knew, all this happened. Mom came to see me and told me that if I want to die, I should just die and not worry her, and now I feel like I'm some kind of juvenile delinquent who tried to commit suicide. But you know how Mom is. Once she makes up her mind about something, you can't argue with her. I'm sick of it! She's always treated me like I'm defective. I'm over thirty..."

I had intended not to say anything, but the words spilled out of me.

Seeing Aunt Monica after all that time made me want to act like a child and throw a tantrum. She seemed to guess what I was feeling, because she tucked my blanket around me like she would for a baby. I felt the secret joy that only grown-ups who are being pampered like a baby can enjoy. Aunt Monica's small rough hand caught my own, and I felt the warmth that radiated from her body. It had been a long time since I'd felt another person's warmth.

"I mean it," I said. "I don't have the energy to die. You know I'm not that kind of person, you know I don't have the will or the courage to die. So don't try to tell me that if I have the will to die then I also have the will to live, or that I need go to church. And don't pray for me either. I'm sure I'll just give God a headache, too."

Aunt Monica started to say something and then stopped. My mother had probably told her everything. I bet she had told her, *Yujeong said yes to the engagement but now she doesn't want to go through with it. Her brother says this man went to the same school as him and graduated at the top of his class from the Judicial Research and Training Institute, so we know he's a good person with a good academic background. He's a decent man. His family isn't much to speak of, but she's over thirty. Where does she think she's going to find another man like that? Go talk to her. She listens to you. I can't stand that girl anymore. I can't believe I gave birth to her. Her father spoiled her because she's the only girl. That's what's wrong with her. Her brothers all went to the best universities, but she could only get into that lousy school. No one in our family has ever had bad grades, so I don't understand how she could turn out that way...*

"I didn't do it because of him," I said. "I never wanted to marry him. He probably didn't really want to marry me either. He'll find some other girl, someone else from a good family with money. Younger, better prospective brides will be lined up for him. He told me the matchmakers have been banging down his door."

Aunt Monica said nothing. I heard the wind rush past outside and the window rattle. The wind was building. The trees outside were dropping their leaves. If only people were like trees and could fall into a long death-like sleep once a year and reawaken. It would be nice to wake up, put out new pale green leaves and pink blossoms, and start over.

"You know what? His ex-girlfriend who lived with him for three years came to see me. She said she'd had two abortions. Her story was so predictable. I bet she gave him spending money, bought his books, cooked for him. On the day of the bar exam, she probably took him out for barbe-cued ribs and toasted to his success. And then, that son of a bitch, after all that, he had a change of heart and went after me, the little sister of the chief prosecutor. Probably factored in my share of the inheritance as well. I'm sure he likes our family because it's full of doctors, lawyers, PhDs... all those stuck-up professionals. Aunt Monica, do you know what I hate the most? Clichés. If only he had dumped her in a less clichéd way, or wanted to marry me for reasons that weren't so clichéd, I would have closed my eyes and looked the other way. I mean it. I couldn't stand what a big cliché he was. That's it! You have to believe me. It's the first time I've told anyone this. Not my mom, not my brothers, no one in this family. No one knows about it. They all think I'm being picky, and I prefer it like that. That way, I don't have to deal with them as much."

At the time, I had no idea why I was telling my aunt things I hadn't told anyone else. Nor did I understand why I hadn't just explained to my family why I wasn't going to marry him. His ex-girlfriend's voice had trembled faintly over the phone: *Is this Miss Mun Yujeong? I'd like to talk to you.* When we were sitting face to face, I was surprised to see how rough her hands looked wrapped around the coffee cup. Her face was pretty, but her face and hands were completely different, like they were serving two different masters. Though her inviting eyes and the contours of her oval face were soft, she was deathly pale. *He's everything to me.* The moment she opened her mouth and said those words, my heart dropped. How on earth could one person say that about another, especially a woman about a man, and how could you say those words so resolutely to someone you were meeting for the first time? It's possible I felt a little jealous of her, just as I felt jealous of everyone who had faith and conviction, a sense that what they were doing was right. I don't mean that I was jealous of her for having a man. I mean that I had never had someone in my life for whom it was worth risking everything, even if it did end in a childish, immature, even laughable way. She looked sad but she didn't cry, and that seemed to be because she still held onto some foolish hope that kept her from facing reality. I thought it might kill her to realize that she was a fool for hoping and was therefore worse off than if she had despaired instead. She had a tragic and dangerous glow about her. But as I finished telling Aunt Monica about her, I started to wonder why I had kept it a secret from my family. My ex-fiancé was not good-looking. He was not that tall, and his square jaw and dark complexion showed that his childhood had not been an easy one. There was nothing sentimental about him. But I wasn't expecting him to give me butterflies. I was old enough to know that when you've made up your mind to get married rather than keep playing the field, then that's how it is. The first time we had met, introduced by my older brother Yusik, I asked him if he had dated a lot of women. He looked down and smiled shyly. I felt a flash of pleasure at the thought of being the first to conquer virgin soil where no others had trod. I could see why men sought out virgins. But I also knew that if I gave in and married this eligible fool who spent all of his time with his nose buried in books, my family would give me a gilded passport into the kingdom they had constructed and never again bring up my past. And when I thought about it, hedonism, self-indulgence, and debauchery—in other words, booze, sex, and other vices—were becoming clichés to me, too.

He told me he'd had a crush on someone once. *We didn't get past the second date. I must have bored her. After that, I was too busy studying for exams. I take responsibility very seriously. For a man, it's important to have a good job that enables you to support a family. Marriage and love are secondary; you have to make something of yourself first.* He didn't hide the fact that he wanted to make a good impression. I thought it was cute. I said, *So, what you're saying is that, even though you're over thirty, this will be your first time going on a date and kissing a girl and taking her back to a hotel room? You're a good liar.* I laughed. He looked shocked, as if he had never met a girl like me before. But I could also tell from the look in his eyes that he was not entirely repelled by feisty women like me. In a way, it was curiosity toward a different species. It bore a trace of the longing that a hick with sunburn and a buzz cut and wearing a wifebeater—and in this case it *would* be a wifebeater and not an undershirt—can't help but feel when he meets a girl from Seoul who is dressed in white lace socks and fancy black shoes tied with ribbons, a girl who doesn't know the meaning of the word obedience. It was probably true. I think I even considered using him as a foothold from which to elevate my life. It was tempting, the idea that he could make a proper woman out of me. Stepping out of my dirty shoes in a muddy courtyard and placing my feet on his stepping stone, being lifted onto a clean, polished wooden porch... standing strong and balanced so the arrow can find its target. I was probably longing for exactly that.

Because there was something a little too bashful about his smile, I assumed he wasn't telling me the whole truth, but I did sort of fall for it. Or was it that I wanted to trust him? Was I trying to convince myself to believe him, telling myself to trust someone once more, to do whatever it took to trust someone just one last time? If I'm really honest about it, I didn't have a problem with the fact that he had lived with a woman, and I was not some innocent virgin who had something to lose. I had lived with men as well when I was studying abroad in France. They had lasted about a month each. But even if he had abandoned her, the woman with the big rough hands that didn't match her face, in order to marry me, the rich girl who returned from pretending to study art abroad and was nagged by her mother into holding a so-called solo exhibition and was given a full-time teaching position that she was unqualified for at a metropolitan university run by her family, I had no right to criticize him. As far as I knew, there was no reason for his actions to be all that strange or especially immoral.

Everyone I knew got married the same way. But I couldn't do it. It became clear to me that if I couldn't marry my first love—the man to whom I could not bring myself to say, *I love you, I love you to death*, the man whose last memory of me was me standing in a crowded intersection, crying and screaming, *Leave! Leave and never come back!*—then I couldn't very well marry this man I felt nothing for.

Disappointed at the thought that I would not be able to gain citizenship in the kingdom my family had built, I started drinking myself into a stupor again. It wasn't because of that woman. The streets overflowed with pathetic people, pitiful victims. Was there any unhappiness that didn't have a story behind it? A sadness that wasn't unfair? To say those people were pitiful meant that justice had already turned its back on them. So even if it had killed her to be abandoned by him, it wasn't my problem. Come to think of it, both she and I were clichés. If there was any kinship between us, it was that we had tried to get ahead in life not on our own but through a man.

"That's right, our Yujeong isn't the type to die over something like that," Aunt Monica said and stroked my hair.

"Aunt Monica."

"What?"

"What took you so long to come see me? I called the convent several times after I got back to Korea, but they always said you weren't there."

"That's true, I've been busy. I'm sorry. I guess my excuse is that since you're over thirty now, I thought you were all grown up and didn't need me."

When I heard the word *sorry*, I felt taken aback. She had no reason to apologize to me. I was the sorry one. Sorry that I was over thirty and still not a grown-up. But I had never been good at saying things like *I'm sorry, thank you*, and *I love you*. Other than in sarcasm, I had never used those words when I really needed them, never used them when no other words would do.

"Aunt Monica, you're so old. You never had a pretty face, but at least the last time I saw you, your skin wasn't this wrinkled. You've gotten so old."

She laughed.

"That's right," she said. "We all get old with time. Nothing lasts forever. Everyone dies. It may not happen right away, but we do all, eventually... die."

Aunt Monica stood up as she spoke. She paused before the last word and then spat it out, as if it were difficult for her to say. She went over to the mini-fridge, took out a can of juice and drank it. She must have been thirsty because she downed the entire can. She sighed and looked out the window. Outside the window opposite the bed, the branches of the sycamore were shaking in the wind. I copied Aunt Monica and stared out the window. *Drop them, drop them*, I thought, *and let the wind take them.*

"Aunt Monica, I didn't want to die. I was just bored and tired. Fed up with everything. I thought if I kept living, I would only be adding one more boring day to a boring life. Because we live one meaningless day after another until, as you said, we eventually die. I wanted to shove my whole life in the garbage. I wanted to shout at the world, 'That's right, I'm trash! I'm a failure! And I can never be redeemed.'"

Aunt Monica stared at me. To my surprise, there was no emotion in her eyes. I had always been afraid of that indifferent gaze and, as with any true fear, it was mixed with respect.

"Yujeong," she asked me carefully, "were you in love with him? The lawyer, Kang, or whatever his family name was?"

I burst into laughter.

"That hick?" I asked.

"He hurt you."

I didn't respond.

"Would you reconsider it?"

I paused for a moment and then said, "I couldn't forgive him. But Aunt Monica, I thought about it, and I don't think it was love. When it's love, your heart is broken. But mine wasn't. When it's love, you're supposed to want the other person to be happy even if it's not with you. But I never had that feeling. I didn't hate him. What I hated was the fact that I took one look at his background and trusted him right away. I hated that, despite fifteen years of rebelling as hard as I could, I still wanted to be like my brothers and my sisters-in-law and people like them. And I hated the fact that even my own hatred failed me."

Aunt Monica nodded.

"Okay, I believe you," she said. "But listen, Yujeong. I saw your uncle, Dr. Choi, right before I came here. He said this is already your third suicide attempt. He told me you have to stay in the hospital for a month for treatment, but I said I would take care of you instead. He wasn't sure at first, but then he said if I really wanted to, it would be okay with him. It's technically against the rules, but he trusts me. So, what do you want to do? Stay in here for a month and go through therapy again? Or help me with something?"

I could tell from the tone of her voice that she wasn't joking. There was no reason for a nun in her seventies to joke with a niece who has just attempted suicide, but I laughed anyway. I always laughed when I wanted to get out of doing something difficult. But when I heard the firmness in my aunt's voice as she said the words *third suicide attempt*, I couldn't help but think that I, too, was a cliché. I wanted a cigarette.

"What kind of help would I be to you? I drink and smoke

and cuss, so other than making people uncomfortable, I'm not good at anything."

"So you're aware of that," she said drily. "There's someone who wants to meet you. They want to hear you sing."

"Aunt Monica—excuse me, *Sister* Monica! You're not asking me to sing in a nightclub, are you? Did the convent run out of funds and now you need a has-been to perform at your café?"

I laughed. I knew I was overacting, but the habit was so ingrained in me, as if I had become a method actor, that it could have fooled someone more naïve. Aunt Monica usually did me the favor of pretending to fall for it, even while being shocked at my behavior. But this time, she didn't laugh.

"Someone wants to hear you sing the national anthem," she said slowly.

"What? The national anthem?"

"Yes, the national anthem."

I laughed again. This sounded like it might be fun.

If you treat someone like a monster, they will become one.

– Criminal psychology

BLUE NOTE 4

After school ended, I went home to find my father eating instant ramen next to Eunsu. When I checked on Eunsu, asleep in the corner of the room littered with *soju* bottles, his body was feverish. I tried to shake him awake, but he only groaned in response.

"Daddy, Eunsu's sick. He's burning up."

My father poured *soju* into a metal bowl, took a swig, and stared at me through bloodshot eyes by way of response. Looking back on it now, can I really say that our father was alive then? He must have been in his early thirties at the time. Never able to look at him without terror and shuddering in fear since my first moment of life, I had nevertheless long learned the devil's tricks in that hell.

"Daddy, I'll buy you more *soju*. You're all out. I'll run to the store."

The belching beast of a man pulled a five-hundred won bill out of the pocket of his sweat- and piss-soaked pants and handed it to me. I ran. The cold medicine Mom used to take—the only thought in my head was that I had to buy those small pills that came in a bottle.

The rain had stopped, and the world was flushed with the light of spring. To this day, I still don't know why all that dazzling green everywhere as I raced to the pharmacy affected me so deeply. For a long time afterward, whenever I saw the different shades of green that dyed the mountains in spring, I was overcome with an inexplicable sadness. The villagers planting rice seedlings in the paddies watched casually from a distance as I ran past. I used the money to buy Eunsu's cold medicine and returned home.

The moment he saw the bottle of medicine in my hand, my father's eyes flashed. He wrenched the bottle from my hand and began hitting me. The ramen bowl flipped over, and I was caught in his strong hands and flung onto the narrow wooden porch outside. If it were not for Eunsu, I would have run away. I did not know where, did not know if there was a place on this earth for me to run away to, but that's probably what I would have done. Each time my father's fist came down on me, flames seemed to shoot up from my eyes. Then I passed out. When I came to, the woman from next door was feeding Eunsu and me broth. She told me she had saved some medicine made by an older man from a neighboring village and that she had given it to Eunsu. My father was passed out drunk, and I could hear the worried murmurs of our neighbors coming from the side porch.

Eunsu was fast asleep beneath a blanket. The room had been straightened up. Eunsu's lips and cheeks were flushed, and he kept muttering something. I didn't want to hear what he was saying. I, too, wanted to call out for our mother. I wanted to ask why she had left us behind. Several nights passed, and then it was morning. I think maybe it was the third day. I decided to go to school, so I went over to check on Eunsu. His fever had broken.

His curly black hair was damp with sweat and sticking to his pale forehead. After a moment, his eyes opened and he spoke.

"Yunsu, the house is full of smoke. It's full of smoke."

After that day, Eunsu's eyes could not make out anything other than a faint light. My little brother had gone blind.

CHAPTER 4

I could see Aunt Monica in the distance. She looked angry.
I was almost half an hour late. When I pulled up to the
entrance of the subway station in front of the Gwacheon
City government complex, she got into the car carrying a
large bundle. It was so cold outside that the cool air rising
off of her black veil eerily made me feel as if I were in front
of an open refrigerator. Her lips were blue.

"I didn't know how I was supposed to dress for this,"
I said. "If I'd known we were going to a prison, I would
have bought a nun costume. I'm running late because I
couldn't decide what to wear. You should get a cell phone.
Even monks and priests all drive nowadays. You should get
a car, too."

I was making excuses for being late. Aunt Monica didn't
say a word.

"I offered to pick you up at the convent, but you're so
stubborn," I said, trying to shift responsibility as I always
did whenever I felt guilty about something.

"They wait all week for me," Aunt Monica said. "Those
boys don't get to see anyone all week long. Because of you,
thirty minutes of their precious time are gone. Wasted on
you!"

She paused, too angry to speak. Then she swallowed hard and started talking more slowly.

"Those thirty minutes that you shoved in the garbage without a second thought could be their last thirty minutes on this earth. They are living this day like it might never come again! Can you understand that?"

Her voice was low, but it was firm and hinted of tears. The words *shove in the garbage* got caught in my throat. Even though I used those words all the time to refer to how I was wasting my life away, it didn't feel good to hear them from someone else's mouth. Since it was true that I was late for our appointment, I thought I had better not say anything. At any rate, it was my first day accompanying my aunt to the prison. But it was not shaping up to be a happy first day. Though I was the one who had brought up the idea of shoving my life in the garbage, it was the first time she had ever used my own words against me with such force. I told myself that Aunt Monica was just emotional because she was getting old.

I had read about my aunt's prison visits in the newspaper before I left for France. My second-oldest brother, a doctor, had come to the house to check on my mother after she'd called him in the middle of the night complaining that her head hurt. He opened the newspaper he brought with him and told us, *Aunt Monica made the papers.* Since it was a liberal newspaper, no one in our household would ever have known that our aunt was famous enough to be in the news if he had not brought it over himself. My mother, who started each day by yelling at the cleaning girl the way other people might say good morning, had given the girl her usual morning greeting and was sitting at the table. My brother said that Aunt Monica was visiting death row inmates, and my mother replied, *How noble of her. That's the kind of sacrifice you have to make when you're a nun.*

So noble. Can you make an appointment for me with a neurosurgeon at your hospital? I need another check-up. Something must be wrong because my head is killing me. I didn't sleep a wink yesterday. Those pills you gave me last time didn't work. Whenever I take them, my makeup flakes. I must be getting old because I can't sleep and I can't take any more pills that are bad for my body. My skin is a mess.

My brother, quiet as usual, didn't say a word, while I ate a sandwich made with ham and lettuce on organic wholewheat bread next to our hypochondriac mother. My brother's eyes met mine. *Don't worry, Mother,* he said, his voice untiringly sympathetic. *They ran several exams but didn't find anything wrong with you.*

I added, *Mom, he's right. How on earth could modern medicine ever fathom a nervous system as sensitive and exquisite as yours? A refined woman such as you has no choice but to bear it.*

Breakfast that day ended as it always did, with my mother shouting at me. It was a typical morning. She screamed at me to quit my awful cabaret gigs and go study abroad or something. I said I would be happy to do so. By then, the fun of being a pop star for a year had been losing steam, and I thought if I left home, I would be able to enjoy a quiet morning for a change. I had grown tired of bellowing in harmony to my mother's octave.

"Sorry," I said to Aunt Monica. "I messed up. I said I'm sorry." Surrendering seemed better than continuing to stand my ground. I wasn't sure why I thought so, but I was afraid she might start crying. "But Aunt Monica, you're not really taking me to see those... is that right?... death row inmates? They're not going to ask me to sing the national anthem, are they?"

"That's who we are going to see. If they ask you to sing

the anthem, sing it. Is there any reason not to? Better to put that voice of yours to some good use rather than shove it in the garbage. Make a left at that fork in the road."

She'd said it again. Garbage. It felt mean of her to take the maudlin words I had said in the hospital and use them to provoke me, and I started to get a little angry. When I turned left, as instructed, I saw a sign for the Seoul Detention Center.

Would singing the national anthem be better than sitting down with the young psychologist my uncle had brought along with him at that boring hospital and answering questions like, *What are you so angry about?* and *Why did you get angry?* and *Did you have similar thoughts when you were a child?* As usual, I calmed myself down by thinking, *Who cares? Don't think too much about it.* At least the detention center would not be as boring as the hospital.

We showed our ID cards at the front and stepped through a barred door. As we passed through, the door shut behind us. The moment the cold clang of metal against metal rang out in the dark, empty hallway, strange thoughts came into my head.

The temperature inside that place was always a few degrees colder than outside—the chill lingered for a long time after. This was true not only in the winter but even at the height of summer. It was, as someone had once said, a place inhabited by darkness. We passed through another door and it too closed behind us. There was a large inner yard that didn't look as if it were used by anyone. Several men dressed in blue prison uniforms were pushing a handcart on the other end of the yard, and further away, beneath a white plaster of Paris statue of the Virgin Mary, stood a small tree. Christmas tree lights in gaudy colors were blinking on and off in the winter sun. When I saw it, I realized Christmas was coming. I thought of Gaudete Sunday in Paris. Christmas lights filling the Avenue des Champs-Élysées, girls selling flowers on the street, red wine and the futile charm of soft, savory foie gras melting on my tongue, ending a night of drinking with arguments and vomiting...

We turned several corners and were guided into a small room. Just a few square meters in size, the room had a crucifix on the wall next to a copy of Rembrandt's *The Return of the Prodigal Son*. It was a simple room with one small table and five or six chairs. Aunt Monica set down her bundle and turned on an electric kettle. After a moment, we heard a knock at the door. I caught a glimpse of a light-blue prison uniform through a small glass window in the barred door.

"Come in! You must be Jeong Yunsu." Aunt Monica went over to the man who was being brought into the room by a guard and hugged him.

Death row. He was on death row. A red nametag was sewn to the left side of his shirt. Except it was not a nametag. There was no name on it. In black letters, it read *Seoul 3987*. He seemed very uncomfortable with my aunt's embrace. He looked like he was about five foot seven in height and had curly black hair and light skin; his eyes behind their horn-rimmed glasses were wide and penetrating. But the curly hair, which looked softer and darker than other people's, spilled over his broad, pale forehead and lessened the sharpness of his features.

To my surprise, the dark shadow that hung over his face reminded me of the young professors I had met at university. The look on his face was the same as the one on theirs when they complained about the school: *Damn it, what does the foundation think it's doing?* Or when they had to listen to the chairman of the board say ridiculous things during faculty meetings: *Our university's primary goal this year is to create a university that studies. We need better students. Our foundation created this school for that purpose.* The kinds of things that anyone in their right mind would laugh at. I momentarily deluded myself into thinking that the red tag on his chest meant he was a political dissident who had violated the National Security Law. It was probably the air of intellectualism that I had glimpsed in him for a moment that caused me to assume this. He looked like the kind of guy you would see in Paris wearing a T-shirt emblazoned with the grim face of Che Guevara.

How could I describe it? He was a being who transcended death, glimmering with some feral quality possessed by those who swear themselves in their youth to a lonely death in the wild. And it seemed to suit him better. To be even more honest, he didn't look like what I had always imagined convicts to look like. But I enjoyed having my own clichéd ideas shattered without mercy. I began to feel curious about him.

"Let's sit down. Please, have a seat. I'm Sister Monica, the one who has been writing to you."

He sat down awkwardly. I noticed then the shackles that bound his wrists in front of him. They were fastened to a ring that hung from a kind of thick leather belt around his waist. It wasn't until later that I even remembered they were called *shackles*, but when I saw them, my heart sank.

"Please, Officer Yi, I brought some pastries for him to eat. Could you... Would it be possible to remove his shackles?" Aunt Monica asked carefully.

The guard called Officer Yi, who was assigned to the Catholic prison ministry, smiled uncomfortably and did not answer. The look on his face said he was a man who played by the rules. Aunt Monica unwrapped the pastries. Cream buns, butter buns, sweet red bean buns. She poured hot water from the kettle to make instant coffee and set a cup in front of Yunsu. Then she put one of the pastries in his shackled hand. He lifted it wordlessly and stared at it for a moment. He looked like he was wondering if he was really allowed to eat it; at the same time, he gave off the sadness of a person gazing upon a food they have long hungered for. He stuffed the pastry into his mouth with difficulty. Because of the shackles, he had to bend over to get a bite. His body curled like a snail's shell. He kept his eyes fixed on the table as he chewed.

"That's right, eat up. Have some coffee, too, to wash it down. And let me know if there's anything you would like to eat next time. I don't have children of my own, so you can think of me as a mother. I've been coming here for thirty years. You are all family to me."

He paused mid-chew to crack a forced smile when Aunt Monica said she didn't have any children. Though I was probably the only one who saw it, there was a hint of mockery to his smile. I guessed that his weapon of choice was a scornful look, just as I smoothed over conflicts by laughing at people. Of course, I might have been imagining everything, but from the moment I first saw him, I felt like he and I were from the same family, in the Linnaean sense. My instincts were rarely wrong, but it nevertheless made me feel a little strange to think I might have something in common with a death row convict. I was hungry for a pastry, having skipped breakfast after oversleeping, but watching him eat with his body hunched over and his hands clasped together like a squirrel made me lose my appetite. I felt a flash of pity. I wondered what had happened to bring him to this point. Aunt Monica urged the guard and me to take a pastry but only drank coffee herself.

"So, how is it in here?" she asked. "Are you getting used to it?"

He had been cramming the food into his mouth, but he

immediately stopped. A tense silence settled over the four of us; in the office where we sat, winter sunlight slanted in through the window. He slowly finished chewing.

"I got your last letter," he said. "I wasn't going to come today, but I thought I should tell you in person. Officer Yi told me you've been coming here by subway and bus for the last thirty years, rain or shine. If he hadn't told me that, I probably wouldn't have come. So that's why I'm here."

He raised his head. At first glance, his was a very tranquil face. But upon closer inspection, that tranquility looked as hard as a mask.

"Okay," said Aunt Monica.

"Please don't come to see me again. I won't read your letters. I'm not worthy of them. Please, just let me die."

He clenched his teeth on the last words. From the way his chin quivered, he seemed to be biting down hard on his back teeth and grinding them together. It was alarming. The skin around his eyes had a bluish tinge. I felt a sudden fear that he would grab me by the throat and take me hostage, and I remembered seeing his name in the newspaper. He had killed someone and run away and then broken into a house and held a woman and child hostage. I could remember only the general details. I stared at the guard and my aunt. The sturdy shackles on his wrists were somewhat reassuring.

"Yunsu... I'm over seventy years old now, so I can call you by your first name, right?" Aunt Monica was not ruffled in the slightest and spoke slowly and calmly. "Show me someone who hasn't sinned. Even if you searched high and low, who would be worthy? I just want to spend time with you. We can meet once in a while, share a snack, talk about how your day was. That's all I want, but—"

"I don't—" He interrupted her. He had the unusually calm voice of one who has thought for a long time about what he is going to say. "I have neither the hope nor the will to go on living. If you have the strength to spend on that sort of thing, then save it for someone else. I'm a murderer. It makes sense for me to die here. That's all I came to tell you."

Yunsu rose as if to say he had no further business with her. The guard stood up, too; he didn't look surprised. Yunsu's impassioned appeal seemed to say, *I may have to hunch over to eat like an animal eating food dropped on the ground, but I am still a man.*

I stupidly thought to myself, *I guess even death row convicts have their pride.*

"Wait a minute, Yunsu! Wait!" Aunt Monica anxiously called out to him.

He turned to look at her. Tears were pooling in her eyes. He must have seen them, too, because I noticed that one side of his face looked contorted. It wasn't so much a grimace as a kind of buckling, like one corner of his stiff mask had been torn away. But then it disappeared and the mocking look returned. Aunt Monica took something out of the bundle she had brought with her and handed it to him.

"It's almost Christmas, so I brought you a present. It's cold in here, isn't it? I brought you some long underwear. Since you went to all this trouble to meet with me, I can't very well send you away empty-handed. This will only take a moment, so won't you sit for a little? I told you, I'm very old, and my legs ache."

He stared at the package in her hands. A muscle in his jaw quivered. His brow was furrowed, and he looked irritated. He was probably thinking, *Why the hell are you giving me a Christmas gift?* But he sat down as if to say he would give her a chance since she was elderly and a woman.

"I'm not giving you a Christmas present to make you feel

obligated. I'm not telling you to go to church. I'm not here to talk about religion. Who cares if you believe or if you don't believe? What's important is that you live each day like a human being. I'm sure you don't hate yourself, but if you do, then you're exactly who Jesus came for. He came to tell you to love yourself, to tell you how precious you are, to tell you that if in the future you feel warmth from someone and think, *Ah, so this is what love feels like*, then that person is an angel sent to you from God. I've never met you before, but I know you have a good heart. No matter what your sins are, they are not all of you!"

When she finished speaking, he smiled. It was a sneer. The look on his face said it was ridiculous to tell a person who has killed and who could be hanged tomorrow for that crime how precious they are. But then, a nervous energy unique to those with strong emotions passed over his face. To my surprise, I felt like I understood him. Whenever I got a phone call from Aunt Monica after yet another stupid fight with my family and she spoke to me in the same tone she was using with him, it made me angry. In a way, it was like the body rejecting a blood transfusion. Whether it's different blood or different emotions, we are only at peace when there is just one type present. Right or wrong, life makes sense only when the bad guys are bad and the rebels are rebellious.

"Don't do this to me," Yunsu said. "If you do, I won't be able to die peacefully. Let's say I do meet with you and go to Mass and obediently do everything the guards tell me to do to make them happy, and I sing hymns and pray on my knees, and I become a perfect angel. Are you going to save me then?"

It was unexpected. He bared his white teeth like an animal and spat the last words out. Aunt Monica's face paled.

"So please," he said, "stop coming to see me."

"Okay, you're right, I want to save you, but it's not in my power. But just because I can't keep you from being executed, that doesn't mean I don't need to meet with you. I don't know how you feel about this, but we are all on death row. None of us know when we will die. So why is it wrong for someone like me, who doesn't know when she will die, to meet with you, who also doesn't know when he will die?"

Aunt Monica was no pushover. He stared dumbfounded at her.

"Why?" she repeated.

"Because I don't want to hope," he said. "That would be hell."

Aunt Monica did not say anything.

"I don't know how much more I can take," he said. "I might go crazy."

Aunt Monica started to say something and then stopped. After a moment, she asked him calmly, "Yunsu, what is bothering you the most right now? What do you fear the most?"

He looked up at her. A moment passed. His eyes were filled with animosity.

"The mornings."

He sounded like he was being forced to confess to a crime before some final conclusive evidence proffered by a vicious prosecutor. His voice was quiet. He sprang up, as if he did not need to hear any more, bowed to her, and stalked out. Aunt Monica, who had been as stiff as a plaster statue, followed him.

"Wait a second! I'm sorry. Don't be mad. If it's hard for you, you don't have to meet me. You can just go. It's okay if you go, but at least take this. The pastries aren't fancy, but I brought them for you. They're not so bad. Officer Yi,

I know it's against the rules, but please, let him sneak in a couple inside his clothes."

Aunt Monica held out a handful of pastries to Yunsu. Officer Yi gave her a look that said she shouldn't. But Aunt Monica's stubbornness was powerful, like the will of the Father being done on earth as it is in heaven.

"He must be so hungry all the time, alone there in his cell. A healthy young man like him must need a lot to eat. Please, Officer Yi!"

It was absurd: Who was the criminal and who was the rehabilitator? Who was pleading, and who was rejecting their pleas? I saw Yunsu look directly at Aunt Monica for the first time. His gaze seemed to quiver with the anxiety of being unable to grasp who she was and what she was doing. Aunt Monica stepped closer to him and shoved a pastry inside his shirt.

He looked shocked. He lurched his head back as if to keep her as far away from him as possible.

"It's okay," she said. "I'm glad we met today. Yunsu, I'm so happy to have met you. Thank you for coming to see me!"

She stroked his shoulder. He looked pained, as if he were being tortured. As he quickly turned away, I got a closer look at him and saw that he had a limp. Aunt Monica watched from the door until he disappeared down the long hallway. She looked as lonely as a goat standing on a cliff above the sea. She pressed her hand to her forehead. She looked fatigued.

"It's okay. They're all like that at first. That's where hope begins. Saying he's not worthy—that's a good start."

Aunt Monica was not so much talking to me as mumbling to herself. My tiny aunt looked like she was going to wither away and vanish on the spot. She looked like she needed to reassure herself. I absentmindedly glanced up at the print of *The Return of the Prodigal Son* hanging on the wall. In the story of the prodigal son, the younger of two sons brashly demands his share of his inheritance from his father. The son then squanders that fortune, and after being reduced to doing demeaning work on a pig farm, he returns home, even though he knows that he is no longer worthy of his place as his father's son. Upon his return, he says, "Father, I have sinned against heaven." He would have meant it sincerely. It was a Bible story. The painting depicted the love of the father forgiving his son and the son kneeling in repentance. I remembered learning in art history class that Rembrandt drew the father's hands differently: one was a man's hand, and the other was a woman's, which represented the idea that God embodied both femininity and masculinity. But as for why that painting was hanging in this room, the reason was all too obvious.

"Is he still causing a lot of trouble?" Aunt Monica asked the guard.

"He'll be the death of me. Last month, he started a fight in the yard. Grabbed the lid off of a charcoal brazier that was sitting to one side of the yard and threatened to kill one of the gang leaders. Spent two weeks in solitary and just got out yesterday. He acted up the entire time he was in there, too. If we hadn't stopped him right away, he would have gone back to court. Not that it makes any difference. He's already sentenced to death—they can't very well increase his penalty. I don't know why I'm telling you this, but these death row inmates will be the death of me. It makes no difference to them if they kill another person while they're in here, because they know it won't change their sentence. They're on death row, so what difference does it make *how* they die. The other prisoners are scared of them, so they act like kings. There hasn't been an execution since last

August, and they can tell another one is coming. That's probably why they get more violent at the end of the year. That's when the executions usually take place. Afterward, they quiet down for a few months. But Yunsu is the worst of them all."

Aunt Monica was quiet for a moment.

"Nevertheless," she said, "he came to see me today. And though he doesn't write back very often, he does write back."

Aunt Monica was like a detective desperately clinging to a tiny clue. The guard smirked.

"To be honest, I was surprised he came to see you. Last month, the pastor gave him a Bible. He ripped it apart and has been using the pages as toilet paper. I think he's gone through three Bibles that way."

I burst out laughing. If Aunt Monica hadn't glared at me, I would have kept on laughing, but I shut my mouth and tried to look serious. It served her right. I felt like Yunsu had gotten revenge on my behalf for the way Aunt Monica kept mentioning the word *garbage* to me on the way there. He had torn up her favorite thing in the whole world, the Bible, and turned it into something even worse than garbage. But I couldn't let on how satisfying it was to hear that. They both looked so serious.

"This morning, I went to his cell and told him you were coming and asked what he wanted to do. He thought about it for a moment and then asked how old you were. I told you were in your seventies. He hesitated again, and then for some reason, he said he would come meet you."

A look of joy stole over Aunt Monica's face.

"Did he? They say good things happen when you get old. I guess it's true. But, has anyone been to see him?"

"No. He might be an orphan. I think he said his mother is alive somewhere, but no one visits."

Aunt Monica took a white envelope from her pocket.

"Please add this to his commissary account. And please, Officer Yi, don't think too badly of him. Guards are also supposed to help rehabilitate them. You're not trying to kill him faster, are you? Aren't we all sinners in the end?"

Officer Yi took the envelope but did not say a word. On the way back to the subway station, Aunt Monica adamantly refused my offer to drive her all the way to the convent. I didn't understand why she insisted on taking public transportation on such a cold day, but it was probably the pointless stubbornness that she and I shared.

While we were waiting for the light to change at an intersection, I asked, "What did he do?" There wasn't anything else to talk about. She seemed lost in thought and did not answer.

"Did they put those shackles on him because he was meeting with us?"

"No, he wears those all the time."

My heart sank just as it had when I saw him hunch over to eat the pastry. In the old folktale Chunhyangjeon, when the title character Chunhyang sits shackled in a wooden cangue, she looks plaintive and wistful, and perhaps even dignified. But that was just a narrative device, the more tragic the better, to set up the dramatic turn of justice when her beloved Mongnyong returns as a secret royal inspector and saves her from the lecherous local magistrate who imprisoned her for refusing his advances. Nowadays, with the twenty-first century just around the corner, the idea of keeping someone shackled around the clock was shocking.

"What about when he sleeps?"

"He wears them when he sleeps, too. Their only wish is to sleep with their arms outstretched just once. Some inmates have even broken their arms from rolling over on them while sleeping. After they receive their death sentence, they spend up to two or three years in shackles before they die."

"How do they eat?"

"They can't use chopsticks, so they lift the bowl to eat, or if there are several of them in a room, someone else mixes their rice for them so they can eat with a spoon. What's more, the guard said he was in solitary for two weeks. When they're in solitary, they don't see so much as another person's shadow. Their hands are shackled behind their backs, so they have to bring their mouths down to the bowl to eat. That's why they call it 'dog food.' Since he was in there for two weeks, he must not be in his right mind. Sometimes they can't even use the toilet. They just go in their pants. Two weeks..."

I sighed and resisted asking if they really had to live that way. I had been clueless before, but it was different now that I knew and had seen it with my own eyes. I felt a sense of foreboding, like when you accidentally take a step into a neighborhood where you would never want to live.

"He murdered someone, right? He said so himself. Who did he kill? And why?"

"I don't know."

Aunt Monica's response was so simple and forthright that I doubted my own ears for a second.

"How did he do it? How many people did he kill? He was in the papers, wasn't he?"

"I said I don't know!"

Her tone was stern. I turned to look at her. She was staring at me as if there was something unusual about my questions.

"How can you not know? I saw that you're a member of the prison ministry. Didn't you bother to check his records when you started writing to him?"

"I met him for the first time today, Yujeong. Today

was our first meeting. That's it. When people meet each other for the first time, they don't ask, 'So what kind of bad things have you done?' If he talks about it, then I listen. But I never saw him before today. To me, what we saw of him today is all there is to him."

She sounded resolute. It felt as if each word struck me in the chest. I was reminded anew that she was a nun.

"Light's green. Pull up next to that station entrance on the corner. I'll call you later tonight."

With that, she got out of the car.

O King! Do not weep. There are none who have not longed for death more than once in this short life.

– Herodotus, *The Histories*

BLUE NOTE 5

Misfortune poured down like a sudden rain shower. One day, I came home from school to find Eunsu as white as a sheet and crying. I asked him what was wrong, but he suddenly started to gag.

He said, *Father made me drink something weird. I keep throwing up.* I went into the room, and a strange scent pricked my nose. The smell was coming from a bottle of farm pesticide that our father had spilled while trying to feed it to Eunsu. I screamed at our father, *Die! If anyone should die, it's you!* I don't know if it was the force of my wrath, but he paused in the middle of drinking and silently turned to look at me. To my surprise, he didn't try to hit me. He just looked at me through bloodshot eyes—eyes that bore a strange mocking gleam. It might have been a smile, or it might have been a look of bitter agony. I didn't know if he was going to change his mind and come after us with a stick, so I grabbed Eunsu's hand and ran away. We went to the same place we always did, a barn behind an abandoned house near the entrance to the village, and we spent the night there. When I went back home in the morning, the person that I used to call Father was dead. The bottle of pesticide that he had drunk was lying empty beside him.

CHAPTER 5

That night, after returning from that place, I didn't exactly sleep soundly. I had met him, and I had looked at him. He had left, and I had dropped Aunt Monica off. Afterward, I had headed downtown, where I shopped for a few things that I needed for Christmas, and was getting back into my car in the department store parking garage when the image hit me: his shackled hands. It was like a pill that you took in the morning but that didn't kick in until nighttime. Was it because the cold parking garage made me look in my purse for my gloves? I pictured the tips of his ears red with frostbite, the dark red scars on his wrists from where the shackles bit into his skin, and the way his firm lips had twisted into a sneer whenever he spoke. When he said he lacked the will or the hope to go on living, the nervousness in his voice struck me as familiar. I probably sounded that way all the time, too. I had said the same words to my family, screamed it at them, in fact: *Just let me die!*

The department store was packed. Men and women with more shopping bags than they could carry were loading purchases into their cars and leaving while more cars kept coming in. Christmas was on its way. I thought

about how Aunt Monica had pleaded with him: *If you hate
yourself, then you're exactly who Jesus came for. He came
to tell you to love yourself, to tell you how precious you
are.* I swallowed hard. I didn't want to acknowledge the
fact that he was not the only one who needed to hear that.
If we had met him in the department store instead, Aunt
Monica would have jokingly added, *Jesus did not come
to earth to tell you to shop.* I thought about how I used
to go to church when I was younger. Back then, I was a
good kid. I wore the frilly clothes my mother dressed me
in, politely helped my teacher, and never missed a day of
Sunday school. I memorized every passage in the Bible and
won awards at catechism competitions. And then, that day
came when everything changed. The sun hid its light and
never again shone brightly over my life. The sun rose and
fell, but it was always the same night for me. I didn't know
why I was reminded of it while standing in a brightly lit
department store parking garage after having met Yunsu.
But after that fateful day long ago, I went to college, albeit
not a good one, appeared on Daehak Gayoje, and won. It
was a nationwide singing contest for college students, and
winning it launched my career. The glory was brief, but I
got to do concerts all over the country. Then I left to study
art in Paris without a single worry about money, and when
I returned, I was made a professor. Though the fact that
I was so unqualified to be a professor was a secret known
only to me and my family, I was nevertheless a decent
member of society and, with the exception of my advanced
age, good enough for a snobby lawyer to want to marry,
even if he was a liar. At least, that's how it looked to other
people. How easy it was to fool others!

I drove out of the garage. The streets were packed
with cars. Fancy Christmas lights twinkled from every
tree, making it look like golden flowers had blossomed

on the bare branches. In the seven years that I was gone, Korea had changed. It looked glamorous and wealthy and crowded. But if I walked behind the buildings that towered nearly high enough to block the sky, the wind was as strong and cold as ever.

When I returned home, I looked up his name online.

Jeong Yunsu. As soon as I searched for his name, news reports popped up one after the other. Judging by the date, it had happened a year and a half ago, while I was still in Paris. He was the main culprit in the so-called Imun-dong Murder Case. He and an accomplice had murdered a woman they knew named Bak, raped and killed her seven-teen-year-old daughter who was sleeping in the next room, and then killed the housekeeper who was just returning from market.

When I read that he had raped a seventeen-year-old girl, I stopped breathing. A sour, metallic taste, like blood seeping from between my teeth, filled my mouth. This was the person I had to visit with Aunt Monica for the next month? I felt humiliated to have thought that he and I had anything in common. I wondered why the government couldn't hurry up and kill those people when they asked to be put to death. And I thought I would rather sit through therapy again than have to visit that ungrateful piece of trash who shamelessly demanded to be killed. I suddenly loathed Aunt Monica for giving him long underwear and packing pastries for him, and pleading, *You have a good heart. No matter what your sins are, they are not all of you.* I got up, went to the kitchen, poured a tall glass of whiskey, and drank it in one gulp. My racing heart seemed to slow a little. I went back to the computer, as if drawn to something, and sat down. *Raped a seventeen-year-old girl...* Her screams echoed in my ears. The terror and shame she felt were as clear to me as if I were watching them on a movie screen.

After he and his accomplice left with the money and valuables and ran away, the accomplice turned himself in, while Yunsu broke into a family's home and took them hostage. Then the police shot him in the leg.

There were more articles. Editorials, even the society pages, went on and on about the case: "Murder Case Grows More Savage: Criminal Jeong Yunsu killed an older woman who had been helping him, stole her money and valuables, raped and killed her daughter, then killed the poor, innocent housekeeper, and still he shows no remorse." My computer screen filled with the tut-tutting of sociologists, psychiatrists, and journalists who naturally understood all of the problems facing our society and therefore had no end of things to say when handed a microphone. I kept clicking.

The article about his hostages included a photograph.

In the photo, he was wailing, his arm wrapped around the neck of a middle-class woman who looked like she was in her thirties. I took a closer look. His features were the same, but he looked completely different. He wasn't wearing the black-rimmed glasses, and his hair was very short. During the half-day standoff, the police had sent in a Buddhist monk who made prison visits. An interview with the monk was included in a separate text box.

"I told him my name was Beomnyun and that I was a monk, and I was going to step inside. I asked him to let the woman go and said, 'What has she done? If you want to kill someone, then kill me.' Then he said, 'Who the hell are you?' So I told him again, 'My name is Beomnyun, I'm a monk,' and he said, 'Well, nice to meet you. You monks and pastors and priests—it's assholes like you that made me this way. Come on then, if you want to die! Come on! I'll kill you, too, and then I'll die, too!' That's what he said. The moment

I heard those words, my heart jumped. I was ready to rush in there, but the police officer held me back."

I forgot all about how I had thought of him as trash and laughed to myself. I had already emptied half of the whiskey bottle. Even if he were trash, I was intrigued by what he said. I thought, *He thinks the same way as me!* I would never be able to forgive my family members, who were oblivious to even one-millionth of what I'd gone through, for turning their backs on me. My mother, who lied and said, *She must have had a bad dream.* My father, who didn't want to hear any more about it. My brothers. The priests and nuns, who took my confession and pressured me to forgive. God, who ignored my desperate prayers to be rescued. Thanks to them, I was falsely accused of the sin of lying and of not forgiving. The only person who did not say anything to me at the time was Aunt Monica. I clicked on the next article. After Yunsu was arrested and taken to the hospital, he was questioned by reporters and said, "I regret not killing more. All those rich people in their fancy houses, I regret not killing more of them!"

The reporters blamed the gap between the haves and the have-nots and the extravagance and self-indulgence of the wealthy in our country. At the same time, they said that such anger was misguided. Everyone seemed shocked by the audacity with which he had brazenly said that he regretted not killing more people. The all-knowing scholars and experts each gave their two cents, saying that someone like him had to be given the severest punishment possible— it had to be the death penalty—in order to send a message to the criminals who were growing more shameless by the day. I poured the rest of the whiskey into my glass. I pictured him holding a knife. What would I do if he took me hostage to try to rape and murder me? Goose bumps stood out on my arm as I raised the whiskey glass. I would probably grab the knife and kill him with it. Though I hadn't had these thoughts since that fateful day long ago, I realized they had always been in the back of my mind. But would I grab the knife and think, *Uh oh, if I do this, I'll get the death penalty, so maybe I shouldn't,* as everyone who knows everything that's wrong with our society seems to think people would do? Of course not! I would do whatever I had to do in order to get the knife away from him and kill him with it. I swear it. I would kill him using the cruelest method I could come up with. The old me would not have been able to do that, but the new me could. Back then, I was just a dumb kid, but now, I was someone who had long since stopped caring about death.

The phone rang. It was Aunt Monica. She asked me if I got home okay and suggested we return to the Seoul Detention Center after the holidays. I didn't respond. I wanted to ask why we had to visit, of all people, someone who had raped a little girl? Did she really not know what he had done?

"And Yujeong, promise me one more thing."

"What is it now?" I asked bluntly.

The fumes from the alcohol I had downed so quickly were rising into my nostrils and making me hiccup. If it were not Aunt Monica on the other end of the line, I probably would have lashed out drunkenly and said, *Well, aren't you a saint? Go to heaven without me!*

"Are you drinking again?" she asked. I said no. "Okay, that's good. Since you agreed to help me out for a month, you have to promise you won't kill yourself before then. It wasn't easy getting your uncle to agree to this. Can you do that for me?"

I wanted to tell her, *No, I can't.* I wanted to say I'd be better off in a mental hospital. But there was always something in Aunt Monica's words that came from some familiar place. Something that disarmed me. Was it the love that she had always shown me? Or was it the sadness of an aunt who wrapped her arms around me and cried? When sorrow is unmasked, it contains something mysterious and holy and urgent. It is both a thing wholly unto itself and a key that opens strangers' locked doors. I could tell that Aunt Monica had been praying for me for a long time. For fear I would die—or rather, for fear I would try to die again. That was why she had been calling me every night and every morning for the last several days.

When I thought about the fact that someone genuinely wanted me around, a slow ache passed through a corner of my heart. It burned like coarse salt sprinkled on rotting fish. I did not want to admit it, but it had occurred to me nonetheless: the reason I couldn't kill myself, the reason I could not finish the job and kept making failed gestures, the reason I never picked something truly fatal from among the various methods of suicide, like throwing myself off of the fifteenth floor of our apartment building, was all because of Aunt Monica. I was going to tell her no, but I was trying to keep from hiccupping and the word would not come out.

"Okay," I said finally. "I promise. Even if I do decide to kill myself, I'll wait until the month is up so I don't let you down. Then I'll do it."

"Sure, that's how we all live, one month at a time, until we die. I die, and then you die."

I was speechless. I realized that I had never thought about her dying. What would I do without her? It was strange that I had never once thought about it even though she was over seventy. I didn't think I could stand it. If she were gone, the only person who genuinely wanted me around would be gone. In other words, the only thing in my life that gave me hope would be gone. The thing that kept me from jumping from the fifteenth floor would be gone.

The person who was the first to rush to my side and hold me the first time I had tried to kill myself in high school. She had held me and cried and said, *You poor thing, you poor thing*. But if I were around to see her die, I still didn't think I would be able to cry.

"Pray for me, Aunt Monica. Pray to keep me from wanting to die." I said.

"I do. I pray every morning and every night. I'm old now, Yujeong, so you have to stop worrying me. Understand? You have to forgive. Not for anyone else's sake, but for your own."

It was the first time she had ever mentioned forgiveness. She must have sensed how tense I was, because she seemed to hesitate before speaking again.

"What I mean is that you have to stop letting what happened to you rule your life. You need to vacate that room inside your heart that he has occupied. Move out of that room. It's been fifteen years, so everything is in your hands now. You're over thirty."

Aunt Monica said the word *thirty* like she was saying it to a fifteen-year-old child. I didn't say anything.

He who has never eaten his bread with tears, who, through nights of grief, has never sat weeping on his bed, knows you not, heavenly powers.

– Goethe

BLUE NOTE 6

Eunsu and I were sent to an orphanage. From that day on, I had to fight like a wandering warrior, and my nights were as sleepless as a guard's in the demilitarized zone. I would come back from school to find that blind Eunsu's food had been stolen by the other kids and his body was covered in bruises. I would track down the kids who beat and tormented him and punish them until their noses bled, and then I in turn would be beaten by the housemaster until my nose bled. I was a juvenile delinquent, the black sheep of the orphanage. While I was at school the next day, Eunsu would become the target of vengeance for the kids I'd beaten up, and upon my return, I'd get my revenge again. Then the housemaster would beat me even harder. None of us—not me, not the other kids, nor the housemaster—ever tired of it, and each day was another cycle of punishment and revenge. They were days in which I drew forth all of the blood and violence and screams and lies and defiance and hatred that I had inherited from my father and that flowed through my veins and put them to practical use. I was an animal. I would not have known how to survive otherwise. If I had not at least been an animal, I would have been nothing. And then, one day, our mother came to find us.

CHAPTER 6

I realized I didn't keep my promise.

A letter from Yunsu arrived at Aunt Monica's convent the following week, before our second visit to see him at the Seoul Detention Center. Aunt Monica was stubbornly intent on going, regardless of whether he agreed to see us or not. The old year had ended; it was 1997.

Aunt Monica looked ecstatic as she handed me the letter. As for me, I was beginning to think that I wanted to face him for a different reason. Was that because I was sensing that the person I really wanted to face was myself? I still can't say.

> *I completely forgot that I wrote Sister Monica a letter a long time ago and told her I wanted to meet that singer, the one who won Daehak Gayoje and sang the national anthem at the opening ceremony for a baseball game in 1986. My little brother, who's no longer with us, loved her voice. He was really fond of the national anthem. I thought that if I could tell him I met her, he would feel happy up there in heaven. But I didn't recognize her when she came that day. When I got out of solitary, I was feeling*

hopeless again and wanted to destroy everything and end it all. After I got back to my cell, though, I thought, my little brother wouldn't have liked how rude I was. I used to think that everything ends when you die, but now I think I might be wrong about that. I'm sorry. Also, the long underwear you gave me is very warm.

It was a short letter. Aunt Monica was in a hurry to get to the detention center. She couldn't very well show up without me—the one-time singer, the one he said his brother had liked, the motivation behind that letter. We waited for Officer Yi to come meet us at the entrance, and the three of us walked into the detention center together.

"When I met you last time," said Officer Yi, "I wasn't sure if it was really you. I'm excited to meet you. I was a huge fan back in school. When I was taking Yunsu back to his cell, he told me you were that famous singer who sang *Toward the Land of Hope*. It's such an honor."

Every now and then, when I was walking down the street, or applying for a credit card at a department store, or boarding a plane, people would recognize my name or face. Around ten years ago, I had performed a song called *Toward the Land of Hope*. The records flew off the shelves like they had sprouted wings, and I did appearances anywhere and everywhere I was called. Now, ten years later, I didn't mind being recognized. But I wasn't so sure I liked being recognized at a detention center.

"I told my wife that you came with Sister Monica. She was so impressed. She said you're such a good person. She said she knew you were glamorous but didn't know you did good things as well."

As far as I was concerned, I was never going back to that prison again once the month was up, and I was far from being a good person, but still, I couldn't bring myself to say, *Well, this is what really happened.* I didn't know what to say. If he was going to keep it up, then I would have no choice but to act like a good person. It would take too long to explain to him why I wasn't who he thought I was.

"By the way," I said, changing the subject, "why are some inmates wearing light-blue uniforms and others are wearing dark blue? The dark-blue ones look cold."

"The dark-blue uniforms are provided by the state, but they can buy the light-blue ones for themselves."

"It's so cold. Why don't they buy the warmer ones? Are they expensive?" Since there wasn't really anything else to talk about while walking down that long hallway, I kept asking him questions.

"They cost twenty-thousand won."

"That's not that expensive."

Officer Yi looked at me as if he were taken aback.

"We have four thousand inmates here," he said. "We check their commissary accounts periodically. There are usually about five hundred who don't have a single cent for half a year at a time."

I stopped and stared up at him.

"It makes sense," he said. "They made their living off of crime, so now they have nothing. In those cases, we have to assume they also have no family. Or that their families have turned their backs on them."

"Five hundred without a single cent?"

"There are just as many who have less than a thousand won for six months. But think about it. Why would people with money wind up in here?"

I thought about how much I had spent on liquor at the department store a few days ago. I felt like saying, *But when I was in Paris, the plazas were packed with more and more Korean tourists every day, and every summer, the other Korean students and I would joke about how we had to head for the countryside to get away from them. I assumed Korea was wealthy because all those tourists refused to stay anywhere but five-star hotels...* But I kept my mouth shut. Five hundred people with less than a thousand won to their names, for six months or more at a time. How were they able to buy toilet paper and long underwear? As I followed Aunt Monica down the hallway, I felt as if my feet weren't touching the floor.

We passed a short, bald man dressed in a light-blue uniform walking in the custody of a prison guard. Just as I noticed that he also had a red tag on his uniform, he stopped and said, "Sister Monica."

Aunt Monica said, "Look who it is!" and hugged him. They looked like an aunt and her nephew greeting each other after a long time apart.

"I heard you met Jeong Yunsu."

"Word gets around fast. How have you been?"

"We don't have any secrets from each other in here. My sister is here to see me. I'm on my way to meet her. But how is Yunsu? He must be in pretty bad shape after solitary. Is he giving you a hard time? Don't give up on him, Sister. Just think about the first time you met me, how I used to scream and cuss at you." The inmate laughed bashfully.

"That's true," Aunt Monica said. "You were a handful."

"Sister, someone told me his accomplice framed him. He must have made a false confession. That accomplice of his, I heard his family is rich. He only got fifteen years, and now he's been transferred to Wonju. None of the guards like Yunsu, but we think he's a good kid. You know that money you put in his commissary account? There's an elderly man here who's serving a life sentence. Yunsu gave all of his money to him. The old man had nothing in his account, so he couldn't even get proper medicine. But Yunsu told him to use the money to get medicine from outside the prison if he had to. It's hard for Yunsu, too, to get by without any money."

"Is that so?" Aunt Monica's face brightened.

"I bumped into him yesterday in the prison yard, and he asked me if I had a Bible. So I loaned him one right away. I did good, didn't I, Sister?"

"Yes, you did. You did really well, my boy."

Aunt Monica patted him on the back, and he beamed proudly, like a child. I watched him and my aunt from a few steps away and thought, *Is that really a death row convict who has killed people?* There was no end to the unexpected and surprising. Not in this place.

"By the way, did Father Kim get that operation?"

"Yes, he did. That's what I heard."

The inmate's round eyes darkened.

"Me and the other guys on death row were talking about it the last time we were together. We decided to pray. We prayed to God to take those of us with more sins first, instead of him. What did he do to deserve it? We also decided not to each lunch until his cancer goes away. We wanted to make a sacrifice. We found out that he kept coming here to offer us Mass right up until the day of his surgery. He never said anything to us about it."

His eyes were wet with tears. Aunt Monica bit her lip.

"That would be an enormous sacrifice for you to make. Eating must be your only pleasure in here... A great pleasure and a diversion... Thank you. I'll tell Father Kim about it. God, too, will look favorably upon you for giving up your lunches. Keep up your promise to Him, but make sure you sneak in some snacks from outside. I'll take the blame for that one and ask Him for forgiveness."

The inmate laughed out loud. The guard who was with him looked uncomfortable.

"I should get going," the inmate said. He started to walk away, his hands shackled and the tips of his ears red with frostbite just like Yunsu's, but he turned suddenly and said, "Officer, wait! Sister, I miss you. Sometimes I miss you more than I miss my real sister. Even more than I miss my mother, who passed away when I was young. Come see me. I'll write to you."

There wasn't even the slightest trace of pretense to his words. Was that the power of someone facing an impending death? When I saw how easily, how like a child, he said the words that I was too embarrassed to say, I was struck by the feeling that he, not I, was Aunt Monica's true kin. And, to my surprise, I felt a little jealous. For a moment, I wondered, if I were Aunt Monica, whom would I have cared about more, me or them? Had they hogged the love that I should have been receiving while squandering my life for the past thirty years? When they cried out, begging to be left alone to die, did Aunt Monica cry, too, and cling to them the way she did with me, and say, *You poor thing, you poor thing*?

The inmate was led away by the guard. Aunt Monica paused in her steps and sighed heavily, as if it was too much to bear, and muttered to herself, "I wish I had three bodies, or that I could just move in here and live with them."

We waited for Yunsu again in the Catholic meeting room. Unlike on my first bewildering visit, this time, I felt like I had come armed with a well-honed knife. When I thought about the fact that I was meeting the type of man who had raped and killed a young girl of seventeen, the desire to die went away and a strange will to fight surged up in me. My whole body was trembling with electricity, but I didn't mind the feeling. Even if it was just hatred, and even if there were an evil intent to my observing him, it had been a very long time since any kind of desire had welled up inside me. When I had woken that morning, profanities that I had never before uttered were buzzing inside my mouth. An unfamiliar pleasure seemed to have raised my body temperature a degree. I felt like I had been looking forward to this day with the heart of a trapper awaiting a snared animal. Maybe I had finally started to realize that the murderous impulse I had been pointing at myself all that time was actually intended for someone else.

"They're all like that at first," Aunt Monica said. "But Yunsu is a little bit better. There used to be one here named Kim Daedu. He was the so-called serial killer of his generation. He tore up ten different Bibles given to him by a pastor. But when he died, he turned to God and went like an angel. Then there was the Geumdang murder case. What was his name? That one spent his final years living like Buddha. And the one you just saw in the hallway cursed up a storm and refused to come into the room the first time the guard brought him."

"No wonder you come here," I said.

My words must have sounded barbed. Aunt Monica stared at me incredulously, as if she had felt their sting.

"You like it when sinners turn into angels. You and the other clergy members wave the word of God like a magic wand and see how it changes people, and that makes you feel godlier, right? There's nothing weird about that. From where they stand, they could die at any time, so of course they're afraid. They weren't afraid when they killed another human being, but now that it's their turn to die, they're scared, so they turn good as fast as they can. I guess the death penalty is a good thing. Everyone gets a little bit nicer when they're facing death. Like you told the guard last time, it really is the best way to rehabilitate them."

Aunt Monica slit her eyes at me. I stared back at her at first, unwilling to back down either. But people's faces, and the eyes especially, contain so many stories. They say so much more than any number of words can. Aunt Monica seemed to be saying, *Think about your father when he died. Think about the tantrum your mother threw right before her operation. Most of all, think about yourself when you decided to commit suicide and end your own life. Being human does not mean that we change in the face of death*, her eyes told me, *but because we are human, we can regret our mistakes and become new people*. I couldn't stare into those old eyes any longer–those small and wrinkled, yet dark and impenetrable eyes–and I dropped my gaze.

Because of our argument, I wound up flustered and unprepared when Yunsu came in behind the guard. While Aunt Monica was taking him by the hand and welcoming him in, I was trying to remind myself of the humiliating fact that a murderer who raped a young girl had watched in thrall as I sang the national anthem at a baseball game. I thought about how I had ground my teeth all night because there was no reason scum like him might not have jerked off to the pictures of me that were printed in magazines back in my pop star days. But something kept blunting my anger. I couldn't erase those stories from my mind: five hundred without a single cent and just as many with less than a thousand won in their accounts; making do with less than a thousand won for six months; a man on death row fasting until a priest was healed; his saying that God should take those with more sins instead; Yunsu giving all of the money Aunt Monica had given him to an elderly prisoner serving a life sentence... Every last grain of those millet-sized words rolled toward me like a gathering ball of snow and blotted out the words *rape and murder of a seventeen-year-old girl*. They faced off inside of me: on one side, a snowman lying on its side; on the other, bulls readying their horns.

His face looked paler than last time. A faint but awkward smile flickered around the corners of his eyes, which had not yet entirely lost their murderous gleam. I had zero intent of cooperating in this trite parade of so-called rehabilitation that Aunt Monica had been engaged in for the last thirty years, but I also didn't want to agonize over it. After this, there were just two more meetings, and then I would never return to this place again. I had promised her a month. Afterward, I would go to my uncle and tell him that I had met with death row inmates in accordance with Aunt Monica's program and freed myself of the neurosis of death while spreading the Gospel to them. Then my uncle would be happy. Because he was a good man. And because it was so easy to fool good people. The less they deceive others, the more they think others never deceive them. But I wasn't sure if he was going to stare right back at me and say, *I wish you would cry.* If he did, then I would tell him I was sorry. Sorry, because, in any case, my uncle was a good man.

Just like last time, the four of us, including the guard, sat in the Catholic meeting room. Aunt Monica took out the pastries she had brought and set them on the table. And just like last time, she put one in Yunsu's hands, and he hunched over to take a bite. Since he always had his hands bound like that, whether sleeping or eating or going to the toilet, I thought it was not unreasonable to think death might be preferable.

"Did you stay out of solitary this time?" Aunt Monica asked.

He stopped in the middle of chewing and hesitated. Officer Yi spoke for him and said, "He took it easy this week." The two of them laughed. Yunsu laughed, too, but only briefly.

"Thank goodness. Don't go back there, Yunsu. It's no

good for you or for anyone else. But most of all, it's hard on you."

He ate the pastry without saying anything. The look on his face said that the meeting would be too difficult to get through if it weren't for the pastries. Aunt Monica sat close to him and touched his frostbitten ear. He grimaced from the pain.

"Poor thing. I brought you two blankets so you can bundle up at night." Aunt Monica clucked her tongue and mumbled to herself, "Those judges and prosecutors should try spending a few nights in those unheated cells. Must be so cold."

Yunsu swallowed a bite of pastry and coughed. Aunt Monica picked up his coffee and brought it to his lips. He reared his head back shyly.

"Drink it. It's okay. If I'd married and had children, you would be about the age of my youngest. I wish we could unshackle you, but we can't. It must be so hard. You're holding up well, though. If you can endure this place, then you can endure any place."

To my surprise, Yunsu obediently replied, "Yes, ma'am." Aunt Monica carefully fed him the coffee as if she were giving milk to a baby. He drank the coffee she offered him just as a baby would. But he looked like he was in agony. I don't think he could have looked more pained if I had been holding a piece of burning charcoal to his head.

"I got the books you sent me," he said.

"You did? Did you read them?"

"Yes. I mean, I didn't have anything else to do, and I was glad they weren't Bibles."

Aunt Monica laughed heartily. She seemed to have no intention of telling him what the other inmate had told her.

"That's right," she said, considerably more relaxed than

the last time we had visited. "Don't read the Bible. Stay away from it."

"That's... the first time anyone has said *that* to me."

"I know you won't read it even if I tell you to, so what's the point of wasting my breath? So, even if you feel like reading it, resist the urge!"

Aunt Monica laughed. He laughed along with her. The half-eaten pastry was still in his hand.

After a moment, he said hesitantly, "The judge sent me a Christmas card."

"The judge? You mean Justice Kim Sejung? The one who presided over your case?"

"Yes."

"Oh really?"

"The card said, 'As a judge, I sentenced you to death, but as a human being, I pray for you.'"

He cleared his throat. I wondered if some judges were really that nice. It seemed like a kind thing to say.

"What did you think about that?" Monica asked, her face brightening.

"When I got the card, I thought... To be honest, I thought, 'Why is everyone acting so nice all of a sudden?'"

He let out a long laugh that sounded like a tire going flat. He looked scornful. While I was thinking that it made perfect sense and was not at all clichéd, Aunt Monica was biting her lip and staring at him.

"It's weird," he said. "Right before the judge sentenced me, he asked me how I felt. So I told him I felt good. I could hear the reporters and the other people in the courtroom start whispering about that. I told him I knew I was going to get the death penalty, so I was glad that the state would kill me since I never managed to do it myself all those years, and I said that no one had ever paid any attention to me my whole life, so it felt good to have them scrutinizing my every move now. After I was placed on death row, the registrar told me to pick one: P, B, or C? I asked him what he meant, and he explained that the prison had to assign a clergy member to all death row inmates. P, B, and C meant Protestant, Buddhist, and Catholic. He said the other inmates pick either church or temple and attend services for a year or so, but I said no. I said it shouldn't be like separating trash into plastic, bottles, or cans."

"That's right! It shouldn't!" Aunt Monica chimed in. He looked at her for a moment in surprise and then kept talking.

"After you told me last time that meeting with you didn't mean I had to convert, I did a lot of thinking. To be honest, I don't need religion. I don't believe in it, either. I've lived fine until now without it. Well, no, I haven't been fine. I've lived like a dog, actually. But if there really were a God, a God of love and justice, then I wouldn't have turned out to be a murderer."

He swallowed hard and continued.

"A long time ago, I went to a Catholic service. It was after my little brother died and I was in jail again for maybe the third time. Probably about five years ago. I said I wanted to be baptized and was taking catechism classes. I liked it because the women who volunteered there treated us really nicely. They wrote us letters and gave us Bibles. They even brought Choco Pies and gave us good things to eat on holidays. One day, after Mass ended, an elderly death row inmate who was sitting next to me grabbed the hand of one of the volunteers. He did it before the guards could stop him. I saw the look on her face when that happened. That look said, *I will feed you, I will give you some money, and I will come to this prison in the dead of winter and hold Mass for you, but I will not hold your hand.* She didn't say the words out loud, but the look on her face was clear to me and to that inmate and to everyone around us. She looked like she was looking at a bug or a filthy beast that wasn't even the same species as her. That night, I heard that old man crying like an animal and raging in the cell next to mine."

He sneered again.

Officer Yi interrupted. "They don't have that many opportunities to see other people, so they're much more sensitive to outsiders."

"That person, that so-called *sister*, probably went home and told everyone that she does volunteer work for the unfortunate. She probably thought she was a pretty good person. But she has no idea how badly she sinned against that old man. He may have taken someone's life, but she trampled on his soul. He's slowly dying in here day after day. After that, I couldn't bring myself to go to another Mass. I made up my mind then that if you're not one of us, then you better not talk to us and pretend that you care about us. It sickens me more than being looked down on or getting beat up. Since then, I've stopped trusting people who have money. We live in two different worlds. And even if there is a God, that God only watches out for the rich. He doesn't live here with us, and He doesn't so much as glance at people like us. Whenever I saw another churchgoer, I just wanted to throw up. They're all hypocrites."

No one spoke for a moment. I studied him carefully so as not to miss the expressions that crossed his face. He seemed like he had calmed down a lot since last time. If the looks that crossed his face then were icy, this time they were merely cool. I imagined him holding a knife. Then I tried to picture him lifting the skirt of a scrawny seventeen-year-old girl and raping her. But the actors in my head would not play their roles properly and just sat there vacant-eyed. I couldn't stay angry.

"I'm so sorry," Aunt Monica said, grabbing his shackled hands.

"Sister, it wasn't you," he said and tried to pull his hands free.

"No, but it could have been. It doesn't matter who that woman was, she was still me. It was my fault. Yunsu, I apologize for her. I'm sorry, too, about the other man. When I think of how your heart must have ached to listen to him crying all night, my heart aches, too. I'm sorry for not paying any attention to you all those years, wherever you were in the world, and for waiting so long to come see you."

He stared incredulously at her for a moment and then looked away.

"I don't know if you're doing this on purpose," he said, "but you're making me very uncomfortable. This is going to bother me all day, even after I go back to my cell. So please, don't do this to me."

He clamped his lips together and struggled to pull his hands free from her grasp. But Aunt Monica held on stubbornly with tears in her eyes. He was not the only one who would continue to be bothered by this. I was angry. I muttered to myself, "What a great way to reha-bilitate someone. Let's raise the flag high and pledge alle-giance to it, then sing the national anthem while we're at it." I couldn't look at them anymore and turned my head away. There was the Rembrandt again. When I saw it, I was reminded of a passage by my favorite writer, Jang Jeongil: "We must kill the prodigal son. He brings worse things with him. Nothing makes us feel quite so small as the son who has returned. The true prodigal son must go, with nary a drop of water nor a crumb of bread, without even a camel, he must go to the ends of the desert and die there. And not just there, but everywhere!"

He was right. I hated hypocrites. It was better that Yunsu remain a murderer, beautifully, to the bitter end. I wanted him to die mocking everyone, just as Gary Gilmore had before his execution in Utah. Gary Gilmore... While I was studying in France, President Mitterrand had abolished the death penalty, despite the public opinion polls that showed the majority of citizens wanted to keep it, and the political fallout was felt for a long time after. Everyone at my school in Paris talked about it, which was how I came to read the writings of people like Victor Hugo and Albert Camus, who vigorously opposed the death penalty, and how I learned about Gary Gilmore. He had shot and killed two complete strangers, and in interviews with the press, he smirked and said calmly, *If you kill me, then you will be assisting me in my final murder*. He was beyond the reach of the system. He mocked the incompetence and contradiction of trading a single murder for all of the violence that he had committed. Many young people wrote songs and made films in his memory after he died because of what he represented. And they weren't clichéd about it. The shock of his execution moved us and made us think. But this trite scene playing out before me would have merely bored us and, to be honest, it would have bothered us a little, too, deep down inside. I wanted to get up and leave.

Tell me what kind of person you are. And I will tell you what kind of god you worship.

— Nietzsche

BLUE NOTE 7

There were two other boys at our mother's house, three and four years older than Eunsu and me. Our stepfather was quiet most of the time, but whenever he drank, the house would be turned upside down and smashed to pieces. What was wrong with our mother that she couldn't free herself of the fetters of violence and alcohol? Her face was as black and blue as ever. The one good thing was that our step-father got up every morning, strapped rolls of wallpaper to the back of his bicycle, and went out to wallpaper houses. But that was just the beginning. It was as plain as day that the two boys, the ones who had been living in that house from the start and who were now our mother's so-called stepsons, did not like us. And I was already like a wounded porcupine, my body bristling with electricity, quills rippling like ears of rice in an autumn field at the slightest touch. Our mother started hitting us, too. Even when they beat up Eunsu, she hit us, and when I punched them back, she hit us some more. One day, our stepfather packed up our things. We were tossed back into the orphanage.

We were taken back, as crushed as empty cardboard boxes. The morning we left, I watched the way our mother shoved Eunsu toward me and stalked off into the kitchen as he cried out for her, flailing his arms around, trying to find her through his blind eyes. We were abandoned again, and this time, it was different. It was, in a word, irreversible. Now we had nothing left to wait for. All of the light in the universe blinked out, not just for Eunsu, but for me as well. No sun would ever rise for us again.

Chapter 7

I was having a relaxed breakfast when the telephone rang. It was Aunt Monica. In an urgent voice, she said she had to go somewhere and asked me to pick her up. I checked the clock. It was not yet noon, and there was plenty of time before I had to be somewhere that evening. I picked her up at the convent in Cheongpa-dong, loaded a side of ribs that she had purchased into my car, and together we headed for Samyang-dong. There was nowhere to park, so I left the car in a pay lot near the entrance of a marketplace, and we began to walk. Since I could not ask my elderly aunt to carry the ribs, I was soon huffing and puffing. We walked quite a way through the market, but the address she had told me was nowhere to be found. In every alleyway, the snow that had fallen a few days earlier had lost its luster and was dirtied; in some places, it was mixed with the beige ash of used coal briquettes.

I knew without asking that it was a poor neighborhood. Was this really Seoul—part of the same city I had marveled over after returning from France and thought of as even more beautiful than Paris? Even in a place that looked like it was stuck in the 1960s, there were still swarms of people! I wasn't entirely unmoved by it, and yet strictly speaking,

I felt nothing, and even if I had felt something, it was still just one part of a larger landscape.

Aunt Monica explained that we were on our way to visit the family of the housekeeper Yunsu had killed. She had tried to visit them several times after the incident, but they refused to see her. She said they seemed more open to meeting now, and so she wanted to bring them some meat since the Lunar New Year was approaching. That was why she was in a hurry.

I was dressed in a short skirt for a party with my old school friends later that evening and was walking uphill carrying a side of ribs, so I did not appreciate the looks I was getting from men passing by. I couldn't help but wonder what the hell we were doing. It seemed like all murderers and all murder victims were poor.

"Why do they do that, Aunt Monica?"

"Why do they do what?"

"Why do they always talk about killing the rich when all of their victims are poor? I'm not saying it's okay to kill rich people, but why do they do that?" I asked, panting for air. "What kind of justice is that? If they meant what they said, then they would load up bombs in trucks like the Arabs do and go blow up rich neighborhoods."

Aunt Monica paused while making her way up a narrow flight of stairs and stared at me aghast.

"Load up bombs and blow them up? Then you'll be the first to die. You and your mother and your brothers."

"That's not what I mean. They claim to be some kind of apostles of justice, doing what others can't, but really they're just killing people who are as poor as they are. It pisses me off."

"You know the term 'high-crime area'? That's what they call poor neighborhoods. Rich neighborhoods have guards standing watch."

"But don't those guards live in these places? So while they're guarding the rich, their wives and daughters are working late at night and getting attacked in these dark, narrow alleys on their way home. I hate that guy, Yunsu, but I agree with him on one thing. Even if there is a God, He doesn't live here, and He only cares about the rich. I've had the same thought. What Yunsu says makes sense. That's why I hate the clergy. Church, too."

"My, you have all sorts of reasons not to go to church, don't you? Do you really think you were both talking about the same thing? The comparison is preposterous. Wait a second. Is this 189-7?"

We had just come down an alleyway barely big enough for a person to pass through. Aunt Monica stopped in front of a building and knocked on the door before I had a chance to clarify whether she meant it was preposterous for me to compare him to myself, or myself to him. The door opened, and I saw a tiny kitchen and sundry household items scattered about. It was cold inside and smelled bad. The smell was like rotting fish or old kimchi. We were greeted by an old woman. She had barely a handful of hair left on her head, but it was pulled back into a bun and held in place with a traditional hair stick. She was not that short, but she was so thin that I could have wrapped my hand around her whole waist. Her eyes were swollen as if from too much crying, and her lips were cracked. I awkwardly held out the ribs, and her swollen eyes lit up.

The room was dark. It was maybe thirty-five square feet, and it was packed with discarded papers that she was in the process of tying into bundles. A stack of folded blankets in the corner looked as if it would collapse at any moment, and a window near the ceiling, no bigger than the palm of my hand, was covered with green masking tape as if to keep the cold out at all cost. But it was a window nevertheless, and a faint ray of light made it through. Below that was an old, beat-up chest of drawers with a Virgin Mary figurine standing on it. As with all Virgin Mary figurines that you find in poor people's houses, it had an ugly face. It was true. It was not the elegant kind of figurine that part of me wanted to buy when I was in Paris or when I traveled to Italy, despite having long lost my faith, but rather the ugly kind, the kind you hope no one ever buys you for a present, standing there with a face as dark as the house itself.

"Should I turn on the light?" the old woman asked.

"No, it's okay," Aunt Monica said. "It's fine."

The old woman laughed and said, "Electricity is expensive, Sister." Her laugh contained a kind of abjectness that had to have been with her for a long time. We squatted in the dark like the people in Van Gogh's *The Potato Eaters*.

"Times have been hard, haven't they?" Aunt Monica asked.

The old woman pulled a cheap cigarette from her pocket and put it in her mouth.

"I'm still alive. The church helped out for a while at first. Lunar New Year is coming, so they'll probably bring me a bag of rice. But what brings you to this humble abode?"

She blew out a long plume of smoke. Aunt Monica glanced at the ugly Virgin Mary figurine, and the old woman was lost in thought for a moment.

"My daughter was Catholic," she explained. "She never tried to convert us, though, and she hardly ever made it to church since she had to work every day, even Sundays. But every morning, she would sit there and mumble to herself before she left. After she died, I kept a black cloth over the face of Our Lady for a while. At first, I wanted to smash it to pieces. But the grandkids stopped me, and I couldn't bring myself to do it. So I covered her up instead and only uncovered her again a few days ago."

The three of us filled the room. The smoke from her cigarette dispersed like dust particles into the hazy sunlight coming through the bars. The Virgin Mary just sat there, as if to say her hands were tied.

"I see. So what made you take the cloth off?" Aunt Monica asked.

"I had a bone to pick with her."

The old lady laughed, revealing uneven teeth stained black from cigarettes. Aunt Monica laughed too but seemed taken aback.

"And did Our Lady give you a response?"

The old lady laughed again and even smiled shyly.

"You have to have faith to get a response. They say faith can move mountains, so faith should be able to make a Virgin Mary figurine talk, too, right? That would be easier than moving a mountain. No one would be surprised by it, and there'd be no inconvenience to the owner of the mountain. That's why I've started taking catechism classes."

"You have quite the sense of humor," Aunt Monica laughed. "I know you've been through a lot, but it's good to see that you can talk about it now."

I had to agree with her. I remembered learning the same thing in Sunday school as a child. Did I believe it back then? When they said that faith can move mountains? But when I was crying like a young swallow in that man's clutches, God didn't listen to my frantic prayers. I know I had faith back then. I believed in heaven and hell and angels and the devil. But that day, the only one by my side was the devil.

"I'm not joking, Sister. I'm going to church because I think she might answer me if I learn the catechism and get baptized. And that way, I'll feel less sorry about the priests who've been helping me. By the way, I heard the Father has cancer?"

"Yes. His surgery went well, and now he's convalescing."

"Things like that make me wonder if there really is a God. Why do all the good people get sick, and only the bad people live well? When I think about that, religion makes no sense."

The old lady must have noticed the look on Aunt Monica's face, because she stopped speaking her mind and quickly changed the subject. The obsequiousness of one who has spent her whole life surviving on seeds, walking on eggshells around others, like a slave sensitive to even the slightest gesture from the master, returned to her face.

"That sweet child lost her husband when she was only twenty-three, and she worked her fingers to the bone every single day after, sleeping no more than three hours a night, doing everything except selling her body to make sure the children and I had something to eat. Even if she had to die, why did it have to be at the hands of that man? That's what I want to ask Our Lady. And Jeong Yunsu—I'll never forget that name. I want to kill him, tear him apart with my own hands, make it more painful than what he did to my baby, more terrible, more shocking. Sister, I won't sleep peacefully until I get to kill him with my own hands. I don't care if it means I'll go to hell. I'll sleep well in hell. I'm doing all of this because I plan to ask Our Lady permission to kill him. If God has a conscience, then He will tell her to answer me. If God has a conscience..."

Her voice grew agitated, and her hand trembled as it clutched the cigarette. Her hands were like two rakes, dark and coarse. Her servile attitude had vanished and was replaced by something like the dignity of a roaring animal. Aunt Monica looked miserable.

I felt sorry for Aunt Monica. I hadn't realized it, even when we went to the detention center and she threw herself at Yunsu's feet to apologize, but I pitied her. Last time, she had begged for forgiveness on behalf of bourgeois hypocrites, and today, she was like the team captain for murderers everywhere. She kept bowing her head like a special emissary from a cruel and unjust god. According to my mother, if Aunt Monica would just keep quiet, she could become the head of the convent and spend her time praying in a garden overflowing with beautiful, elegant hymns, or she could be the head of a Catholic-run hospital. I felt like asking the Holy Mother myself why my aunt had to be so feisty at her age.

"You've tried to contact me several times, but that's why I didn't want to see you. Each time you called, I couldn't sleep afterward. I couldn't stop thinking about it. The police made me look at her face to confirm who she was. There wasn't a single spot on her body that wasn't sliced up. I kept picturing it and thinking about how bad it must have hurt and how scared she must have been. It was so unfair. Just the thought of it makes me so angry."

Her tears were nearly dry, but she wiped hard at her eyes, as if they were bothering her.

"I don't know what we did wrong—me or her or the grandkids—what kind of sins we committed in our past lives that God should be punishing us like this. It was only her third day working at that house. She used to work for some rich family, but those bastards claimed they were broke and didn't pay her a single cent, not even any of the back pay they owed her. So she had no choice but to go to work on a construction site, putting up wallpaper. She hurt her back doing that and couldn't work for several months. Then someone introduced her to that widow. It was such a good job. The widow had a bad temper, but still, she said it was better than doing wallpaper. The night before it happened, she didn't sleep a wink, complaining that her back hurt. I told her to stay home, just one day, but she said it was her duty to go, and she left. And then that happened to her. She should have skipped work that day to rest her back, and instead she died so senselessly."

The tears started falling from the old woman's eyes again. She wiped them away with fingers stained yellow from nicotine.

Aunt Monica waited a moment and then asked, "How are your grandkids?" She seemed to be trying to calm the old woman. The woman sighed and carefully extinguished the cigarette in a brass ashtray. I could tell from the way she carefully balanced the cigarette butt on the edge, despite her tears, that she planned to smoke the rest of it later.

"The youngest one, my grandson, is studying. He went to the library right after breakfast."

"Your oldest is around twenty now, right? A girl?"

A dark shadow passed over the old woman's face. Her lips trembled as she spoke.

"After her mother died, she left home. She sends me money once a month. I don't ask what she's doing. Even if I did ask, what could I do about it? She was doing so well in school, but after her mother died, she dropped out. She's probably working as a bar girl now."

Aunt Monica sighed. The old lady picked up the cigarette butt that she had so carefully stashed on the edge of the ashtray and relit it.

"Sister, I have a favor to ask."

"Go ahead."

"It's that son of a bitch. I want to meet him."

It was an unexpected request. Aunt Monica's face hardened.

"Let me meet him. I'm not joking."

"Ma'am, he's having a hard time right now, too. I'm not going to ask you to forgive him. God will understand. But please give it some time, a little more time, until you are both a little more settled."

Aunt Monica sounded like she was pleading with her, but the old lady kept on talking as if she hadn't heard her.

"It's been almost two years. The priest who used to visit the prison came to see me once, and he told me about him."

We were silent for a moment.

"The priest told me he was an orphan. He said that he had a younger brother who was blind and died in the streets, and that he lost his mother and father when he was young, so they grew up in an orphanage. That means he has no family of his own. After the people from the church left, I thought about it for a long time. I thought and thought, and then I thought some more. My daughter's kids are also orphans, now. I know that even if I tell people my granddaughter works in a bar because she's an orphan, they won't be any more sympathetic toward her. I know how alone we are in this world. I'm an orphan, too. That man grew up without a mother. His little brother was all he had. Sister, I've been setting a little bit of rice aside each time I cook. Since it's the holidays, I want to make a little rice cake from it and take it to him."

Aunt Monica looked like she was trying to find somewhere she could back away to in that tiny room. I couldn't believe it, either. Aunt Monica made a face to say it was a difficult favor to fulfill. The old lady grabbed her hand.

"Sister, I'm not planning on doing anything bad. I just want to meet him before it gets any later and the state executes him. I have no education, and I don't know anything, but I want to go to him and say, 'I'm the mother of the woman you killed!' I want to forgive him."

Aunt Monica's face looked ashen. I probably looked the same.

"I want to meet him so that I can forgive him. I grew up as an orphan, too. I had no flesh and blood to call my own. I didn't even have a husband. It was just the kids and me, so I know how he feels. I know how lonely the holidays can be. A holiday is still a holiday, even to a murderer. And this could be the last holiday he ever sees. No one knows whether he will die today or tomorrow. When I think about him dying, I think, *Good riddance!* If killing him meant bringing my child back, I would kill him myself, even if it meant getting the death penalty a hundred times over. If killing him meant my grandchildren's bruised hearts could heal, I wouldn't be afraid of anything. But that's not how it works. That's why I want to see him. I hate the thought of him dying peacefully, but still, if he could, even if he were the only one who could..."

"The thing about forgiveness," Aunt Monica said, "is that it's not as easy as you think."

I had never seen my aunt so flustered. I had never seen her stumble for words. She looked as if she was going to start flailing her hands around. The old woman looked at Aunt Monica and made an expression that I could not decipher. Suddenly, she raised her voice.

"Isn't that what Jesus told us to do?" she yelled. "That's what the priest told me to do. And the nuns. And all those people who keep coming to see me and handing me Bibles and singing hymns. They know everything, and they listen to God, and that's what they told me to do. That's what you all told me to do! 'Forgive! Forgive your enemies!' Seven times or seventy times, if you have to. That's what they said!"

Aunt Monica closed her mouth and pressed her hand against the floor as if she had lost her balance. I went to her side to help her, but she shoved my hands away. She was crying.

I said to my soul, be still, and wait without hope
For hope would be hope for the wrong thing; wait without love,
For love would be love of the wrong thing.

– T.S. Eliot, "The Four Quartets"

BLUE NOTE 8

Abandoned once again in the orphanage with Eunsu, I was still the most violent, still a troublemaker, but I had no more problems because of my brother. That's because I was big and had ganged up with the other bad kids, which meant that as long as I was in the gang and was strong, they wouldn't mess with me—or rather, they wouldn't mess with Eunsu. Sniffing glue was my Bible, and jerking off was my hymnal. The shoulders of my fellow gang members were my law and my nation. By the age of thirteen, I was already taking girls who had run away from home and putting them up in rooms with boys. I kept a lookout while the older boys took turns raping them. But one day, an older boy who was stronger than me started bullying me and trying to push me out of the gang because I wouldn't steal things for him from the supermarket. They were too strong, and I couldn't protect Eunsu, or even myself, for that matter. We were hungry, and with each day we were becoming the butt of the other kids' jokes. So one day, I made up my mind. While all of the other kids were asleep, I beat the oldest boy to within an inch of his life, grabbed Eunsu by the hand, and ran.

The night we ran away from the orphanage, we wandered the streets of Seoul. We were hungry and cold and hopeless. I had stopped beside a trashcan in a corner of a marketplace and was rummaging through it in the hopes that there was something we could eat, when Eunsu said he was scared. He said he wanted to go back. I got mad, but I bit my lip and suggested that we sing something instead. He liked singing. Since he was blind and never got to go to school, the only song he knew was the national anthem. That's because we used to sing it during the morning assembly at the orphanage. So we sang the anthem. *Until the East Sea runs dry and Mt. Baekdu wears away, God save us and keep our nation...* Eunsu could remember all four verses. I remember how, on that cold night, the stars floated in the sky like cold popcorn as we raised our faces to the sky and sang the anthem. When we finished, Eunsu laughed and thought aloud, *It's a great country, isn't it? Whenever I sing this song, I feel like we're good people.*

CHAPTER 8

When I woke up, my head was splitting. Yellow rays of sun passed through the white lace curtains and shoved their way deeper into the blankets. For a moment, I wondered where I was. I could see a tall magnolia outside the window. But the first thing on my mind wasn't what I was doing in my old room at my mother's house, but rather that I was thirsty. I thought about the first time I tried to commit suicide: I had slit my wrists in this very room. Of course, I knew then that what I was doing was wrong. Ever since I was young, I had been going to church, and I never hesitated to mark the box for *Catholic* on the questionnaires they handed out in school. When I was christened in the church that my father carried me to in his arms right after I was born, I was given the name Sylvia in addition to Yujeong. In those days, the Catholic Church was still so strict that they did not allow a funeral Mass to be held for suicides. People who committed suicide were regarded as murderers who mistook their God-given lives as their own to take. During catechism class, the nun explained to us why suicide was murder.

Raise your hand if you decided to be born, was how she began the lesson. *Raise your hand if you decided whether*

97

you would be male or female. Raise your hand if you think you can die whenever you want to. In the throes of puberty, I was ardent on the subject of suicide. I had drawn my own conclusion about it, which was that I did not have the right to kill myself. Above all, my life was not created by me. I didn't know why the hormones I had learned about in biology class were released at certain times and went away at others, or why my stomach was refusing to digest food, or why my period had to start. I didn't know why I got diarrhea, or why my stomach hurt, or why my heart was beating. The territory I governed was smaller than my own brain. Back then, I had a folder with a Descartes quote printed on it that said the only thing about ourselves that we can control are our own thoughts. So I, too, had come to the conclusion that since I did not own myself, it would be murder to kill myself. But then I slit my wrists in this room. Back then, I felt only one thing: knowledge could not ward off despair. And I realized something else: Descartes was wrong. Not even my own thoughts were under my control, and I had even less control over them than everything else in my life combined.

I got up and headed downstairs to get some water or juice to drink.

Around the time I started high school, my father bought land in this neighborhood that was now towering with high-rise buildings and built a house on it. Back then, there weren't that many high-rises yet, and it was the kind of out-of-the-way spot that was crowded with cheap motels bearing old-fashioned names. Yusik, my oldest brother, had moved out of the house with his wife. It was right around the Lunar New Year, so I had gone on an errand for my mother to the head family's house, where my father's eldest brother lived. I went alone. That wouldn't seem like a big deal nowadays, but at the time, I had already grown to my full height and was very tall for my age. Once, I had even been approached while out running errands. It was summer, and I was wearing a dress. I think I was in the seventh grade at the time. An army officer in full uniform came up to me. His breath reeked of alcohol, and he said, *Excuse me, miss, care to join me for a drink at that café?* I told him I was only in middle school, and he looked flustered for a moment and then looked up at the sky and laughed in amazement. I laughed, too. When I got back home, I told my mother, *Someone flirted with me. But he was a soldier.* I don't remember what my mother said. I'm sure it wasn't nice. My brothers teased me about it: *He must have been really drunk. He was blacked out, wasn't he? Maybe he deserted his post and wanted to take a kid hostage to keep from having to go back.* Now that I look back on it, I was as tall as a grown woman. I had hips and, though they were not yet full, my breasts were showing. Since I was no longer a child but a young lady, I didn't mind being approached by a man, but I felt strange that it had to be a drunk soldier. Was that to be my fate?

On my way downstairs, I kept thinking about the man who had made me want to kill myself. Each time I walked down those stairs, I used to think about all the ways I could die. What if I did it this way? What if I did it that way? At the bottom of the stairs, the telephone was ringing.

"Yujeong? I think she's still asleep. Oh, no, here she comes."

My mother saw me coming down the stairs and shoved the phone toward me. It was my brother Yusik. When I said hello, he let out a long sigh. I couldn't help but sigh as well.

"Do you remember what happened last night?"

He sounded as if he had been waiting a long time to ask me that.

"Yeah, I meant to thank you."

He sighed again.

"I was planning to give you a piece of my mind, but since it's Mom's birthday today, I'll hold off. It's only been a month and a half since her operation, and I'm worried she might collapse again. I didn't say anything to anyone else in the family."

"Thanks."

"Also, since we're both grown-ups, I didn't want to say anything to you, but let's talk again later, around dinner-time. Mom's sick, so don't throw another one of your tantrums. Just hold it in until dinnertime. I called Aunt Monica. I don't think you should keep meeting those death row—or whatever—inmates. Stop going there."

"What are you talking about?"

He hung up without answering me. Despite thanking him, I didn't actually remember what had happened the night before. As I poured myself some juice, I tried to call up all of my memory circuits. I had met my old friends from elementary school for drinks, and we went from one bar to another, and another. I remembered getting into my car and insisting that I could drive, even though someone tried to stop me. Then I remembered the police station, and yelling my head off. A detective, a short man who looked to be over fifty, had said to me, *What kind of woman goes out drinking in the middle of the night? Girls like you should all be rounded up and shot.* That was when I lost it. I think I must have screamed at him, *So what? Yeah, so I broke the law, but at least I have character. You want to shoot me? Is that what a police officer of the Republic of Korea's "Civilian Government" is supposed to say? Take my blood! Take my blood!* I remembered screaming my head off in the police station. It all came back to me: I must have called my brother. Then he showed up and I asked him how he knew I was there. The other people in the station clucked their tongues at me from behind my brother's back and said I was crazy, so I got mad at them. When I thought about it, I couldn't believe that was me. As much as I enjoyed complaining, I wasn't the type to get drunk and make a scene in public, let alone a police station, of all places. I would never be able to show my face in Itaewon again. As the alcohol in my blood receded like the tide, standing in its place were memories, as stark as rocks on the seashore.

It must have been close to dawn when he picked me up. I think I cried... I say I *think* I cried because all I could remember was having heard a woman crying in the car. My brother and I were the only ones there, and since my brother isn't a woman, the crying must have been coming from me. Did that fit into my uncle's definition of the crying he wished I would do? I don't know if the tears helped to sober me up, but I chose that moment to pick a fight with my brother. I think I started babbling, without any sort of preamble, about prisoners who had to survive on less than a thousand won for six months at a time, and how I was going crazy. I told him, *They're driving me crazy, Yusik. Help me! I'm dying because of them!* My brother could not have felt good about having to pick up his little sister from the police station—his little sister who was nearly booked with drunk driving, who had broken off an engagement with his younger colleague, and who had attempted suicide not long ago. After my father, Yusik cared about me the most. We were so far apart in age that he doted on me as if I were his niece; when I was little, he used to carry me on his back. I could still remember his warm, strong, young back.

Whenever I see those guys in my line of work, my brother had said, *guys who rape children and kill old*

*people, and don't show even the slightest remorse in court,
I hate the idea of having to breathe the same air as them!
The death penalty is too good for them! I look at them and
wonder whether they're even human or whether they're
just animals. That may be a bad thought, but it seems like
there really is a devil, and those people are marked from
birth. They don't deserve to live. They're animals.*

It was just an inference, but as I drank a glass of cold
juice and stared out at the warm sunlit garden of my
mother's house, I figured my brother had said what he did
because his little sister who never cried had suddenly fallen
apart and bawled that she was losing her mind because of
death row prisoners. He was probably worried that I would
go into further shock while following Aunt Monica around
and die for real. I told him the men on death row were
killing me and, to try to calm me down in my drunkenness
and my indignation, he said in return that Aunt Monica was
killing him.

I understand what she's feeling, he said, *but she keeps
coming to see me to ask why he can't get a retrial, and she
pressures me to petition the minister of justice to commute
his sentence. She'll be the death of me.* I knew he was only
saying that to calm me down.

He was a good man, too. A conscientious prosecutor,
he was famous for never accepting favors of any kind. He
had made a name for himself faster than any of his peers.
Though it was just the effect the alcohol was having on me,
the way he called them all animals weighed on my heart.

"Back when I was in college," I said, "I visited you at
work one day at the public prosecutor's office. But I didn't
go into your office. As soon as I got to the door, I could
hear someone inside screaming. Do you remember that?
I found out later what the sound was. Someone had been
hung upside down from the ceiling, spun around, and

tortured into confessing. You were surprised to find me shaking outside your door. You took me to a teashop on the first floor and tried to tell me you weren't one of *those* prosecutors. I asked you to put a stop to it, and you said it was 'that damn section chief' again. But Yusik, you didn't run back upstairs to tell him to stop torturing that person. At the time, I wondered whether you, the section chief, and the prosecutors—the ones you said you weren't like—were people or animals."

He stared at me in shock.

"I've had that question a lot, whether men like that are human beings or animals. I think about it every time I see those men who go to room salons and do things in front of others that should only be done in private—not that it has anything to do with intimacy between human beings—like shamelessly shoving their hands up girls' skirts and feeling them up just because they paid for it, and throwing their money around. I think about it every time I see them at school, too. Those professors who get up in the morning and drone on and on about the sanctity of education and the unequal division of wealth with the smell of a whore's genitals still on their lips. They swarm to brothels and use those poor young girls who have to sell their bodies for cash. They strip their clothes off and stick them on top of tables and watch them slice bananas with their vaginas or open bottle caps—anything and everything that can be done with the human genitals. When I lived in Paris, I felt so ashamed every time a French person asked me if it was true that democracy activists in Korea were being taken away and tortured by the KCIA—or the Agency for National Security Planning, or whatever it was—having their arms dislocated or being stripped naked and beaten and, since that wasn't enough, female students just a little older than me being tortured sexually. Back then, as well, I wondered whether they were people or animals. Murderers? Animals, of course. Why even ask? Of course they're animals. But now it's your turn to answer. Of the types of people I just described, which one is the most likely to evolve into human beings?"

Like a typical drunk, I must not have been paying any attention to my brother's reaction. He didn't say a word to me. I kept going.

"I'll give you a hint. One at least acknowledges that they did something wrong, while the other not only refuses to acknowledge it but thinks they are decent human beings. The first are punished for the rest of their lives for a small number of sins, while the second repeat those sins over and over, all the while believing that they are pretty good people. So, who do you suppose are the ones who think they're innocent?"

"You haven't changed a bit! How old are you?" my older brother said angrily.

"Fifteen."

I laughed out loud. He looked at me with pity, just as the cops had at the station, and lit a cigarette. I grabbed it from his mouth and took a puff. He sighed and said nothing.

"Fifteen years ago, on Lunar New Year, when I went to the head family's house to run an errand for Mom, and that thing happened to me, no one in the family cared. Do you know why I'm like this? Why I swallowed pills and cut my wrists three times? The thing I could not understand, what I really could not forgive, was the fact that everyone acted like nothing happened—Mom, you and our brothers, even Dad! It was swept under the rug, the same way my drunk driving charges never happened because my big prosecutor brother showed up and made them go away. I thought I was going to die—I wish I had died—and meanwhile everyone just closed their mouths and pretended that nothing happened. It didn't take me long to figure out why you all did that. If it hadn't been for our uncle— Dad's brother, the big-shot National Assembly member for the ruling party—the family business would never have survived. If he hadn't been watching out for us, Dad wouldn't have been able to embezzle all that money and commit malpractice and put in illegal bids and evade taxes. That's why!"

"Enough!"

I could tell he was holding back. He yanked the cigarette from my lips and crushed it out hard in the car ashtray. But it wasn't in my nature to back down.

"I was only fifteen. Do you understand now why I tried to kill myself, and why I'm still trying? Our family, Mom, Dad, our brothers—you all thought that was more important than me. Do you know now what you did to me? What made me even more miserable than dying? And yet you have the nerve to call those men animals? I think *you're* the animals!"

He yanked hard on the steering wheel, pulled the car around, and started heading toward our mother's house. I couldn't speak from the force of the U-turn. It seemed like his way of saying, *No, I will not leave you on your own tonight. If I do, something bad will happen again.*

⋆⟐⋆

I could hear my mother playing the piano. It was Chopin's *Tristesse.* My mother was sitting with her back to me at the grand piano in the middle of the living room. There was a time when my mother would have paid any amount of money to lose weight, but now she was as gaunt as if someone had stripped a heavy coat from her body. I thought about the fact that, with or without cancer, it would not be long before I would have to say goodbye to my mother, who was in her seventies, and I felt sentimental. What cannot be reconciled in the face of death? What in this life is worth clinging to? Especially if that thing is hatred. I had once overheard her telling her friends that it made her feel ashamed as a woman to have one of her breasts removed. She said that she had no idea what caused her cancer, and that it would cost twenty million won to reconstruct her breast. I had taunted her, saying, *What are you going to do? Try out for Miss Old Korea?* As I listened to her playing the piano, I thought, *Twenty million won would mean ten thousand won for each inmate who has nothing in his account half the year.* I was surprised at myself for thinking that. Why was I making that kind of comparison?

Over a pink silk blouse, my mother wore a silk scarf draped long in the front, and her shoulders were moving quietly. I didn't know if it was my sentimental mood, but for once, her piano playing didn't make me want to plug my ears the way it used to. When the song ended, I clapped. I could hear the housekeeper in the kitchen clapping, too. My mother smiled as if deep in thought, to make herself look as elegant as a real pianist on stage, and began playing another song.

The reason I hated my mother and the rest of our family was not that they fancied themselves to be cultured and artistic, wearing looks on their faces that said they weren't all about money, camouflaging their own snobbishness in that all-too-typical way. I hated them because even though they all felt vulnerable and lonely as hell whenever they found themselves sitting alone at night, they had too many tools and opportunities at their disposal to help them disguise their own feelings and thus deprived themselves of the chance to face their own loneliness, their pitifulness, and their isolation. In short, they were missing out on the chance to face life head on.

I went over to the piano. It used to be so hard for me to listen to my mother's playing. After that fateful day, whenever my mother played a romantic song like this one, I would plug my ears, put on some rock music, and turn the volume up as high as it would go. I probably did it because of her. Had she been a pop singer, I would have listened to classical. *Turn it off! Turn that noise off!* she would scream, and race up to my room on the second floor, whereupon I would quickly turn the volume down and open the door with a peaceful look on my face.

What's wrong?

Turn it down!

I did.

You're driving me crazy. Why did I have to give birth to you only to suffer like this? Why did I ever give birth to you? I should have gotten rid of you when the doctor suggested it, when he said I was too old for another pregnancy! But your dad insisted. He claimed you were a gift from God.

I always won those arguments, since I was the one who remained calm, but my mother had no idea how much my heart bled each time. Back then, I cursed our religion that forbade abortion. What was it Job said? *Curse the night I was conceived? Why did I not die at birth, come forth from the womb and expire?* I liked Job's earnest voice. I would wait until I heard my mother's footsteps reach the bottom of the stairs, and then I would crank the volume back up again. It was my way of getting revenge for the blood I lost each time she wounded me.

When did I ask you to give birth to me? I had resorted to that sort of mud flinging once.

You think I made you because I wanted to make you? If

I'd known it would be you, I wouldn't have! I should have gone to the hospital anyway, despite your father. That was her response.

Since you couldn't kill me when I was inside of you, I told her, *I'm trying to finish the job now. So why do you keep stopping me? Why are you stopping me?*

That's when she said, *Then die somewhere where I can't see you! Die somewhere where I can't stop you!*

Those were our mother–daughter talks. When they were over, I would smash all of the innocent records and flower vases in my room. But now that I was over thirty and watching my mother who was now in her seventies, as she played Chopin's Piano Concerto No. 1, I wanted to ask her something.

"Don't bother me! This song requires all of my concentration!"

It was the same thing she always said. It reminded me of something that happened when I was little. We had guests over, and my mother had seated them all in a row and was wearing a pretty lavender concert dress, probably playing this same song, when she suddenly burst into tears and ran out of the room. She was muttering something as she went. One of the guests asked, *What on earth is wrong with her?* Someone else said, *I think she said she's too sad to keep playing.* My dad explained, *My wife is an artist, so she's very sensitive. Just reading a poem can make her cry.* And then he laughed. A few of the guests laughed politely. I was embarrassed. I could tell my father was tired of dealing with his pianist wife. It made sense. My mother had attended a top-tier girls' high school, but my father only graduated from a commercial high school. I had no idea what *top-tier* meant.

I waited quietly for the song to end. My uncle might have been right about crying, as I felt different after having cried my eyes out the night before. I thought maybe that was why I was able to stand there and watch my mother without getting upset, like a ray of sunlight shining down on good people and bad people alike.

"Happy birthday, Mom. I didn't get you a gift. To be honest, I didn't know it was your birthday. But happy birthday for now, and I'll give you your present later."

"You don't have to say anything or buy me any gifts. Just don't worry me!"

"Still, happy birthday. Isn't it better to say something even if I do worry you, rather than say nothing and worry you anyway?"

"Now what's gotten into you? You scare me to death. Last time, when you smashed your IV bottle in the hospital and glared at me, I thought you were possessed by the ghost of your dad's mother."

There she went again. It was never a good sign when she said I resembled someone on my father's side of the family. I used to wonder all the time what she prayed about when she went to church. I told myself to hang in there. It was her birthday, after all.

"Mom, what was the happiest time of your life?"

She smirked.

"Wasn't there a time when you thought you felt really happy?"

I guess I just wanted to talk to her. I wanted to talk to my mother who was facing her death, a mother who might spend her final days in the hospital as cancer cells spread through her body again. I wanted to have a real conversation on my mother's birthday, a conversation between a mother and a daughter who had returned to her old home after a long time away, to look down at a warm sunlit garden together and have the kind of real conversation that mothers and daughters have. I wanted to tell her, *Mom,*

I don't have any memories of being happy. I've had all of the things that other people don't get to have, and I've eaten all of the things that other people don't get to eat, but I don't remember ever feeling happy. Either my tone was softer than usual, or maybe it wasn't really in her nature to be so severe, despite the arrogance that came from having ridden to school on a palanquin carried by servants when she was young, but she surprised me by responding gently.

"How could I have been happy? You know I was busy taking care of your grandmother and putting up with her senility when I was younger. I was afraid your father's business would go bankrupt. Then, after raising three boys, I was ready to start playing piano again, but you dropped in and I had to give up piano entirely. You gave me so much trouble. And today's my so-called birthday. I just had surgery and could have a relapse and die at any moment, but do you see those three sisters-in-law of yours anywhere?"

I sighed to myself. Here we go again. Nothing was good enough for her. She had every nice thing you could possibly own, but it was never enough. When my father was alive, he kept her from having to wash even a single cup. He said she might damage a finger while doing the dishes and wouldn't be able to play the piano that she loved so much. Nevertheless, nothing was ever good enough for her.

"They have important things to do," I told her. "A pianist, a doctor, and an actress! The first one's nerves are on edge because of her recital. The second one is working at the hospital. And I hear the third is pregnant again? But Mom, whenever you meet your friends, all you do is brag about them. 'My sons married a pianist, a doctor, and an actress.' And your friends all envy you for it. But at least you have one stupid daughter, and since she's not busy, she has the time to wish you a happy birthday in the morning. What luck."

"Go away! You stay out all night drinking and have to be carried home on your brother's back, and now you're starting up with me first thing in the morning? All I wanted to do was play one song after such a long time. Why do you have to torment me?"

"When did I torment you? All I did was say happy birthday!"

"Just looking at you gives me a headache. Now I've lost my appetite! And while you're here, let me ask you this. Why on earth don't you want to marry that prosecutor, Kang?"

I laughed out loud. As I laughed, I had to acknowledge once again that people never change, that even I never change. What my brother had said last night was right. You can be facing your own death and have your cancer operated on, and be eating breakfast with your daughter who has come back from the dead herself and is home again for the first time in a long while, and still, people never change. Maybe that is the only thing that doesn't change in this world.

"I'm just like you, Mom," I said through clenched teeth. "I, too, hate men whose families have no education. Admit it. You always looked down on Dad and Aunt Monica. So maybe I take after you."

Mom stopped moving her shoulders in time with the music and stared at me. She looked as if she was staring at something foreign.

"You're just like your aunt!" she said.

I tried to hold it back, but I could feel all of my childhood emotions surging up inside me. That stern voice! There was no point in sticking around. Even though I tried to remind myself that it was her birthday, not even a birthday was enough to tear down the fortress walls erected by our pasts. It would take far longer than that to dismantle them.

But then again, how was time of any use when no one was willing to try? Even if I had been even slightly willing to try, my old habits all too easily took down that willingness. It didn't matter that it was her birthday, and it wouldn't have mattered even if it had been the anniversary of her death.

I walked away from the piano and cried, "I'm just like you. I thought I was like Aunt Monica, but I'm not. I'm just like you! And that's why I hate myself!"

Clang! My mother slammed her fists on the piano as if she couldn't take any more.

As always, I was playing the role of the unfilial daughter. Later, at the dinner table, my mother would explain to my brothers *ad nauseam* about how I had come home and hurt her feelings and ruined her birthday and shortened her life and made everything worse for them. My sisters-in-law would hide the bored looks on their faces and pretend to chew their food, while my brothers would make an effort to hear her out with the patience and filial devotion befitting the birthday of an old, weak mother who has had a breast cancer operation. Not that they had much choice since she wouldn't let anyone else get a single word in. Meanwhile, the meal would end, and once it did, someone would make this or that excuse, like students who have just finished a class they hate, and someone would get up first, and they would all file out. Then my mother would end the day by shouting at the cleaning girl, as if that were her way of saying good night. She would leave out all of the words that said she really just wanted to be loved and wanted to give love, and that she was lonely and wanted someone to be with her, and instead she would say that the dishes were chipped and the cupboards were dusty. There was no way I could stay in that house until dinnertime. I purposefully stomped all the way upstairs to get my bag, still no further away from being that teenager who had run away from home after fighting with her mom. I was on my way out of the house when I felt something inside of me burst. I could tell that something was happening on the inside.

Everyone is sad. Sadness is a wealth that you cannot give away. That is because you can give everything else to other people, but you cannot give yourself to others. Everyone is tragic. Tragedy is a scar that you alone carry forever. River of tears, river of sadness, river of wailing. Unlike wealth, sadness is shared among all people evenly.

– Ven. Bak Samjung

BLUE NOTE 9

Then we lived on the streets, like wet garbage, using the city's back alleys as our pillows. There were other kids like us. They were looked after by a man who looked like he was in his forties. He offered us a place to sleep, and in exchange, we fanned out across the subway stations and marketplaces to beg for money. People were more generous to us since Eunsu was blind. We sat up all night making flyers that read: *My little brother went blind after taking some bad medicine in the countryside when we were younger.* Kind-looking men and women gave us money. Then, one day, it was Eunsu's birthday. I asked him what he wanted to eat, and he said cup ramen. The man, whom we all called Blackie, fed us instant ramen, but never the kind that came in Styrofoam cups. It was too expensive and not filling enough. So one night, I stole a box of cup ramen from a corner shop in the market that I walked past every day, and I got caught.

The moment the owner shouted at me, I grabbed the box and ran, but in the confusion, Eunsu, who had been standing nearby, got caught instead. The owner started beating him for no reason. My brother cried and called out to me over and over. If I had been alone, I would have run as fast as I could, but I couldn't bear to leave him behind. I went back, returned the box to the owner, and tried to plead with him. The owner said it was the tenth time a box of cup ramen had been stolen from him, and he took us to the police substation. They said brats like us needed a good thrashing before we would wise up, and no matter how we tried to tell them that it wasn't us and that this was our first time, we were sent to juvenile detention centre for stealing ten boxes of cup ramen. Eunsu was my accomplice. Right then, I made a decision.

Never again would I beg. Never again would I plead. There was only one way to survive in this world, and that was by having money and having power.

CHAPTER 9

It is amazing how memory reveals things to us that were not apparent when the original events happened. Like a pin light that shines on an extra who is making small gestures off to one side of the stage, memory not only brings that moment back to life but adds to it. And that addition can sometimes contradict what we have believed to be our memories.

Now I must return to the visitors' room. The place where I have been meeting him. The place where our meetings would continue to follow the same script since we would never meet anywhere but that place. The place where life and death cross paths, where a single ray of light shines in the darkness. That place where crime and punishment and hope spill their blood on a lost battleground to defend a dying castle, where those who hold all of the power battle for supremacy, though that battle cannot be perceived with the human senses. It was my third visit to the prison with Aunt Monica. It was also the day that the old woman from Miari or Samyang-dong, or wherever it was, insisted on coming with us and bringing the rice cake she had made.

We were waiting for the guard to bring him. No one spoke. Aunt Monica was slumped in her chair and biting her lips. The old woman was dressed in a light-blue *hanbok*. The color of the traditional dress clashed with her dark, wrinkled face. Inside a light-blue cloth wrapper on the table sat the still-warm rice cake. Outside the window, it was winter, but rays of sunlight as warm as the cake were shining down. Yunsu did not show up until thirty minutes after our appointed time. I have no idea what happened during that time between Yunsu, who was trying to avoid seeing us, and the guard, who was trying to make him come out. I could have guessed, but I didn't have even a fifty-fifty chance of guessing correctly.

Yunsu came in, and Aunt Monica stood up. I could tell from the fact that she didn't greet him that she was nervous. The old woman fumbled with a gauze handkerchief, her body stiff, as if the dress were binding her. It looked as if she hadn't worn it in a long time. I realize now that the three of us were probably all wondering if we were doing the right thing.

Even Aunt Monica, who had devoted her whole life to love and forgiveness, was afraid of what was happening. We could tell that it was a frightening reality for her, regardless of whether the old woman said to Yunsu, *Your sins are forgiven, rise up and walk*, like a young Jesus from two thousand years ago, or whether it was all an act and she tore at his throat instead and raked her nails over his face as he sat there in shackles.

Yunsu looked pale. I could not find any trace there of the memory of our first and second meetings, when his face seemed to say, *I'm a human being, too*. I doubt he would have looked any more afraid if he were looking at the gallows noose. His lips looked blue and were twitching slightly.

This may not be the best expression, but the old woman was eyeing Yunsu as if he were a lost son who had returned:

she looked as if she didn't want to miss a single detail of his face or body. Everyone—the old woman, Aunt Monica and I, Yunsu, and Officer Yi—stood around awkwardly.

"Please have a seat."

Officer Yi was calmer than the rest of us. He filled the kettle with water and turned on the switch. He had a certain sense of virtue about him, the kind you often find in public servants who have studied hard for the civil service exam. When I saw him do that, I realized that Aunt Monica had skipped her usual step of preparing hot water the moment she stepped into the room. The silence in the room was so heavy that we were all grateful for the beeping of the electric kettle when the water reached a boil.

"Have you been well?" Aunt Monica asked.

Yunsu looked dazed. He said yes and started to smile, but his face crumpled like tinfoil. The old woman had her gaze fixed on Yunsu's shackles.

"It must be so hard to be tied up all the time like an animal."

The woman mumbled but the room was so quiet, and she was not composed enough to control the volume of her voice, that it sounded loud. It might have been the word *animal*, but everyone became even more uncomfortable.

"This lady is..." Aunt Monica stuttered. Her next words should have been, "the mother of the person you killed," or to put it a little more precisely, "the mother of the person you murdered." But she paused and swallowed hard.

"The person... whose death you caused..."

Aunt Monica swallowed again. I swallowed, too, in reaction to her. Sometimes words can be so concrete and so real, and therefore so cruel. Maybe that's what they meant when they said the pen is mightier than the sword.

"This is the mother of that housekeeper."

Yunsu's head dropped as if his neck had snapped.

They say people on death row die six times: when they are caught, when they are sentenced at their first, second, and third trials, and when they are executed. The remaining death happens every morning. When the wake-up bell rings, they ready themselves to die. If they receive rations and get exercise time, it means they are not dying that day. They say that if footsteps ring out in the hallway before the morning exercise, men on death row turn pale. But Yunsu looked like he had already been executed. To put it another way, because this stubborn old woman was the mother of his victim, he was already burning in the fires of hell. He was sitting right next to me, and I could see his chin quivering. For the first time, I understood that crime, like words once they are uttered, does not go away. It does not vanish like a breeze that swells and then disappears.

"I came to see you!" the old woman said.

Yunsu's shoulders were shaking. His entire body was trembling like a twig in a small breeze. A human being—that's all he was. It occurred to me that all of us, even murderers, must tremble and shake, and I felt a little sad.

"Since it's the holidays," Aunt Monica said, "she saved up some rice so she could make you rice cake."

Yunsu mumbled something with his head down.

"What was that?" asked Aunt Monica.

"It was a mistake," he said. "I'm sorry. I made a mistake."

I still think that human beings are a queer breed. Strictly speaking, the woman was the victim and Yunsu the attacker—and an attacker who had committed the worst crime one person can commit against another, at that—so there should have been no shame in him saying those words to her. But in that moment, I suddenly felt like Yunsu was the victim. At the same time, I thought about the man I had told my brother about when I was drunk, the one I had unearthed from my memory. Even when I imagined myself killing him, he was still my attacker. I did not feel even the slightest trace of sympathy for him. Yet I felt the pain that Yunsu was going through as someone who had attacked another person.

"I didn't know what kind of rice cake you like."

The old woman slowly stood up and unwrapped the cake. The soft, flimsy sound of the cloth coming undone seemed to echo like thunder in that room. When I took a closer look, her hands were shaking too hard to untie the knot. Officer Yi got up to help her. When the wrapper opened, we saw white *baekseolgi* in a nickel bowl. She picked up a piece of the rice cake, which she had cut into bite-size pieces, and turned to Yunsu to give it to him, but she collapsed back onto her chair instead. Her lips were trembling like his.

Officer Yi's eyes grew tense.

"Why did you do it?" she said. "Why? Why did you have to kill her? You bastard, you son of a bitch, you'll die for this!"

The expressions on our faces said that the moment we had all been dreading had finally happened, and Aunt Monica's turned to a look of regret. But there was nothing anyone could have done about it.

"Please, calm down." Aunt Monica got up and tried to restrain her. The woman's face had turned dark.

"How could you? You should have just taken the money and left her alone. Take the money, and let the person go. You can always make more money, but people don't come back from the dead. They never come back. Our lives are so short as it is. Don't take that time away from us."

The old woman started to cry. Her sobs turned to a wail. Clutching her crumpled handkerchief and the piece of rice cake that she had not managed to hand to Yunsu, she curled over until her small body was even smaller. It hit me then that she and Yunsu were wearing the same color. And they were both hunched over. It was a coincidence that her dress was that shade, but I found myself thinking that they were bound together by the same curse. Yunsu kept shaking. His hair looked as if it was glued to his forehead. He had broken into a cold sweat. If I had to use one of those clichés that I detest so much, I would say he was sweating buckets.

Officer Yi stood up. He looked as if he was planning to take Yunsu back to his cell.

"Wait. Please, just wait," the old woman said.

Officer Yi sat down again, looking uncertain. Aunt Monica tried to get the woman to drink some water. Despite her own distress, the woman kept saying, "I'm sorry, Sister. I'm so sorry." It was as if she had lived her whole life having to cater to others' feelings first. Apologizing seemed to be a reflex for her—I had no idea what on earth she was sorry about. The woman slowly sipped the water and looked at Yunsu. His face was wet from the sweat sliding down his temples, and both armpits were soaked. The woman lifted the handkerchief that was damp with her tears and tried to wipe the sweat from his face for him, but a shriek snuck out from between his clenched teeth. *That's right*, I thought. *That's the cry an animal makes when it's being dragged to the slaughterhouse.* A sad look stole over the woman's face. She closed her eyes for a moment and then slowly started talking again.

"I'm sorry. I came here to forgive you. Sister Monica told me it was too soon, but I was stubborn and came anyway. I'm sorry. I can't do it yet. I'm sorry, kid. When I look at you, I keep picturing my daughter, and I want to hate you. I couldn't sleep at all last night. I promised myself I wouldn't do this. I'm sorry. I want to grab you by the throat and ask why you did it. Why did you have to do it? Will you pray for me? Kid, you look so kind and handsome, and you keep trembling, which only makes it harder for me. But I'll come back. I will... until I'm ready to forgive you. It's a little far and the bus fare is expensive, so it won't be often, but I'll come back every holiday. I'll bring more rice cake. So you can't... die... yet."

She was shaking. Sweat was running down her face, too. During those few minutes, her hair seemed to have turned even whiter until her whole head was covered in gray. Aunt Monica also seemed to be ageing faster along with her for that brief moment.

"Sister, I'm sorry. I'm sorry to put you to all this trouble," the woman said, bowing her head again. Then she turned to the guard. "Sir, I apologize. I made such a fuss and caused you all so much bother."

Officer Yi was shocked. His face was contorted with misery. It was probably the first time in ten years of being a prison guard that he had witnessed something like this.

Yunsu got up to follow the guard. His head was still down. The old woman paused in the middle of wiping her tears with the crumpled handkerchief.

"Don't die yet," she said to Yunsu. "Not until I can forgive you!"

Yunsu's face was a mess of sweat and tears. As he turned and walked away, his limp was more pronounced than usual.

⚬══◯══⚬

"You've done enough," Aunt Monica said, clasping the old woman's hand. "You can't forgive him any more than that. Even the greatest person could not do better. You did so well. I'm a nun, and I could not have done that."

The old woman didn't say a single word on the drive back. She seemed to have retreated into a room of deep silence that she had built herself, and like any human being deciding whether to face themselves honestly before a grave undertaking, she bore a look of dignity and poise that had nothing to do with her appearance or education or anything like that. After today, she would go back to stooping over to collect empty bottles and old newspapers and adding 3,150 won or 2,890 won to her bankbook, and if she saw people who had a lot of money and they brought her a bag of rice or a package of meat, she would have no choice but to lower herself, but for now, her face had a glow more radiant than that of any empress. In contrast, Aunt Monica looked very ordinary sitting next to her. The woman had, as naïvely and fearlessly as a child, taken on the word that Jesus, the Son of God, had barely squeezed out in his final moments—*forgiveness*. She had failed as a person, and she knew that arrogance was the reason she had failed. But at that moment, in my mind, she was already crowned with the laurel wreath of a saint. It had nothing to do with her past or with her future. Had I ever seen that in another person? The people I knew never changed but just kept on living the same way they always had. Including Aunt Monica.

What on earth made this old woman who, in her own words, had no education, no faith, and knew nothing, try to forgive him? What sort of foolhardiness made her take on something that human beings have never gotten past, though a million theologians could shout until the veins popped out on their necks, and a million books could be published calling for people to *forgive, forgive*? Was it a kind of grand simplicity?

The following week was my final visit to the prison with Aunt Monica. The Lunar New Year had passed, and the weather was warming up as if spring were already on its way. Officer Yi tried three times to get Yunsu out of his cell, but he refused to see us. When he came back from his third trip to Yunsu's cell to try to convince him, he shook his head sadly.

"I think it would be better if you just go home for today. That last meeting must have been really hard for him to take. From what I've learned about him, he's a very simple guy. After you left last time, he refused to eat, and when the head guard checked on him, he was pretty sick. The day before yesterday, they took him to the infirmary and forced him to accept an IV. The registrar got mad at me, too. He said it was because I made him meet that old lady. They have him on a twenty-four-hour suicide watch now. I took some heat from my colleagues as well."

"I'm so sorry for the trouble we caused you. Has Yunsu started eating again?" Aunt Monica asked weakly. Officer Yi laughed.

"Yes, he's eating a little bit. First time I personally saw someone on death row go on a hunger strike. It was more common back when there were political dissidents who had violated the National Security Law. It's rare, now."

It wasn't until later that I realized the comedy of sticking an IV in someone sentenced to die in order to keep him from dying. I thought to myself, 'They saved him so they could kill him.'

First kiss the earth which you have defiled, and then bow down to all the world and say to all men aloud, "I am a murderer!"

– Fyodor Dostoevsky, a former death row convict,
spoken by Sonja in *Crime and Punishment*

BLUE NOTE 10

I was surprisingly relaxed when we were put in the juvenile detention centre. It seems strange to me now, but maybe that was because, at the time, I thought I would no longer have to rack my brain for ways for us to survive each day. Nor did I have to worry about where we would sleep. No more standing with Eunsu in ragged tennis shoes and no socks to elicit more sympathy from people getting off the subway, people who scattered in all directions in a mere second or two, leaving us to feel like every last person on earth had vanished and it was just Eunsu and I left behind in this empty world. No more thinking about how we had nowhere to go. No more getting up in the morning and worrying about what we were going to eat that day. And maybe, too, it was because I thought there would be others like us there, kids who had been abandoned by their mothers and beaten by their fathers. But as usual, my hopes betrayed me.

It happened our first night, when I went in holding Eunsu's hand, right after the warden finished roll call. The kids surrounded us. I was afraid because, once again, we were among the youngest ones. I was accustomed to fighting, but we were locked up in there, and I did not yet know how everything worked. There were those who gave orders and those who did their bidding. One of them pointed at Eunsu.

"I bet I could lift that runt with one finger. What do you think?"

The other kids snickered. I didn't know what he meant. In a flash, two boys grabbed my arms. I had a sinking feeling. One of the kids spread out a blanket and laid Eunsu down on it. The moment I tried to resist, their fists flew at me.

"Hey kid, calm down. The boss is only going to lift him up a little."

The kids pulled off Eunsu's pants. I had no idea what they were going to do to him. He was stretched out in front of them like a fish pulled from a tank. The one they called the boss proudly held up his forefinger and said, "One finger!" Eunsu, poor blind Eunsu, called out for me over and over. The boy put his finger on Eunsu's pepper and started rubbing it. As Eunsu called out to me, the vowels and consonants began to drop out of his voice. His pepper swelled and rose, and the hushed cheers from the kids egged it on. Splayed out in front of everyone, my thirteen-year-old brother's hips began to jerk up and down. Then a cloudy burst of semen shot from his pepper. He looked as if half of his body was off the ground. While the kids were busy snickering, I saw my opening and attacked the boss. I started strangling him without any warning. If the guards had not busted in just then and pulled me off of him, I might have killed him. I looked back as they were dragging me away to see a dazed-looking Eunsu staring into space with unfocused eyes, tears streaming down his face. I didn't mind taking a beating, and in fact I was used to taking one, but the thought of leaving my blind brother alone in that room with those animals made me crazy. And like an animal, I howled.

CHAPTER 10

My meetings with Yunsu ended without me singing the anthem for him. I told Aunt Monica, and myself, that school was starting again and I had too much to do. Aunt Monica looked hurt, but I decided I'd had enough.

But when Thursday rolled around again, I found myself waking up earlier than usual. The sky outside the window was overcast. I looked out and saw that it was snowing. It was a full blizzard. I wondered if Aunt Monica was having trouble getting to the prison. She had to take the subway to Indeogwon Station, transfer to a neighborhood bus, get off near the detention center, and walk the rest of the way. I wished my stubborn aunt would just take a taxi. What if she went all that way on a snowy day like this, and Yunsu refused to see her again? My head was so crowded with thoughts that I didn't even have my usual morning cup of freshly ground coffee. It had gotten much colder, so I turned up the heat and filled the bathtub.

I thought about the prisoners in the detention center—showering once a week for barely five minutes at a time, Yunsu's clothes drenched in cold sweat. I undressed and slowly got into the tub. All at once, I remembered something I had seen while living abroad. I had gone to a party at the house of a Korean friend who was studying in Germany. Playing on the television was a show about four women living together in a kind of row house. It looked like an ordinary house with two bedrooms and a small kitchen. Each of the rooms had a bunk bed, and the women were cooking and laughing. They smoked constantly, and they were even filmed doing their makeup. When my friend told me it was a prison, I couldn't believe my eyes. One of the people at the party took a swig of beer and said, *What kind of prison is that?* Someone else asked, *Isn't that the new model prison? No,* my friend said, *that's a regular prison.* Then, one of the women was shown being escorted to the door by a guard and going out. My friend explained that the woman visited her daughter once a month. *She's got a better life than we have,* someone said. The woman met her daughter, and they ate hamburgers and played with dolls. Then she returned to the prison. Someone else asked, *If our prisons were like that, wouldn't one out of three Koreans want to be put away?* The show cut to a scene of the woman crying after coming back from seeing her daughter. *Right now she's saying she doesn't want to be there anymore,* my friend translated. *She said she wants to hurry up and get out of there so she can go back to her loving family.*

Just then, the telephone rang. I wasn't going to answer it, but whoever it was seemed to have a lot of patience, as it showed no signs of stopping. I rushed out of the bathroom. To my surprise, it was Officer Yi from the Seoul Detention Center.

"I imagine you're surprised to hear from me. I got your number from Sister Monica. You had better come right away."

Even though I was concerned about Aunt Monica, the moment I heard the words *you had better come right away*, I felt annoyed and put off. Especially since I had just been relaxing in a warm tub. I asked what was wrong, and he hesitated before telling me.

"Sister Monica had a little accident. Nothing serious, but she seems to have slipped on the ice on the walk here. I tried to call her a taxi, but it's snowing really hard. I told her she should go to the hospital right away, but she insisted that I call you. If you show your ID at the front and wait for me there, I'll come get you."

I had no choice but to get dressed and leave. Spring was supposed to be on its way, but winter had launched a surprise attack. Luckily there were not many cars on the road.

I was normally an aggressive driver. I would slam on the brakes and pass other cars without a second thought. When I first started driving, truck drivers used to roll down their windows and shout things at me that I cannot bring myself to repeat. It was not that long ago, but even then, there weren't many female drivers on the road. Feeling as if I'd just had garbage dumped on my head, I would try to avoid making eye contact with them. It made me scared and angry. Sometimes, I would squeeze past other cars, barely avoiding a collision, and a strange pleasure would rush over me.

But that day, I drove very carefully. I didn't know how badly Aunt Monica was hurt, but I had a feeling that if something happened to me as well, everything would be ruined somehow. I knew, too, that it was the first time I had ever thought that way: *This car is on its way to transport the most precious passenger in the world. I can't be careless. Those men are relying on Aunt Monica. The half-hour that I can just shove in the garbage could be the last thirty minutes of their lives.* I realized that I was picturing Yunsu's face. I could see him covered with sweat and trembling. Though I didn't care about him, my heart ached when I pictured him. Was that the first time I'd ached like that and felt bad for anyone other than myself? I was gentle with the brakes and avoided overtaking anyone if I could help it. When other cars came racing up from behind with their blinkers on, I let them pass. I was in a hurry, but I reasoned with myself that the more impatient I felt, the more important it was to slow down. By the time I reached the detention center, my body was stiff. I realized then just how tense I had been the whole time I was driving.

I followed Officer Yi into the meeting room. Yunsu and Aunt Monica were sitting across from each other. Aunt Monica had a handkerchief wrapped around her veil. From another point of view, it could have been a comical sight: an elderly nun with a pink floral-print handkerchief tied over a black veil. On the back of her head, the blood had dried to a dark patch. She looked like a militant labor unionist who had gone on the attack. The first thought in my head was, *You win, Aunt Monica.* Then I laughed. When they saw me laughing, Yunsu and the guard laughed too. So did Aunt Monica. My eyes met Yunsu's for the first time. Without a moment's pause, I thought, *It feels good to laugh.* It seemed like the first time that Yunsu and I were meeting as two ordinary people. I saw that when he laughed, a dimple appeared in one cheek. At the same time, I could tell from the look in his eyes that he had been waiting for me. But I was more worried about Aunt Monica. When I touched the matted blood on the back of her head, she winced in pain. I let out a long sigh. She looked at me and told me to sit down. From the way they all waited impatiently for me to take my seat, it was obvious that I had interrupted them in the middle of an important conversation.

"Keep talking," Aunt Monica said.

"So I was thinking..."

Yunsu glanced at me as if my presence made him a little uncomfortable. I dropped my eyes. I did not enjoy feeling like an interloper. It was my original sin, the one I had committed by being born to a mother who already had three strong, beautiful sons. My mother said it was because of me that she'd had to stop performing on stage. Outside the barred window, a late snowstorm was turning the air white.

"I realized that you're not just here to try to fill up the church pews. I used to think that every word and every gesture from other people was meant to make fun of me and torment me, and that everyone was using me for their own personal gain. Since that was what I felt, all I thought about was not letting anyone take advantage of me. But now I know that the guards and the other prisoners—I mean, of course, there are still a few I can't stand—they aren't always thinking bad things about me. They've actually been very nice."

"I see. Well, it's true. Even when you were a bad guy, you weren't only thinking bad thoughts all the time."

I lifted my head. I wondered if you could really get away with calling a bad guy a bad guy, and I wanted to see how Yunsu would react. To my surprise, he was smiling. It wasn't a happy smile. It bore a trace of shame, but also the sense of respect or keenness that one feels when an archer's arrow has hit its mark dead-on. Officer Yi and I laughed.

"So what else did you realize?" Aunt Monica looked as if she was listening to the first monk in the world to ever reach enlightenment.

"For the first time, I thought maybe it was all in my head. Maybe I was the one who gave others a reason to treat me that way, because I thought others were bad and started those fights first. To my surprise, that made me feel better. And I also thought about that volunteer I told you about. The first time you grabbed my hand without asking, I was caught off guard, too. So maybe she wasn't looking at the inmate like he was a bug. Maybe she was just startled. Maybe I was just making things up the whole time."

Aunt Monica smiled brightly.

"I really enjoyed the book you sent me, *Greek and Roman Mythology*. At first, it was confusing because the names were so difficult, but once I got used to them, I was staying up all night to read it."

"Really? Who did you like best?"

"Orestes."

"Orestes? I don't quite remember him. You didn't like the stories about Zeus killing bad guys with wind and lightning?"

Yunsu smiled again.

"So why did you like Orestes?" she asked.

Yunsu hesitated a moment. He looked at me again, so I did my best to look like I was completely fascinated and couldn't wait for him to keep talking. That was when I noticed that his shackles had been changed to handcuffs. The prisoners called them "steel bracelets for your trip to hell."

"The other names were too hard. Orestes was some kind of a prince. His grandfather conspired to become more powerful than the gods, so the gods cursed Orestes' family for several generations. The first to receive the curse was Orestes' father, Aga—"

Yunsu hesitated.

"Agamemnon? Oh, so Orestes was the son of Agamemnon," said Aunt Monica.

"Yes, and Agamemnon was murdered by his wife, Orestes' mother. She and her lover had conspired to kill Agamemnon. Back then, according to the laws of the land, it was a son's duty to kill his father's murderer. So Orestes killed his mother for killing his father. But the Furies despised people who killed their own parents. The Furies started sending bad noises and visions to Orestes. All day long, he hallucinated about killing his mother and had to listen to the curses sent to him by the Furies, until finally he was nearly insane with guilt over killing her and wandered all over the world."

Yunsu paused in the middle of talking and glanced at me. I knew what he was doing. I knew he was doing his best to get on Aunt Monica's good side, and that he had practiced this story over and over again last night. At the time, I thought it was kind of pathetic and also comical. But in the light of memory, it strikes me now as sad.

"Apollo—he's the god of the sun, right?—he called a meeting with the other gods and defended Orestes. He said that Orestes had been cursed by the gods, and that they were being too cruel because his grandfather was the one who had sinned. Orestes never had any choice in the matter. Apollo said that since they had cursed him, it was up to them to forgive him. Orestes was there when this all happened. He looked at Apollo and said, 'What are you talking about? You're not the ones who killed my mother. I was!'"

Yunsu bowed his head.

Outside the barred window, the snow was still falling. When Yunsu lifted his head again, his eyes were bloodshot. He looked nervous. He swallowed and kept talking.

"I never wanted to be a god, but ever since I was a child, I wanted to be strong. If you're strong, you can do anything. You can kill all the bad guys. That was what I used to think. But then I met you. I wondered why a nun would bother to come to a place like this and cry and plead with someone like me. That old woman who came with you that day—I wouldn't have blamed her for killing me. But to see her cry and apologize for not being able to forgive me—I would rather hurry up and die than have to see that. If someone asked me if I would rather die or see her again, I would prefer to go to the gallows. If there is a God, then He has given me the worst punishment of all. Death doesn't mean anything to me. I'm not afraid of dying. I never was, not even when I was a little kid. But for the first time, I started thinking that maybe I had it all wrong. I used to think life wasn't fair, that my environment made me the way I was, that anyone would have done the same if they were in my shoes, and I wanted to say to everyone, *Let's see how well you do.* But Orestes—even though he only did what the gods made him do—he took the blame."

Yunsu stopped. Aunt Monica grabbed his cuffed hands and closed her eyes. She stroked the backs of his hands as she spoke.

"I'm so proud of you," she said. "That was a lot for you to think about. But you really gave it a lot of thought. I'm proud of you. Yunsu, those are wonderful thoughts."

Yunsu's face fell, and his bloodshot eyes filled with tears. He pressed his lips together and closed his eyes.

"I wanted to kill my father," he said. "My mother, too. I thought I was cursed. And as long as I believed that I was cursed, I wasn't afraid of anything. I thought I could end the curse by killing them all and then killing myself. Since I thought of it as ending a curse, I didn't feel any guilt. But now that you say you're proud of me..."

The snow was falling harder but made no sound. The world was very quiet.

"It makes me realize that I have never heard those words from an adult in my entire life. I felt really bad that you slipped and hurt yourself while coming all this way in such terrible weather. I thought to myself, *That must have been really painful.* Then I wondered if I had ever felt that way about someone else before. I don't think I have. Other than my little brother and the woman I was in love with, I've never, not even once, looked at another person and thought, *They must be hurting. I wish they weren't in so much pain.*"

Twenty-seven-year-old Yunsu bowed his head again. His tears fell onto the shiny metal handcuffs.

"But, Sister, the truth is, I'm terrified of what I'm feeling."

I don't believe in miracles. I rely on them to get me through each day.

– K

BLUE NOTE 11

Six months later, my brother and I left the juvenile detention centre. Parents came to take their children home. The children whose parents did not come went with siblings. The children whose siblings did not come formed groups and went their own way. Eunsu and I stood on the street in front of the centre until the sun went down and it was dark.

CHAPTER 11

Aunt Monica leaned back in her seat and didn't speak. The flurries had thinned out, but deep piles of snow lined the sides of the road. The snow that fell in the middle of the road had melted, and the streets were muddy.

"Let's go see your uncle. That's why I asked you to come. His place is hard to get to by public transportation. I would try to take the subway, but I look a fright. You're not busy, are you?"

"You need to go to a hospital. You might need stitches," I said curtly.

Since I had gone straight there without eating breakfast, I was hungry. When I saw Aunt Monica with her head wrapped up, I felt bad for her. I felt as bad for her as Yunsu did. It didn't make me feel any better to hear Yunsu say that it pained him to see her that way. But I couldn't express my feelings other than by being curt. I wasn't someone who cried.

"I've lived a full life. Who cares if I die? I will work until the day the Lord calls me to his side. If I had one wish, it would be to serve the people here until that day. Even if it means dying in the street, I will go happily."

"Die, die, die—all we've talked about since the New Year

is death. Ever since I started following you around, every-thing has been about death! Are you God? Why are you trying to do what even God himself can't? Like that guy said—Yunsu or whatever his name is—do you think you can save them from being executed? If you die trying, you'll only make it worse for them. I hate that. Just the thought of it gives me the shivers."

To my surprise, I was on the verge of tears. I was flustered by these emotions that I didn't understand, and I hated revealing them to Aunt Monica. She didn't say anything. I thought about what Yunsu had said: *I used to think life wasn't fair, that my environment made me the way I was, that anyone would have done the same if they were in my shoes, and I wanted to say to everyone, 'Let's see how well you do.' But Orestes—even though he only did what the gods made him do—he took the blame.* I should have been the one saying that. *I've never, not even once, looked at another person and thought, 'They must be hurting. I wish they weren't in so much pain.'* When I heard him say that, something in me responded. But actually, I did once wish for someone not to be in pain. Shimshimi, who died of old age when I was in middle school. The Jindo dog who was so docile we named him Shimshimi. My brothers told me that eight in dog years was eighty in human years, but when he was dying, I prayed: *Please, no pain. Let him die without any pain.* And I meant it. I was afraid Aunt Monica would notice that I was getting emotional, so I reverted to my old tactics.

"He sure sounded convincing. How can you tell whether he meant it or not? Maybe he thinks he'll be taken off of death row if he can get people to campaign for him. But I don't trust him. It was too fast. Same with that old lady. You're all so gullible. *Forgive and repent, forgive and repent...* That's what I hate the most about Christianity.

You do all the bad things you want and then go to church and say you're sorry, and presto! What hypocrites!"

Aunt Monica kept her eyes shut and didn't say anything for a moment.

"Yujeong," she said slowly. "I don't hate hypocrites."

That wasn't what I had expected her to say.

"When it comes to the people that we think are great—pastors, priests, nuns, monks, teachers, and so on—a lot of them are hypocrites," she said. "I could very well be the biggest hypocrite of all. But being a hypocrite means that the person at least has a sense of what it means to be good. Deep down inside, they know that they are not as great as they pretend to be. That's true whether they are aware of it or not. So I don't hate those people. I think that if you can live your whole life without letting anyone other than yourself know that you're a hypocrite, then that's a successful life. The people I hate are the ones who pretend to be mean. They think they can treat others poorly on the outside while still regarding themselves as more or less good on the inside. At the same time that they act mean, deep down, they're hoping others will realize they're good people. They're more arrogant and more pathetic than hypocrites."

I stupidly wondered if her words were directed at me. I didn't ask. But I felt overcome with shame, as if a private scar that I did not want revealed had been uncovered. I passed a van in front of us. As the car lurched back into the lane, Aunt Monica grabbed for the overhead handle.

"There's another group I hate even more, though," she continued. "That's people who think there are no moral standards at all. People who think everything is relative, who think fair is fair, who think in terms of self versus other. Of course, some things are relative, but one thing is not: human life is sacred. When we forget that, we all die. No matter what, death is never a good thing. Wanting to live is an instinct engraved in the genes of every living thing. When someone says they want to die, what they really mean is, *I don't want to live this way*. And not wanting to live a certain way really means wanting to live well. So instead of saying that we want to die, what we should say is that we want to live well. We shouldn't talk about death because the meaning behind the word life is a command to live."

A command to live? Whose command? Who would order such a thing? And who does he think he is? I wanted to ask Aunt Monica that, but I couldn't speak.

"Sometimes when I think about you, and I could be wrong on this, I think maybe you're only pretending to be bad. It really worries me. My heart aches. Being good doesn't mean being stupid. Feeling pity doesn't mean being soft. Crying for others, hurting because you think you did something wrong—whether or not that's sentimentality— is a good and beautiful thing. Giving your heart to others and getting hurt is not something to be ashamed of. People who speak the truth get hurt, but they also know how to overcome. I've been around a lot longer than you, and this is what I've come to realize."

I almost said, *Yeah, yeah, I know*. It was what I used to say to the psychiatrists who tried to treat me. My uncle had said, *That's right, Yujeong, you know everything. I know you've read a lot of psychology books on your own. But Yujeong, knowing doesn't mean a thing. Sometimes knowing is worse than not knowing. The important thing is realizing. If there is a difference between knowing and realizing, it's that you have to hurt in order to realize.* I said to him, *I'm tired of hurting*. I must have laughed at him then.

We didn't say anything the rest of the way to my uncle's

hospital. When we got there, there was a woman and a little boy waiting in the lobby. The boy seemed to be around ten years old, and the woman looked like she was his mother. When we came in the door, the woman, who had just been threatening to hit the boy, looked happy to see Aunt Monica and rushed over to us. The moment I saw the boy, an eerie feeling came over me. I didn't know what that feeling was. But when I saw the mother and child together, a chill ran down my spine. Looking back on it later, I thought it was because of the mother's unfocused pupils and the scars that covered the boy's hands and face. But no. That wasn't it. It was the boy's restlessness. As if he couldn't set his feet down anywhere in the world. There was something about his presence that troubled me, that seemed to say, *I do not know what I am thinking or where I am or even who or how old I am.* I couldn't tell yet what was wrong with him. The boy's hands were covered with scars, and he kept kicking the chair legs.

"I don't know why my kid has to come here, but they told me at the police station that I have to bring him, so I did. Hey, Sister, what happened to your head?"

The woman, who had a short perm and kept chewing her gum while she talked, suddenly laughed at the sight of the handkerchief tied around Aunt Monica's head. There was something about the way she talked that didn't quite make sense.

"It's just a simple check-up, so it'll only take a moment. Has he been sleeping well?" I could tell Aunt Monica was trying to avoid the woman's curiosity.

"No. Sometimes he screams all night and doesn't sleep a wink. He says that girl shows up in his dreams and says, *You killed me.*"

Aunt Monica looked at the boy and sighed. He had stopped kicking the chair legs and was now sitting upside down on the chair. After a while, the nurse called the child in. I sat in the waiting room while Aunt Monica took the boy into my uncle's office. Nurses with familiar faces nodded at me as they passed by. They smiled brightly at me; in an instant, my mood soured. I wondered what they were thinking about me. Maybe they had all snuck a peek at my chart. I remembered the nurses whispering about me the last time I was hospitalized. A nurse who was changing my IV thought I was asleep and whispered to another nurse: *If she attempted suicide three times and didn't die, doesn't that mean she's just pretending?* At least, I was sure that's what she said.

As Aunt Monica said, just because someone is bad doesn't mean they only think bad thoughts, and the nurses probably weren't thinking that every time they looked at me, but I still felt like getting up and leaving.

"What're you here for? Counseling?" the boy's mother asked me while slowly chewing her gum.

I didn't especially feel like talking to her, but I said yes. Since I would have to talk to my uncle when I saw him, it wasn't that far from the truth.

"You came with that nun?" she asked again. She looked as if she could barely contain her curiosity.

Of the things I had noticed upon returning to Korea after seven years abroad, my least favorite was the way people here thought nothing of prying into other people's private lives, as if they were interviewing them for marriage. They would start with *Are you married? Why aren't you married?* and move on to *So what do you do for a living?* Every time someone asked me those questions, I wondered whether they knew why they were doing it, why they got married, why they had kids, why they were here. I didn't say anything, so the woman kept talking.

"I really don't understand why my kid has to go to a

psychiatrist. But the nun and the police kept telling me to bring him, so here I am. How are people without cars supposed to get to this place?"

I could tell that she wanted to start complaining about how far away the hospital was and how there was no public transportation, as if she wanted me to agree with her. I couldn't stand women like her who had no sense of tact, and I did not respond. She laughed again.

"You're so quiet! Say, how many kids does that nun have?" It didn't seem as if she could control her nosiness.

"Excuse me?"

"She's old, so her kids must be all grown up. Wait, what am I talking about? She must have grandchildren by now."

I frowned unconsciously. We may not live in a Catholic country, but surely everyone knew that priests and nuns didn't marry, just as Buddhist monks didn't marry. To be honest, I was a little shocked. I caught myself wondering if she had even made it through grade school.

"I barely managed to get away from the restaurant today, but I have to get back before the dinner rush. The owner's father-in-law had a stroke a few days ago. It's already his third, but that old man just won't die."

The woman started babbling. She didn't seem to care who she was talking to, or whether that person even wanted to talk to her or not. She didn't even seem to know what she was saying. In fact, she seemed to forget that she was talking at all the moment she opened her mouth. Since I would not respond, she jumped up, hitched up her pants to keep them from sliding down, and started pacing back and forth. While her back was turned, I quietly got up and went into my uncle's office. That crazy woman probably wouldn't notice I was gone.

My uncle was sitting across from the little boy, and Aunt Monica was next to them. The boy was squirming in his seat, not resting his eyes anywhere for a moment. If the boy's mother was the type who couldn't keep her mouth still, then the boy was the type who couldn't keep his body still. They resembled each other.

"So, you stole a thousand won?" my uncle asked the boy.

"Yes."

"But you really just wanted to take the money and go, right?"

The boy yawned.

"Why did you hit her?"

"I thought she would tell."

"Tell who?"

The boy started squirming again. He looked over at me. His constant fidgeting reminded me of a butterfly caught in a spider's web. Just like the first time he had looked at me, his eyes passed right over me without any sign of emotion.

"When you hit her, didn't you think it would hurt her?"

"No!" The boy picked up a cushion from the sofa and abruptly asked, "Who bought this? Was it expensive?"

My uncle sighed.

"You promised you would behave while we talk, didn't you?"

"Then hurry it up!" the boy yelled.

A troubled look passed over my uncle's face.

"Did you know that if you kept hitting her like that, she would die?" he asked.

For the first time, the boy stopped moving and shook his head weakly.

"You were just trying to scare her and make it so she wouldn't tell anyone, right?"

"Yes," the boy said flatly.

"So what did you do with the thousand won?"

"I bought a pastry."

"Did it taste good?"

"Yes."

My uncle's face went blank for a moment, and then he grabbed the boy's scarred hands. The skin looked pockmarked, and the tips of his fingers were red with blood. How did he get all of those scars? Even if I could have guessed where the scars came from, I did not understand the bloodstains on his fingertips. Later, I found out that he had a habit of scratching the walls until his fingers bled.

"Who hits you more? Your mom or your dad?"

"Dad!"

"Who hits you worse?"

"Dad... I'm done now."

My uncle looked upset. The boy jumped up and went out the door. Aunt Monica tried to stop him, but he was already gone. She followed him out to the lobby.

"He killed someone?" I asked. "That little boy killed someone?"

"Yes, he killed a four-year-old girl who lived next door to him. So he could steal a thousand won. The law can't do anything to kids under fourteen years of age. But they don't provide any treatment or custody either. In a word, it's negligence. So your Aunt Monica has been looking after kids like him."

We were both quiet for a moment. An eleven-year-old boy beat a four-year-old girl to death. So he could steal a thousand won to buy a pastry. And he said it tasted good—the end! *Just how far down can this society go?* I wondered. *And how deep are we now?* I didn't understand why these problems that I had never noticed or paid any attention to before were all coming up at once. The cynicism and meanness that I performed so well, but that Aunt Monica hated, was not working for me here. I felt like I was the one caught in the spider's web, not that little boy.

Aunt Monica came back in. She and my uncle looked at each other for a moment as if they were old friends, and then they both laughed at the same time. They sounded dumbfounded. They were like two powerless people looking at each other and thinking, *What the hell are we going to do?*

My uncle sighed and changed the topic to my aunt's head injury.

"That cut looks deep. At the very least, you should let us bandage you up before you go."

"Don't worry. I'll have it looked at later. There's a hospital near the convent. But what are you going to do about that boy? God's looking after my head, so I think I can still use it even if it's bleeding. But the one who really needs to have his head fixed is that little boy."

"He does need treatment. His whole family does. He needs to go to a child psychiatrist and get medication, not just counseling. Otherwise, I really don't know what will happen. What are the cops in this country thinking? Or rather, what are the lawmakers thinking? How can they just send kids like that back home? The kids are like that because their families are like that, so how can they say the kids are too young for treatment and send them back to their parents? When that happens in the United States, the parents and the child have to show proof that they received psychiatric care. It's really dangerous. The boy needs treatment, first of all. That's a given. But also, if the state can treat that child right away, the rest of us won't have to pay so dearly for it later."

Aunt Monica took a look at my uncle's scrawled chart.

"Do you mean it's pretty likely that he'll become a criminal?"

"Not just pretty likely. More like a ninety-nine percent chance."

My uncle stood up and went to the window. Then he started talking, but it wasn't to either of us in particular.

"They're the same. They're all the same. All over the world."

He sounded angry, as if even he didn't know whom exactly he was addressing.

"Behind every person who's committed an unimaginable crime is an adult who committed unimaginable violence against them as a child. All of them, as if it was plotted that way. Violence begets violence, and that violence begets more violence. No one ever says, 'Sure, I could use a good beating,' when their parents threaten to 'smack some sense into them.' I mean it when I say that violence has never stopped violence. I swear! Not once in human history."

A look of despair passed over my uncle's face, and I realized it was the first time I had ever seen him so angry and discouraged.

"Uncle, do you think some kids are just born bad? Like an evil gene, as some people say."

I was not yet over the shock of hearing that an eleven-year-old had killed someone, and then hearing that child say the pastry they bought afterward was delicious.

"No, absolutely not!" my uncle said testily. I had never seen him that tense before.

"Here's the thing about people. We're not born fully made. Colts and calves are fully made while in their mothers' bellies, so they can already run by the time they come out. But humans are born and then made. It usually takes three years. Lately, there is even a theory that says it takes eighteen years. So, to put it in simple terms, God makes seventy percent of the person, and the parents fill in the remaining thirty percent—the rest has to be completed. But that thirty percent, it leads the other seventy percent. If we compare it to computers, that thirty percent is the operating system. But when the brains of people who were abused as children are scanned, five to ten percent of the brain is damaged. It's as if, from the time they were children, they've been driving cars with damaged engines. They cannot control their impulses with that kind of damage. But it doesn't affect the intelligent parts, their intellect. That's why serial killers can have high IQs and be very logical. Ultimately, they are mentally ill people who have not yet been proven to be mentally ill."

"But not being able to control their impulses doesn't mean they always hurt other people, right?" Aunt Monica asked.

"Right. In these cases, the most typical symptom is insensitivity to others' pain. In other words, their ability to empathize is noticeably diminished."

"Ability to empathize?" Aunt Monica asked.

"Yes, when we see someone fall in the street or get injured, we think, *That must have hurt*. But they're not able to do that. In other words, they lack the ability to feel what other people are feeling. They become insensitive to other people's pain."

"So beating a child can lead to such terrible consequences?" Aunt Monica asked. My uncle paused.

"There are several types of abuse. Physical abuse—in other words, violence—is the main type. Then there's sexual abuse, emotional abuse, and neglect. To give you an example, neglect means not feeding the child when he or she is hungry, not changing the diaper when it needs to be changed, withholding physical contact when the child needs to be held, and so on. As for emotional abuse, that can mean acting coldly, not being loving... It's *all* abuse. This is quite painful to talk about..."

My uncle sighed again.

"There was a seventeen-year-old boy who used to come

see me not long ago. He had stabbed a middle-school girl who walked by him one day. Do you remember him? He said the girl looked happy. He thought, *Why do you get to be happy when I am so unhappy?* and he stabbed her with a knife. His mother and father showered him with love. But his father beat his mother every day. Seeing that was worse than being tortured. That, too, is a form of abuse. They don't have the ability that we have to control their impulses with reason. And they can't just overcome it using willpower. How can you have will-power when your brain has been damaged? So, as a result, they're impulsive. They become addicted to alcohol, gambling, sex... They resort to violence or murder, or commit suicide."

My face must have turned pale. My uncle looked at me as if he'd said something he shouldn't have. I didn't say anything.

"Of course, I don't mean that they all become crim-inals. Sometimes it has no effect on their social lives. It has nothing to do with their educational level, either. The people we went to school with all came out of top-tier high schools and universities, but when you see them, there are a lot of broken people. They get by just fine only to go home and beat their wives and kids. Those people are—"

My uncle jokingly circled his index finger next to his head.

"Even if they're lucky and don't commit any crimes, their kids can wind up with problems."

He rubbed his face with both hands.

"But Dr. Choi," interrupted Aunt Monica. She had been listening intently. "Some people are beaten as children and grow up in brothels, and they still turn out to be great people. You're not saying that they're all impulsive and prone to crime, are you?"

"No, of course not. It's like a virus. The same illness can be going around, but only some people catch it while others are fine. Human behavior cannot be explained through a single cause."

"Then, can't a brain that is damaged like that ever recover? Medically speaking, I mean." She sounded as if she was pleading with a doctor who had just diagnosed her own child with cancer.

"That depends on the extent of the damage." He pointed to an orchid on the windowsill. "When I went on vacation, that little guy withered. As soon as I gave him water, he sprang back to life. But if I went away for three years, it wouldn't matter how much water I gave him when I got back. Sister, you have religion. If I were ten years younger, I would have adamantly said that recovery was impossible. Back then, I would have cited hundreds of reasons. But now that I'm old, my thoughts have changed. In a word, I am no longer certain. Things I cannot explain are always happening around us. Sometimes, I think that there are more things that cannot be explained through so-called science or so-called medicine. Human beings are truly mysterious, and only the universe knows the answer. I think that for humans, there are more times when love alone can cure them. But that leaves us with the problem of what love is... It seems this conversation has taken a philo-sophical turn. Or perhaps a religious one. Sister, be strong. You are showing them great kindness."

Aunt Monica looked dizzy. I asked if she was okay, but she seemed lost in thought and did not answer me.

We went back to the lobby. That strange mother and her son were waiting for us. When she saw us, she started babbling again.

"Sister, there aren't any buses around here. I have to get back to the restaurant right away. You know, the owner's father-in-law collapsed of a stroke. It's the third time. But all he ever does is collapse. He refuses to die..."

"Okay, let's go," Aunt Monica said, cutting the woman off. Then she said to me, "I need your help one last time. Let's give her a ride home."

Aunt Monica turned to look at the boy. I followed suit. He was still climbing up and down on the chairs and kicking them. In the past, I would have thought the child wasn't even human. In the past, I would not have deigned to meet or even look at a child who had already committed murder at the age of eleven, a child who said the pastry he bought afterward was delicious. But now, I couldn't help but think that maybe he and I were suffering from the same disease. Maybe we shared the same handicap, with different causes but identical damage. For once, I did not think of myself as a woman who was a painter and a college professor, who thought she was good enough for a snobby lawyer to want her, but rather as a brain-damaged patient who was grue-some and unfocused and talked too much, like that scarred child. I thought, *Maybe I really am a worthless person*, and I got goose bumps. Like Yunsu, I was terrified of what I was feeling.

But what right had I to these highest joys, when all around me was nothing but misery and struggle for a mouldy bit of bread?

— Kropotkin

BLUE NOTE 12

Eunsu and I returned to Yeongdeungpo. Blackie was still managing the kids. We went back to the subway stations and open-air markets to panhandle. Every time I passed the corner shop, I stood outside and glared at the owner who had accused us of stealing. I thought, *I'll get him one of these days.* When I was strong enough, I would make him beg and plead for mercy, just as I had, and when that happened, I would look at him coldly and give him hell, just as he had done to me. If I had one reason to stay alive, it was to get revenge.

Then one day, Eunsu got sick. He had a high fever and couldn't eat anything. I even bought him the cup ramen that he loved so much, but he couldn't eat it. I had no choice but to stay off the streets for several days so I could take care of him, and we did not bring in any money. The day his fever broke, Eunsu opened his eyes and called out to me. 'Yunsu! The person who's singing right now. I bet she's pretty. Isn't she?' I looked at the television playing in that tiny room. Blackie had put us in his own room for fear the other kids would catch Yunsu's cold. It was the opening ceremony for baseball, and a woman in a miniskirt and a baseball cap was singing the national anthem. I said, 'Yeah, I guess she's pretty.' Eunsu asked, 'As pretty as our mom?' Feeling annoyed, I said yes without thinking about it. But then Eunsu started to cry. I knew why he was crying, but I cussed him out anyway and kicked him and punched him even though he was sick. He cried even louder and said, 'I won't cry anymore, Yunsu! I won't cry!'

I stopped hitting him and left the house. I joined up with some street kids I'd met once and passed the time drinking with them and avoiding going back to Eunsu and Blackie. I felt like punching and smashing everything. It was as if I had to knock out everyone I saw on the street—a mom holding hands with her kid, lovers walking side by side, students dressed in school uniforms. I wanted to beat the hell out of anyone and everyone who looked happy. Then I decided to pick a fight with a man who was walking down the street with a woman. I started it by saying, 'Why are you looking at me like that?' I was arrested again, and they let me out after several days. Blackie was furious. When he saw me, he told me to take Eunsu and get lost. 'Damn it,' I said, 'if you want us gone, then we'll leave.'

I went to find Eunsu. While I was gone, he had wasted away to skin and bones, and his face had shrunk to half its size. My heart sank. Blackie acted like he was mad at me, but the truth was that he had sensed something about Eunsu and was trying to get rid of us. I picked up Eunsu and carried him on my back.

It was a spring night. The smell of flowers had spread all over the city, even to our sewer of a neighborhood. The weather felt warm enough for us to be able to sleep in an underground passageway with only a few sheets of newspaper and not freeze to death. Eunsu grabbed my hand just like he used to when we were little, when we used to spread our blankets out on the floor and lie down side by side. 'I'm so glad you came back,' he said. Then he asked me to sing the national anthem for him again. I won't feel as cold if you sing it for me. I told him to go to sleep. He said okay. I was unable to sleep at first and tossed and turned for a while. Finally, I wrapped my arm around him so he wouldn't get cold. But when I awoke at dawn, Eunsu was dead.

CHAPTER 12

I typed in the words *capital punishment* and hit Enter. Countless documents and articles popped up. The first result said, *Capital punishment is the highest penalty as it deprives a criminal of life and permanently removes them from society.* Next to the computer was Yunsu's letter. It read:

The mountains have changed color. Everything is the same, but it all looks tinted yellow, and I can feel the air changing. I guess spring is here. I wondered whether I would see another spring. For all I know, this could be my last spring. But I also can't help thinking that this is the very first spring of my life.

I pictured him writing the letter one word at a time with his hands cuffed. Then I pictured the little boy with the scarred hands. As I moved the cursor over the words *highest penalty*, I kept thinking about how Yunsu cried when he told us the story of Orestes.

If someone asked me if would rather die or see her again, I would prefer to go to the gallows. If there is a God, then he has given me the worst punishment of all. Death doesn't mean anything to me. I'm not afraid of dying. I never was, not even when I was a little kid. I kept thinking about what Yunsu had said, and how he had told us at our very first meeting that he feared mornings the most.

I opened another link: *Origins of the Death Penalty.* According to one amusing article, England used to be crawling with pickpockets, so they were executed in public to discourage the practice. People gathered like clouds to watch these executions, and other pickpockets made a fortune off of them. There was another article that said 164 of the 167 death row prisoners incarcerated at Bristol Prison in England until 1886 were executed in public. The United States, as well, held public executions up until the end of the 1930s. Of the world powers, the United States produced the highest number of death row inmates after China.

I went to the kitchen to top off my coffee and looked out the window for a moment. Just as Yunsu had described in his letter, the hills behind the apartment building where I lived were tinged with yellow.

The letter continued:

After you left, I had a dream. Maybe it's because my little brother died in the spring, but every year at this time, he shows up in my dreams. He got sick once when we were very young. I remember running to buy him medicine. Back then, the whole world had turned pale green—why did that color seem so sad? Yesterday, I prayed before going to sleep. If I saw my brother in my dreams again, I was going to tell him that I met the pretty singer who sang the anthem he loved so much, the one about whom he asked if she was as pretty as our mom, and I was going to say that she is now a wonderful college professor. My little brother would probably have said, See? I told you she would be pretty and wonderful. But last night, for the first time in a long time, I slept well without dreaming. I read the book you sent me. I didn't know books could be so interesting. Lately all I do is read all day. Maybe that's why I miss you. I know you're busy, but I wish you would come by some time with Sister Monica. I hope that's not too forward of me to say.

It looked like the shaky handwriting of an adolescent boy trying to impress a female teacher that he has a crush on. I could tell I was getting sentimental about the fact that he was a man facing death. I shook my head. This was not a good sign. My heart felt like it was bubbling over, like it was filled with soda water. Over the last few days, whenever I was driving somewhere, I kept catching myself thinking about him. I stared blankly out the window. Since he had gone to the trouble of writing me a letter in handcuffs, I had no choice but to write back. But I had no idea what to write. I couldn't exactly say, *So, you were suicidal? What a coincidence. So was I.*

While I was standing at my kitchen window sipping coffee, I saw something strange happening in the park behind the apartment complex. There was a circle of teenagers, around twenty of them, a little too big to be middle-school students, but a little too small to be in high school. Curious as to what they were doing, I took a closer look and saw that they had another teenager surrounded and were beating him up. Even from the fifteenth floor, I could see that his face was covered in blood. An eerie feeling came over me, and my heart started to race. When one of the kids was done punching him, another would step forward and start punching him again. I remembered that I had seen other kids gang up like that and fight in the park from time to time. I think I had also seen fliers posted in the elevator stating that the neighborhood association had passed a resolution and asked the police to increase security in the park behind the complex. In the past, I would have been indifferent to something like that, but not anymore. I felt scared, as if I were witnessing a murder. I picked up the phone and dialed 112 for the police. My family had had to dial 119 for medical emergencies several times because of me, but it was the first time in my entire life that I had ever dialed 112. I heard a voice on the other end.

"Hello? Hello, I'm calling from, um, Gangnam-gu in Seoul—"

"Yes, Seoryeon Apartments?" The operator cut in as I was stammering, trying to figure out what to say. I thought to myself, *Wow, Korea's emergency services are really advanced.*

"Yes, hello, uh, there are some teenagers beating up another kid on the hill behind building Number 109. He looks like he's bleeding."

I took the phone to the window in the kitchen and looked out again. The kid was on the ground.

"He's fallen! Please come quickly!"

"Yes, ma'am."

The operator hung up. I looked at the clock. It was 3:48 pm.

I felt a little bad about the mean things I had said about Korea after returning from abroad. Once, while arguing with a man I had lived with in Paris, I had screamed at him in the street. Not five minutes went by before a police officer came over and grabbed him by the arm. I was shocked, as was the man I'd been arguing with.

The officer asked me, *Mademoiselle, is this man bothering you? Shall I take him down to the station?*

Oh, no, we said. *We were just joking around.*

That's how I remember our fight ending. Someone had looked out their window and reported it, and the officer got the call and was dispatched. The swiftness of it shocked us, and we said, *Let's not tell anyone we're Korean,* and went back into the café for a drink.

Feeling anxious, I stood and watched out the window. Several minutes had passed since the kid had fallen, but he still wasn't getting up. I thought, *What if he dies?* Several of the kids picked him up and started helping him out of the park. Since the fight was over, the police would not be much use even if they did show up. But then two of the kids grabbed another kid by the arms and led him into the circle. It looked like they were dragging a condemned criminal to an execution ground. Another kid stepped forward and began beating him. I checked the road and the path right in front of the apartment building, but the police were not yet on their way. I couldn't even hear any sirens. When I checked the clock, it was past four. I dialed 112 again.

"Hello? I called a moment ago. The kid who was bleeding is gone, and now they're beating up another kid. Why aren't you here yet?"

"Yes, thank you, we're on the way."

They hung up again. This time, the kid who was getting beat up looked like he was putting up some resistance. Several kids surrounded him and, all at once, they started beating him at the same time. He flopped to the ground, and they started kicking him. Like a flock of vultures surrounding a dying animal, the kids would not get off him. I looked at the clock. It was 4:15 pm. The police still had not arrived. My heart would not stop racing, and I felt like I might throw up. It was as though the child's despair was being transmitted directly to me. The police showed no sign of arriving. I paced around the room, and then out of some sort of stubborn pride I dialed the number again.

"I'm the person who called a while ago. Why aren't you here yet? A kid is getting beat up. They have him surrounded and are kicking him. He's already on the ground, and they're kicking him! This is the second kid."

"Yes, ma'am."

The operator hung up again. I went back to the kitchen window. Two kids had picked up the boy who was on the ground and were holding him up by the arms while another kid did a flying kick into the exhausted boy's stomach, like something straight out of the movies. My entire body reacted to the boy's pain. My teeth started chattering, and I felt like I was being tortured. The police did not come; my telephone rang instead.

"Hello?"

"Hello."

"Did you report a crime in progress? This is the police."

South Korea's emergency hotline system is indeed amazing, I thought stupidly. *They even know the phone numbers of the people who call in crimes.*

"Why aren't you here yet? If you'd gotten here sooner, you could have stopped the first kid from getting beaten up. Now they've moved on to a second kid! A bunch of them are ganging up on one kid. You have to stop them. Please hurry."

"Listen, we're on our way to a three-car collision at the Gangnam intersection. So we're going to be a little late. We'll be there as soon as we can, so please stop calling."

The police officer sounded like a friendly car repairman. He was explaining his tardiness and asking for my understanding. Meanwhile, the kid was nearly unconscious. I looked at the clock. It was 4:20 pm. I calmed myself down by saying, "Viva la Korea." After a while, I heard a siren. I waited with my fists clenched for the police to hurry up and punish those bad kids. Several of the kids left the park to stand guard. The strong circle they had formed started to come apart. They, too, had heard the siren. The phone rang again.

"This is the police. The park is empty."

"Where are you?"

"The park at Seoryeon Apartments."

"Do you mean you're in the little park inside the complex?"

I hurried to the front window. The apartment complex had a fountain and a small marble-paved park.

Out front, a police car was parked with its siren wailing. In the toddler playground with its swings and slide, women pushing baby strollers were crowding around and staring at the police car.

"Officer, what kind of madman would be beating someone up in a children's playground in an apartment complex where there are guards on duty? I didn't mean that park. I said the hill behind building Number 109!"

"Lady, why are you yelling at me?" the officer said. "I got it now."

After a moment, the phone rang again. It was the officer.

"Are cars allowed on that hill? I don't see a road."

Before, he had sounded like a car repairman, but now he sounded like an unfriendly removals man. I suppressed the emotions that were welling up inside of me and responded like a friendly operator.

"Park behind building Number 109 and walk up the hill. Please hurry!"

I went back to the kitchen window. At least the police had showed up. They were here now, and no more children would be hurt. A group of kids were standing in formation, like they were discussing something, and then several of them took the blood-covered boy with them and took off on a path through the woods. Their timing was like something out of a script. The police were slowly making their way toward them. They looked like they were out for a walk. Since I was up on the top floor, it felt strange to be looking down on them from the sky, like I was a god or something. The phone rang again.

"Lady, we checked out the area. But no one seems to be hurt."

"What? So?"

I could longer keep my voice calm.

"I asked, and the kids said they were having a middle-school reunion. I ordered the kid who was beat up to step forward, but no one did. If none of them were beat up, then none of them could have been beating up anyone either."

I exploded with rage. I could not think of how to respond to him.

"You asked the kid who was beat up to step forward? Did you also ask the one who was doing the beating to step forward? I guess I made a mistake. It was wrong of me to expect anything from the police in this country. It's already been over thirty minutes since I placed the call. That's enough time for two or three people to die!"

I slammed the phone down hard. I wondered if I would have let them off the hook that easily if it were my son or little brother getting beat up. The phone rang again. The officer seemed to be calling back. I felt like the young Rastignac mumbling at the top of the hill in the final scene of Balzac's *Le Père Goriot*, except instead of saying to the city of Paris, "Henceforth there is war between us," I was saying it to the police.

"Hello?"

"This is the police. Lady, what are you so mad about? We didn't do anything wrong. I'm going to speak now, so listen up. We weren't late because we wanted to be. A handicapped guy fell into Yangjae Stream today. We were late because we had to go fish him out and take him back home. And the kids here said they were just playing. That's what they told me. I don't know what kind of world you think this is, but what were you expecting? For me to torture a confession out of them?"

He made it sound like I was the unreasonable one. It seemed as if he was pleading with me, saying that I didn't understand his job, that there was so much to do and so few people to do it, and that he worked and worked but there was never any end. I felt like muttering, *We got a real comedian here*, but my anger rose.

"Do the police usually get permission from citizens before torturing confessions out of people?" I said. "Is that what you've done so far? If I asked you to now, would you do it?"

"You know we can't."

I laughed. I couldn't help but laugh.

"The very least you could do is teach those kids that they can't just beat someone up in broad daylight, at least not out in the open like that right in the middle of the day in a residential area. That's your duty. We're the grown-ups, so we at least have to tell them that it's not okay. When those kids grow up, they'll commit even bigger crimes and wind up on death row!"

"Who do you think you are? I guess you think that every time someone does something wrong it's the police's fault? You really don't get it."

This time, he was the one to slam down the phone. To him, the only thing that had come of this incident was that I just didn't get it. I wondered if I had gone too far, but then just as quickly I wondered why I had gotten so upset in the first place. I never used to care about anyone, except for our dog Shimshimi when I was in middle school.

The comment about death row was definitely going too far. I sat down at my desk. This was not at all like me. The first thing I had noticed after returning from seven years abroad was the coarse way in which Koreans talked to each other. The words they used had become harsher, and people walked faster on the street. If someone stepped on your foot in the subway, or slammed into your shoulder as they were passing by, they would stare straight ahead and not apologize. I used to get angry because I thought they were being rude, but later I realized that I had stopped noticing anymore when someone bumped into me or stepped on my foot. Everyone was in a hurry to get somewhere. But to where? Neither they nor I had any idea. In the movies, every other word was a cuss word, and though they were well made, they were filled with such cruel scenes that I had to turn my eyes away. I couldn't look, even when the actors were so attractive that I wouldn't have minded dating them. Nevertheless, the newspapers crowed about the fact that Korean movies were drawing international attention.

I missed Aunt Monica. I also thought about buying some kind of potted spring plant and taking it to the detention center to give to Yunsu. I didn't know why he was on my mind. I wanted to ask him how someone who was so moved by the story of Orestes, who ached at the thought of his first and last spring, could have done something so cruel. I felt confused. What did it mean to be human anyway, and to what extent were we capable of being good, and to what extent were we capable of evil? It bothered me to be having these thoughts. The phone rang again. I thought it was the police and worried about what they might say to me. I couldn't call my older brother for help this time, and even if I did, what difference would it make? I answered the phone. It was my older brother. For a brief moment, I stupidly pictured an imaginary line going from the police to the prosecutor's office, and I thought, *The emergency line goes all the way to my brother?* But then Yusik spoke. His voice was heavy.

"Come to the hospital. Mom's had a relapse."

I asked for everything from God so I could enjoy life.
Instead, He gave me life so that I could enjoy everything.
I got nothing that I asked for but received everything that I hoped for.

– Epitaph on the tomb of the
Unknown Soldier in Turin, Italy

BLUE NOTE 13

After Eunsu was gone, I felt like a burden had been lifted.
Physically, at least, I felt lighter. I started hanging around
with a bad crowd. Well, not a bad crowd, exactly. When I
was hungry, they gave me food to eat, and when my clothes
were ragged, they gave me clothes to wear, and when
I was thirsty, they gave me alcohol to drink, and when I
was in jail, they came to see me. I was in and out of jail all
of the time and slowly slipping into darkness. Never
having made it through elementary school, jail provided
me with a comprehensive education. There, I majored
in the criminal arts with a double minor in hatred and
revenge. Inside were thousands of people giving lectures
on how to rid yourself of things like guilt and increase
your brazenness and underhandedness. Whenever I was
on lookout while the others were stealing, the moment
I felt a tug of fear and nervousness, I would sing the

national anthem quietly to myself. When I did that, I didn't feel like a good person, the way Eunsu did, but I didn't feel afraid either.

CHAPTER 13

There were only three of us in the room: Yunsu, the guard, and me. Yunsu kept glancing up at me while eating the pizza I'd brought. I still had not said anything. I couldn't stop asking myself whether I was doing the right thing. I was so quiet that Officer Yi pushed his glasses up then pulled them back down several times. I had not even brought the Bible that Aunt Monica always had with her. All I had in my bag were cigarettes, lipstick, a wallet, and a small compact. Yunsu stared at me as if to get me to say something, anything. So did Officer Yi. But I still couldn't bring myself to start talking. Outside the window it was spring, but all I saw inside were gray cement walls. The bright green sprouts I had seen from the car on the way here, the river rippling and flowing under the bridge like freshly washed hair now that the weather had finally warmed, and the tiny scattered flowers blooming like stars in a green field—none of that mattered here. Spring could arrive, but there wasn't really anything to awaken. Oscar Wilde had said about prison, "With us time itself does not progress. It revolves. It seems to circle round one centre of pain." In a six-by-six meter room, seven or eight healthy young men sat face to face all day. If a young couple in love were put into that tiny room for just a month, even they would probably call off their love at once and start to hate each other instead. As Aunt Monica said, it was a miracle that people who had not always been good could sit face to face all day long and not want to kill each other.

"The weather's really warmed up. I guess the frostbite must be wearing off, because my ears are itching me to death," Yunsu said.

He sounded as if he had no choice but to say something. He lifted his cuffed hands and stroked one ear. His words were no longer barbed but were as mild as the changing seasons, as mild as the breeze that fluttered the hem of my skirt without aggression now that spring was here. Since I had started meeting him, he had been changing day by day, like a willow tree in spring. His growth was as rapid as a baby's after its first birthday. Later, I came to understand that, unlike babies, feelings grow without regard for the rules of time.

"So..."

He and the guard looked at me in unison. I felt like I was standing in front of my students. Or before a priest who was ready to take my confession.

"I'm not here because I want to be here. My coming to see you all this time hasn't been because I wanted to."

He and the guard looked surprised, and I saw his face instantly darken. He lowered his head. He looked like he wanted to say, *So, you're a hypocrite, too.* If I were to exaggerate, I would say he looked like he was thinking, *I'm tired of being hurt by hypocrites like you,* or perhaps even, *I figured as much.*

"I don't want to lie to you. I really hate predictable conversations. I hate clichés more than anything."

I struggled to keep talking. Yunsu kept his eyes down and did not say a word. Then something seemed to occur to him, and he raised his head.

"It's okay. I'm only here today because I thought Sister Monica was coming. I heard she couldn't make it because she had to visit a cancer patient in the hospital. That person is probably going to die soon. So if you forced yourself to come here in her place, you can go ahead and go. You must have other things to do. Thank you for being honest with me, Professor."

When he finished, he stood up and looked at me coldly. A sneer crossed his face. The moment was brief, but the look of regret at having expected anything of me was clear to see. When he spat out the word *Professor*, there was a dark shadow over him that made me think, *That's probably what he was like in the streets*. But it was followed by a pained expression. He looked hurt. Being accustomed to betrayal didn't mean that betrayal didn't hurt, and just because someone was used to falling didn't mean it was easy to pick themselves up again the next time. I did not know until later that because he was locked up, he could not see anyone unless they came to see him, and if it did not take place in the Catholic meeting room, he could only talk for ten minutes from behind a sheet of acrylic with holes drilled in it, even if it were his own mother, and therefore he looked forward excitedly to every Thursday.

But at the time, I felt a little angry and thought, *He's so impatient*. I looked up at him and said, "I didn't mean that I was going to leave. I'm here today in Aunt Monica's place because I asked her to let me come. The cancer patient she went to see, the one who's about to die, is my mother. I told her that since she was going to see my mother, I would come to see you. So she's there, and I'm here."

He gave me the same look of surprise that I had given him. He started to get nervous, unsure of what I was going to say next.

"I hate my mother. I know that if I go see her, I'll want to kill myself again. That's why I'm here instead. It's not that I like you, but I don't hate you either. You and I haven't wanted anything from each other or cared about each other enough to hate each other yet. So, since we can't hate each other, this is comfortable for me. Or maybe I should just say it's better. Please don't misunderstand. That's not the whole reason."

I paused. I could tell he had no idea what I was talking about. Officer Yi looked confused, too.

"This might sound weird, but the first time I met you, I thought you and I were very similar. It's hard to explain why that is, but the first thing that came to mind was that maybe you hated your mother, too, and maybe you'd hated her for a long time."

Yunsu looked at me strangely and sat back down.

"Why did you think... Did you read about me in the newspaper?" he asked.

"I did read about you, but not until after I met you. What I mean is that for people who hate their mothers—let me rephrase that—for people who grow up without knowing a mother's love, the part of us that can grow only when it receives the love that we are entitled to as children remains stunted somewhere deep inside of us. It's like a premature baby that doesn't get to grow up. I think it shows in our faces. And I think that's what I saw in you."

It bothered me that Officer Yi could hear what I was about to say, but I decided to push on. Now he too would know that I was not a good person. It hurt a little. I figured he would go home to his wife again and tell her, *Turns out, her reasons for visiting the prison aren't so great after all.* For a moment, I thought I could understand the fear and sadness that hypocrites must feel.

"I've never told anyone this before. My uncle is a

psychiatrist, but I've never even told him. On the way here, I kept wondering why I wanted to come, and I thought it was because I wanted to tell you. It's not easy for me to talk about it. But if my mother winds up being in hospital for a while, then I'll probably be coming to see you for the time being. If you don't want to see me... then I'll stop coming."

Officer Yi, who was quick to catch on, seemed to be doing his best not to listen in on the conversation. Yunsu's eyes were boring into mine; in them, I could see some emotion arising that I had never seen in him before. I could also tell that he was trying to keep his doubts about me. He was staring at me with his neck craned forward, like a deer alert to every sound, trying to identify whatever was moving. But the doubt in his eyes also told me that he wanted to believe me.

I swallowed hard and looked him in the eye.

"In your letter, you said this could be your last spring... Because of you, I realized for the first time that spring only comes once a year, and that I will have to wait another year to see spring again. So I, too, feel like this is the first and last spring I'll ever have. I never knew that a season, something that comes around at the same time every year, could feel that way. That it could be someone's last. And that therefore every day for that person passes in yearning, like a kind of thirst. For you, it's like you're seeing everything for the first time—from the sap rising in the trees to the yellow forsythias that grow everywhere—and yet the moment you see them, you already have to say goodbye. Things the rest of us take for granted are probably stamped in your heart as both the first and last of their kind. I realized that because of you. I also realized because of you that though I have wanted to kill someone, that someone isn't me. So I don't want to have the kind of obvious, predictable conversation that religious types have on what could be our last spring day together. We don't have time. Since we're already here, I want to have a real conversation."

Yunsu looked nervous again.

"What do you mean by a real conversation?" he asked.

"I don't know yet. If you keep talking, it must turn real eventually. I can't tell you only nice things, the way Aunt Monica does. She talked to the warden about making me a so-called member of the Catholic ministry, so for now I get to walk around wearing this badge. I don't know the Bible, I haven't prayed in fifteen years and, in that time, the only time I've gone into a church was to buy postcards when I was traveling in Europe. Of course, I've never repented for that. I'm supposedly a painter, but aside from a few paintings I did after returning to Korea and a single solo exhibition, I haven't painted anything. And I'm called a professor, but the school I went to in France was worthless, the kind of place that anyone with money could get into. At work, the other professors look at me like they're thinking, *How did she get to be a professor?* The students are more clever that that. They look at me like, 'Her dad's the chairman of the board. When you come from money, you get money and connections. That's how it is.' And when I think about my life, I agree with them. I was arrested for drunk driving recently. The cops said I was crazy. But I'm not crazy. I'm an idiot."

Yunsu had been sitting there nervously but he laughed out loud at the word *idiot*. His laugh sounded like air escaping from a balloon. Even Officer Yi looked down and snickered. I didn't know if it was because of their laughter, but the room suddenly seemed to fill with the yellow glow of spring. Having said the words out loud, it did seem kind of funny. They both looked amused.

"I tried to kill myself three times. The last time was this past winter. I promised Aunt Monica that I would come here with her, in exchange for not having to go through therapy. In other words, I had no choice about coming here. But I'm not crazy. I just hated myself and wanted to die. The reason is that when I was fifteen..."

Why I decided to bring that up, I still have no idea. But at least I was calm and not agitated. I could tell from his attitude that he was listening to me with his whole being. That was because that day could have been both the first and the last day of his life, and therefore I could have been the last person he ever saw. Had anyone in my life ever listened to me with their entire being before?

"An older cousin of mine on my father's side..."

My throat closed up. I stopped talking for a moment so I could control my emotions. A pain, like my heart was splitting in two, ran through me. I waited for the pain to pass.

"...raped me. My mother sent me on an errand to the head family's house, where my cousin lived. He lived there with his wife and kid."

It was the first time I had ever said the words out loud. It was also the first time I had ever used the objective term for it—rape. But if I had to tell someone, I wanted it to be him, the man who was facing his final spring. I don't know. There were so many ways in which I identified with him. It had been that way from the start. The most important thing we had in common, though, was the fact that, whether pushed or voluntarily, we had both longed to board the train of death. Everything had changed the moment I decided I wanted to board that train. Things I'd thought were important no longer were, and things I'd thought were unimportant became important. The desire to die distorted many things for me, but other things became very clear. Death contradicts ownership, which people hold above all other values. In this world, where everyone is crazy about money, money, *money*, death may be the only thing that enables us to laugh at it, and everyone has to face death at least once. I was sure that Yunsu would understand me.

The room was so quiet that it may as well have been empty. Officer Yi and Yunsu were barely even breathing as they listened to me. I didn't think about it until later, but Yunsu was probably more nervous than when the judge sentenced him to death. I had not given any prior thought to how he might react to hearing the word *rape*. It wasn't until after I said it that I remembered he had raped and murdered a seventeen-year-old girl. But to my surprise, he was looking at me calmly, and in his face was a mixture of boundless compassion and sympathy along with the painful regret of being forced to look back on the past. I glimpsed a trace of terrible remorse in his eyes. It seemed that by exposing my wound, I had triggered his own. But I decided to push forward.

"After that, I couldn't have a normal relationship with a man. It was okay if I didn't love him, but I couldn't be with someone if I did. Once I fell in love with someone, I had to let him go. That's why they all left me."

My eyes stung as I told him that. It was the first time I had ever tried to explain myself so concisely. I wondered why I had brought up relationships. My ears flushed red with shame. I thought of myself as someone who was cool and unaffected. When the break-ups happened, I acted like I didn't care in the slightest. I thought that was what I was supposed to do. But it wasn't until that moment that I realized it had hurt each and every time. It was true. I could tell that Yunsu was soaking my words up like a sponge—the truth about me and even the shame that I felt. I could tell because I was used to people not believing me, so I was sensitive to it. When I mentioned relationships, his eyes wavered, and my own heart wavered in response. We were like two people standing at either side of a ravine with a rope stretched between the two of us. If one of us trembled, the other person's hand trembled, too. When I look back on it now, I think I wanted to console him. I wanted to tell him, *You're not the only one who has it hard, so stop acting like you're already dead*. It was true.

"I read all of the articles about you." I spoke slowly, with as little emotion as possible.

"Hold on."

Officer Yi stopped me. Yunsu was grimacing.

"You're not allowed to discuss his case or anything related to his case in here."

Officer Yi looked at me apologetically. We were quiet for a moment. I paused. I felt like asking, *Then what can I talk about*? His *case* was the fatal event that had brought the two of us together, and if it were not for his *case*, he would have had no reason to meet with members of the ministry. But such were the rules. I was in no mood for predictable conversation, for grasping at clouds or saying this was why Jesus came to earth or how precious we all were. What I really wanted to talk about was why Jesus had come to him and me specifically, and who I was and who he was, and exactly how someone like him could be considered precious. Yunsu had his head down, as if he could not yet understand what I was getting at. Behind him was the print of Rembrandt's *The Return of the Prodigal Son*. Since entering the painting, the son had spent every single day on his knees. I stared at his feet. One sandal had fallen off, and his bare foot was exposed. The father was patting his son on the shoulder. Rembrandt had painted the moment of the son's return. He did not draw the father forgiving the son or the feast he threw for him after. The prodigal son had returned and the father was patting him on the shoulder, yet for over a hundred years he had not been able to straighten his knees. He would never rise and walk about his home on his own feet. The sons who knelt in this room like the prodigal one would have the noose placed around their necks while on bended knees in the execution room as well.

"Officer, I was only planning to talk about myself. I'm not a prosecutor or a reporter, and I have no intention of attacking him."

Officer Yi thought it over for a moment and then nodded wordlessly. I looked back at Yunsu. His eyes were filled with the tension and curiosity of a roomful of first-graders. He looked very nervous, and also afraid. He even had the slightly stupid look of someone seeing a tribe of people they have never come across before.

"To be honest, I don't know you. I never thought for a moment that the newspapers would tell me everything there was to know about you. Newspaper articles contain facts, but there's no such thing as a fact created by a fact. The truth is what makes facts, but people don't care about that. Intention precedes action. Let's say that someone tries to stab a man to death but accidentally cuts a rope that's wrapped around his neck instead, and he survives. And now let's say someone tries to cut a rope wrapped around a man's neck, but the knife slips and he kills him instead. The first person would be a hero, but the second person would be executed. The world only judges our actions. We can't show our thoughts to other people, and we can't read each other's minds. So are crime and punishment really that valid? Actions are only facts, and truth is always what comes before actions. So what we really need to pay attention to is not fact but truth. You're the reason I've started thinking this way. I thought about what would happen if someone wrote a newspaper article on me. I would probably come off worse than you. Mun Yujeong attempted suicide three times. She attempted suicide despite receiving psychiatric treatment. Nobody knows why. The end."

His eyes seemed to flash behind his dark-rimmed glasses. If I had never met him, and if I did not have Aunt Monica, I, too, would have remembered him only for what I read in the papers. A bad guy. The end. But there was no end. It was around that time that I was starting to think maybe even death was not an end. As Rilke once said, some people continue to grow even after death.

"We're only three years apart in age. Same generation. We've probably walked right by each other—somewhere, at some point. But when I came to the prison for the first time this past winter, I couldn't believe that the men in here were really born in the same country as me and lived right beside me. To be even more honest, I used to think I was the only one in this world who was unhappy. It made me even more miserable to wonder why everyone else was happy while I was not. But coming here has made me confused, including about myself. I'm unhappy, and yet why am I not locked up, too? I couldn't understand that. This place seems like a gathering point for all of the unhappiness in the world. I was surprised that so many sins could be committed by so many people and that there were so many types of unhappiness as well. I was surprised, too, that every day, without fail, more unhappy people who had sinned were being brought in here. I thought that if we had a real conversation—though I didn't know what that was— about why I was outside and you were inside, then maybe I could understand myself. Maybe I could understand why I was unhappy and why I couldn't be happy. Do you know what I mean?"

Yunsu stared at me, as still as a statue. He slowly nodded.

"I'm not here because I have free time. If I had a class

on Thursdays, I wouldn't have been able to come today. But this semester, as luck would have it, I don't teach on Thursdays, and my mother is in hospital. So I used all of these coincidences to come here. I've never done volunteer work or given to charity. And I don't want to, either. In fact, I don't believe in such a thing as a pure heart. Well, even if some people do have a heart like that, I certainly do not. I don't like to go away empty-handed. So that means it's your turn to talk. If I'm going to come here, I should get something from you, too. That's only fair, right?"

That was how our meetings began that spring day. Every meeting was our last meeting because we did not know when his sentence would be completed. Death row prisoners were technically in limbo, as their sentences were not fully carried out until the day they were executed. That was why they were not sent to the same prison as other criminals but were detained at the center with prisoners who were still on trial. Even the name of the place contained an administrative lie: The Seoul Detention Center was not in Seoul but in Uiwang. Nevertheless, it was still called the Seoul Detention Center.

We kept the words *last time* in parentheses each time we met, but we never forgot that those words were there. Each of our meetings lasted for three hours, from ten in the morning to one in the afternoon on Thursdays. That was 180 minutes that I could have shoved in the garbage, as Aunt Monica would say.

The following Thursday, we sat across from each other again. The world outside was filled with the pale light of spring, like sweetened condensed milk dissolving, but inside the detention center, it was always cold and dark. Someone had once described it as a place inhabited by death and, for all I knew, the brighter the light of the world, the deeper the shadows that covered the prison.

Yunsu looked cheerful.

"After I was sentenced to death by the Supreme Court, they put this tag on my shirt. One day, I was walking down the hallway when I saw someone coming toward me. I saw that he had a red tag, and my blood went cold. I thought he must be really bad if they put a red tag on him. I did everything I could to avoid making eye contact when we passed each other. I was afraid of him. I went back to my cell, ate, and was lying down for a moment, when it hit me. My tag was red, too."

We both laughed. His cuffed hands held his coffee cup loosely.

"No one bothers you when you're on death row. One morning, they served us rice cake soup. It must have been around the Lunar New Year. No one could eat it. Everyone was unhappy and thinking about the families they left behind, nearly crying over the situation they were in. One guy was crying because he had to leave his kids with no mother to care for them, and another guy was crying because his wife was sick. One guy was upset because his girlfriend dumped him for someone else. But then they all looked at me, and their faces changed. It was like they were thinking, *This guy's going to die soon*, so their own worries seemed like nothing. They started to eat and, the next thing I knew, they were slurping it up. That's when I knew: as a death row inmate, I could still do something nice for others. I'd never done anything nice for anyone else in my entire life, but now that I was on death row, I could. So, does this fit your idea of a real conversation?"

I couldn't tell whether I should laugh or not.

"The last time you came, you said you didn't like to go away empty-handed, and that you wanted to do this fairly. I wish you knew how happy that made me. I thought of myself as just an asshole—sorry, I mean, just a guy who had nothing to give to anyone. My hands are bound, I don't have a penny to my name, I don't know anything, and I was taught even less. Not even my life is my own anymore. So to hear you say that you want something from this ass—sorry, again—to hear you say you want something from me, well, I guess you really are an idiot."

All three of us laughed.

"Okay, now I'll tell you something real. I decided to become a hypocrite. Just the thought of being a believer makes me sick to my stomach, but I decided to give it a try. I decided if I was still alive by Christmas, I would get baptized, and I started taking catechism classes. Father Kim was teaching them. You probably already heard—he's the one all the guys on death row here were skipping lunch and praying for—but he had a miraculous recovery and came back. His hair had all fallen out, and he was really thin, but he said he was better. Everyone was clamoring that it was a miracle. More people started taking his classes because of it. Even I started thinking about miracles for the first time in my life. Sister Monica sent me a letter last week. She wrote that when stones turn into bread and fish turn into people, it's magic, but when a person changes, it's a miracle. I don't believe in miracles, but I felt like experimenting a little, to see if someone like me could live a different life. So I guess that makes me an idiot, too."

Officer Yi and I laughed. He had caught us off guard with that.

"But I'll stop talking about religion, since you probably don't care for it. That's only fair. I, too, don't like being left empty-handed, and I don't like when others are either."

"Fine," I said. It sounded like Yunsu had remembered everything I had told him last time.

"After I saw you last week, I thought it over carefully, and I really like the idea of having a real conversation. I don't really know what a real conversation is, but I think I want to try. It's because of you that I realized that there is such a thing as real conversation and fake conversation. It's also the first time I realized that someone can go to school—and in some amazing place like France, at that—and study art and become a professor and be from a rich family, and still not be happy."

He stared at me. He had an apologetic look in his eyes. I laughed quietly. My friends all said the same thing. *What on earth do you have to be unhappy about?* My mother said it, too. And my brothers. The only one who didn't say it was Aunt Monica. Sometimes I heard her mumble to herself, *Those who have everything are the poorest of all.*

"I couldn't even imagine it. I used to hate people like that. I thought you could kill all those assholes—sorry—all those people, and they would die in peace because they'd already enjoyed everything they could possibly enjoy. I couldn't believe a young woman who had so much would..."

Yunsu paused to read my mood. After a moment, he continued, avoiding any mention of the word *rape*.

"...would be in so much pain and want to kill herself."

He sounded like he meant it. He stared at me with compassion-filled eyes. I had never been looked at with so much empathy by a man before. He lowered his head for a moment.

"It wasn't until I met you that I learned a woman of your class could be suffering and wanting to die in a different corner of the same world as me. Even rich people can suffer. You can still know nothing despite being well educated. And forcing a woman... Raping someone can be crueler than killing someone. For the first time, I realized that as a man. I went back to my cell that day and felt bad. For several days I kept muttering apologies on behalf of that man. And when I felt apologetic toward you, I thought of that girl who died, the seventeen-year-old girl..."

He stopped. He brought his hands up to his mouth, the cuffs glimmering around them, and buried his face in them. Since the cuffs forced his hands together all the time, he looked like he was praying.

"I felt so sorry. I know that saying sorry doesn't make up for anything, but I *was* sorry. If I could atone for that by dying, I would die ten times over. I didn't feel sorry back when the prosecutor was snarling at me. I was determined not to feel sorry, even if they were to hang me on the spot. But now I am, in spite of myself."

He closed his eyes. Tears spilled from his closed lids. There was nothing clichéd about it. I had no intention of preaching to him, but he kept saying nice things and making me nervous. I was finding it harder and harder to think of the Jeong Yunsu I knew as the man who was behind the Imun-dong murder case that I had looked up online. I had even surprised myself during one of our meetings by suddenly wondering, *Could he really have raped and killed someone*? Whenever I looked him in the face, laughed, or drank coffee with him, I ached inside. It sounds stupid, but I wanted to ask him, *Couldn't you have not done it*? I wanted to ask Yunsu the same thing Aunt Monica used to ask me: *Why did you have to do it?*

"I don't know if you'll believe me, but when I think back on those times, I have no idea why I did it. It feels like I'm watching myself in a movie. Actually, I felt the same way when I took the woman hostage and when they arrested me, like it wasn't really me. But the problem is that it was. I can't take it back, and now I can't say sorry or ask for forgiveness. Now I get it. It really was me!"

He was shaking hard. Officer Yi grabbed a tissue and handed it to him. He took it and wiped the sweat from his forehead.

"Also," he said, staring down at the sweat-soaked tissue, "I've never used honorifics before. When I called you by the formal 'you,' I realized for the first time in my life that we have a really beautiful language."

I opened the packet of *kimbap* that I had brought him for lunch and handed him the fork I had packed as well in case the chopsticks were too difficult for him to use. He didn't eat much. All three of us just sipped green tea.

"Officer Yi." I changed the subject. "It's your turn to give us some real conversation. Yunsu and I aren't getting paid for this, but you get to listen to real conversation *and* take home a salary."

Officer Yi laughed and said, "I'm no good with words. I don't have anything real to say, but if I did, it would be that—just like you two—I'm a real idiot."

We all had a good laugh. It felt like the three idiots were becoming friends. In that moment, death, anxiety, memories of murder, fear, and times of curses all seemed to pass us by. Though it was clear they were only setting up camp behind us, biding their time until our own time together ended, we avoided talking about them. I was afraid. The season moved on, three hours a week at a time.

It hardly seems to exist, except for the man who suffers it—in his soul for months and years, in his body during the desperate and violent hour when he is cut in two without suppressing his life. Let us call it by the name which, for lack of any other nobility, will at least give the nobility of truth, and let us recognize it for what it is essentially: a revenge.

– Albert Camus, *Reflections on the Guillotine*

BLUE NOTE 14

And then one day, I met a girl. She worked in a beauty salon close to where I lived. She was very popular among the guys in my gang. No matter how hard anyone tried to come on to her, she would not be won over. I went there to get my hair cut and liked her so much that I tried to pay her extra, but she said she didn't take tips from bad guys like me. I had assumed from her crude way of talking that she'd been around the block, but she surprised me.

I fell in love with her. And though she didn't show it, she seemed to like me, too.

I asked her to live with me, and she made a surprising suggestion. She said if I wanted us to live together then we should get married, and was I willing to throw away everything and run away with her and truly start a new life in order to marry her? She said she hated bad guys. I couldn't make up my mind. I had no skills. To be honest, I was worried because manual labor doesn't pay even a fraction of what you can get from stealing a few times. You have to have a home if you want to get married, and you could work for a hundred years as a manual laborer and still not be able to buy one. But I felt like I could go anywhere in the world as long as I was with her. We ran away together. She found work in another salon, and I ran deliveries for a neighborhood market. They were hard but happy times. Then, she got pregnant. That joy, too, was brief. One night, her stomach started hurting, so I carried her on my back to the hospital. They told us it was an ectopic pregnancy. They said they needed three million won to operate. They said I had to hurry because her life was in danger. She looked at me and said she was scared. I was scared, too. I couldn't let her die like Eunsu. I had no choice but to hunt down my old friends while she was in the hospital. I had once made some good money from a job I pulledm, back when I was on top of my game, and loaned it to one of them. My plan was to get the money back from the guy. But he was gone, and instead an older guy he had been close with made me an offer. One last job, he said. I had no other choice. And I was thinking the same thing: just one last job.

Chapter 14

The water in the fountain was dancing in time to music. Children holding ice cream cones were running around the fountain, and people dressed up for a concert were walking by in pairs. I had arrived at the Seoul Arts Center a little early. Since I had time to kill, I was sitting at an outdoor café. The seasons were changing quickly. School had already been out of session for a week. As I watched people walk past me, I reached into my bag for my sketchbook and started drawing them. There were little girls in lace dresses that puffed out around their waists like tutus, little boys dressed in shorts and holding colorful balloons, and men walking hand in hand with women in sleeveless tops that revealed their slender arms. The summer evening was redolent with the heavy scent of trees breathing in the forest where the flowers had dropped their petals. I stopped in the middle of sketching and suddenly wondered if the people around me were happy. The old me would have stared at them like a vagrant looking up at lamp-lit windows from a darkened alley and assumed they must be happy. I used to think that if I could just get inside those windows, happiness would be waiting there like silverware set on a table. I used to toss and turn in bed every night, awash in the sorrow of one cast out alone into the wilderness, walking barefoot along an endless night road. But then I realized all over again that people don't live in either the land of happiness or the land of unhappiness. Everyone is both happy and unhappy to some extent. But then again, maybe that wasn't true, either. Maybe if everyone in the world could be divided into two groups, one group would be people who were somewhat unhappy, and the other would be people who were completely unhappy. And there would be no way of objectively distinguishing which was which. As Camus might have said, there were no happy people, just people who were richer or poorer in spirit when it came to happiness.

I filled a sheet in my sketchbook and turned to the next page. It hit me that Yunsu was somewhere out there on the other side of the mountain behind the arts center. A professor who had spent many years in prison as a political dissident once wrote that while winter is a humane season in prison, summer made you hate the man next to you. I pictured Yunsu's young muscles; him shackled in a tiny room, enduring the body heat of the other men, never able to remove the cuffs except when he was changing clothes. He had told me that he was sensitive to heat, and that it was probably because he had been used to sleeping in cold places for such a long time. The cuffs even got in the way when he tried to wipe away the sweat. The dark-red sores that formed where the edges of the cuffs rubbed against his skin festered in the hot weather. "It's a little better now," Officer Yi had told me while applying the ointment I had brought for his wrists. "An older co-worker of mine told me that one death row inmate's wrists got infected with maggots in the summer." Instead of ice cream cones, children, and the dancing fountain that looked like a symbol of happiness, Yunsu's hands appeared on the pages of my sketchbook. His blue-tinged wrists, so pale that the veins showed because they never saw the sunlight except for thirty minutes of exercise every twenty-four hours. His scar-covered wrists and their gleaming silver cuffs. His eyes that he sometimes fixed on me before hurriedly casting them down. He had written in his letter, *Do you know how much I look forward to Thursdays? I wish every day was Thursday.* He was like a child. His child-ishness left me helpless. After meeting him, I felt bad for every warm ray of sun, every refreshing breeze, and every cool room in the summer. Whenever I drank a lemon soda filled with ice or a draft beer poured into a glass white with frost from the freezer, his face stopped me, and the degree of satisfaction I got from that sensual pleasure plummeted in inverse proportion to the money I had paid for it. There was a mother who had rented a room in front of the detention center after her son was put on death row. The room was as small as her son's cell. She kept the heat off during the winter and the window shut tight during the summer. She was a devout Buddhist: she performed three thousand bows toward the detention center every morning and visited her son every afternoon. Was heaven moved by this? In the end, her son's death penalty was commuted to a life sentence, and his true story became a legend in the detention center. A guy I dated once had told me about it, possibly over drinks one night when he was telling me stories from his time in the army. I remembered that he told me not to look down on the South Korean army. He had served as an intelligence officer while stationed in a forward unit, and he said the number one thing that disqualified a soldier from being assigned to patrol the DMZ, the military tinderbox where tensions ran higher along the border with North Korea, was if he had no mother. Maybe mother, ulti-mately, was just another word for love.

Someone tapped me lightly on the shoulder. It was my oldest brother Yusik, dressed in a dark-navy suit. With his necktie on in this hot summer weather, he looked a little pitiful. This, too, was just another type of uniform. "You're early," he said, but when he saw the wrists and handcuffs I was sketching, his face hardened. I closed the sketchbook. He fanned himself lightly with the envelope he was holding and said, "So you're still seeing him." His voice dripped with contempt. I was not unaware of what he meant by his statement. I took his arm without responding, and we headed into the air-conditioned restaurant.

After we ordered, I glanced at the envelope he had brought with him. It looked like he had reserved recital tickets. He must have noticed that I was looking at them because he said, "Your sister-in-law asked me to get them on the way here."

"I guess Korean prosecutors make good husbands," I said, and he laughed.

"What else can I do? Her nerves are so on edge before a recital that at times I feel like trials are a piece of cake in comparison. Anyway, it's easier to just do what she tells me to do."

The men in my immediate family, including my deceased father, were all nice to women. Or as my mother put it, they were too weak to get out from under their wives' thumbs. At any rate, we were putting off the real subject at hand—our mother—for as long as we could. Our food had not come out yet, and we knew that we couldn't enjoy the food and talk about her at the same time. In a way, we were starting off in our own demilitarized zone.

"Something happened to Yuchan's wife," he said.

Yuchan was the youngest of my brothers. His wife was Seo Yeongja, the former movie actress whose stage name was Lina but whose real name was Yeongja.

"She came to see me at the public prosecutor's office. Didn't even call first."

I dipped a salmon canapé in sauce. Of the people in our family, Yeongja was easier to talk about than my oldest sister-in-law, the pianist, or the next one down, the doctor.

"Someone broke into their house last week, and the burglar has been taken into custody by the police. But she asked me to have him freed."

"Someone broke into Miss Seo Yeongja's house? Why does Miss Seo Yeongja want them to let him go? Was he an old boyfriend of Miss Seo Yeongja's or something?"

He clucked his tongue at me. I decided to be a little more serious.

"The problem is that the kid was caught red-handed stealing her jewelry. But Miss Seo Yeongja—eh, now you've got me doing it, calling her by her full name—"

My brother gave me a stern look and laughed. For a moment, it felt like old times. Like that day long ago, before I turned fifteen, when he had just started working and celebrated his first paycheck by treating me and only me to an ice cream cone. That long-ago time felt like a fairy tale now.

"But she didn't press charges. Not only did she not press charges but she fed him, bathed him, and even bought him a pair of shoes before sending him away. Yuchan had no idea what his wife was up to, and a few days after that incident, he came home to find the kid choking Miss Seo—I mean, our sister-in-law. Anyway, he found him strangling her on the living-room sofa. Strangling his pregnant wife! So Yuchan grabbed the kid and started hitting him. Turns out, he says he's fifteen, but he looks no older than a third-grader. That was when Yuchan found out that she had caught the kid stealing from them the time before. Of course he wasn't going to stand for that. So he dragged the kid down to the police station. And now she wants me to set him free."

I couldn't understand what he was talking about. He laughed and drank a glass of the sherry that had come out as an apéritif.

"What I heard is that she's well known all over the neighborhood. If a beggar walks past their house, she calls him inside, makes him take a shower, and fixes him a meal. If she sees construction workers eating on the ground, she calls them in and sets the table for them. The number of vagrants who've been through that house may not amount to a battalion, but we are talking about a squadron. Once, Yuchan even asked for a divorce and moved out of the house for a while because of her."

My brother paused to light a cigarette.

"When she came to see me at the office, she had no makeup on, was dressed down... I almost didn't recognize her. She addressed me formally as 'Elder Brother-in-Law.' It's hard to believe she's the same Seo Lina who used to be so attractive. Maybe it just happens with age?"

The moment was brief, but my brother seemed bothered that her beauty as a woman had faded. I remembered the day Yuchan, who was an economics professor, had told us, "I'm getting married, and her name is Seo Lina." Our mother had said, "Are you crazy?" but our other brothers were oblivious, their faces filled with awe and jealousy. All they had to say about it was, "When are you bringing her home?"

"She told me something similar happened right after they were married. They were robbed by someone who took all of their wedding jewelry, and he was caught later by the police. But when they went to the station to identify the stolen jewelry, she cried and pleaded for clemency. She said she knew the kid and that she would take responsibility for it, and she asked them to let him go. The cops probably recognized her from her acting days and went along with it because of who she is, and because the kid was so young. Then recently—I think she said it was sometime just last year—she happened to get in a cab, and the driver asked if she remembered him. She said she asked who he was, but he didn't answer. She got to her destination, went about her business, and came back out to find the cab driver waiting for her. He got down on his knees and told her he was the one she'd set free in the police station. He blew off the rest of his fares for the day and invited her to his house. She went with him and met his wife and their one-year-old baby. The guy's wife told her that he talked about how grateful he was to her every single day, and that he said he would never forget the kindness of the woman who had cried and pleaded for the police to let him go. He said it made a human being out of him. After that whenever life became difficult, he was able to overcome it by thinking about her tears. That's what she told me."

The food we had ordered came out, but we were both quiet for a moment.

"She's an unusual woman. I had always thought of her as a glamorous actress turned traditional wife who somehow managed better than the other wives, including handling the ancestral memorial services and putting up with our mother's temper... but this time I didn't know what to think. She kept saying, 'He's so young. Can't you do something to help him? Let him go just this once. What's the point of arresting him and churning out another ex-convict?' So I talked to the other people involved, and then I called Yuchan. I told him, 'That wife of yours is a real saint.' He sighed and then sighed again, and he said, 'Brother, they say you have to destroy ten lives to produce one saint. I'm one of the ten. I'm going to wind up on the street.'"

We laughed. As I was laughing, I realized that I had actually been looking down on her all along as a loser who couldn't even make it through college and as a pushover who only knew how to say yes. At the same time, I realized that I had been looking at her through my mother's eyes. I had been measuring people by the same snobbish scale that my mother used, the one I could not stand—all while despising my family members for being snobs. She clearly had problems and was probably causing danger, and living with her would no doubt, as Yuchan had said, wear you down to the point that you dropped dead, but all the same, I had to acknowledge how wrong I had been about her, and regretted misjudging her all over again.

"This isn't a good family for a prosecutor," I said. "If everyone keeps this up, they'll have to shut down the public prosecutor's office."

He laughed and then looked at me.

"You think prosecutors just throw everyone into jail? We take people's situations into consideration. Recently, there was a woman who was caught stealing with her baby. She was so pathetic that I asked her, 'You're not going to do this again, are you?' And I suspended her indictment."

"I don't believe it!" I said. He laughed. I twirled the pasta around my fork, but I could barely eat anything.

"Mom's been through a lot." He paused in the middle of cutting his steak and glanced up at me. "The doctor examined her again, but he said it's not a relapse. She said she wants to stay in hospital anyway. They put her in a VIP room. She insists it's a relapse, so what can they do? She says she feels better there. You should go see her. I stop by every day on my way home from work. Whether or not it's a relapse, she's definitely not going to last long."

He was trying to reason with me. It caught me off guard. I had assumed that he had asked to meet with me in order to scold me for not going to see her yet. He set his knife and fork down beside his plate, drank the wine he had ordered, and took a deep breath. It looked like we were about to have a "real conversation," as Yunsu and I would put it. I suddenly found myself thinking, *He's been a prosecutor for a really long time*. The look on my brother's face just then—I had never been a criminal looking into the eyes of a prosecutor, but I had a feeling I knew what it would feel like.

"That thing you told me about last time when you were drunk in Itaewon."

My heart sank. I lifted my wine glass and drank as slowly as I could.

"Yujeong, is it true?"

I lowered my eyes. I didn't feel like talking anymore. I could understand why the families of murder victims refused to talk to Aunt Monica, and why she said that talking to the victims' families was harder than rehabilitating death row convicts—the hardest thing, in fact, because the families did not want to listen to anyone consoling them about what had happened. I didn't understand it the first time she told me, but now that I was in their shoes, I did.

"Sorry. I couldn't sleep after you told me. I really had no idea. I didn't. Mom told me that someone had teased you, and that you were sensitive to anything to do with sex because you were going through puberty. But I still can't believe it. Our cousin pretends to be so respectable."

"I don't want to talk about it," I said.

When I picked up my cigarette, my hand was shaking. I accidentally put the cigarette in my mouth backwards and then dropped it once it was lit.

"Mom was right," I said, not bothering to pick the cigarette back up. "I don't want to talk about it anymore."

"So it was true."

My brother was a prosecutor. He had probably dealt with thousands of liars. His eyes were slowly turning red.

"I asked a lawyer friend of mine. If you wanted... a civil suit..."

He stopped talking and puffed on his cigarette. It wouldn't be easy. Sue my cousin for damages for a rape he had committed fifteen years ago? My cousin, the board member of a major corporation known around the world? My cousin, known for being a man of character? My cousin, the devout Christian? There would be an uproar. People would wonder which of us was lying.

The only evidence was my testimony. And since I was on record for having attempted suicide and nearly being an alcoholic, and having therefore received psychiatric treatment, there was a strong possibility I would be charged with libel. My brother couldn't have been unaware of that.

"I gave it a lot of thought. If you want me to, I'll file a suit for you. I don't even care if I get fired for it, not that that would happen. I don't even care if Mom goes ballistic, or if I have to resign and open my own law practice. I'll do it. Yujeong, if it's true, I have to do something. What he did was unforgiveable."

He became overwhelmed with his emotions and stopped talking. I felt bad. I was the one it had happened to—or as my mother put it, I was a grown girl who had wagged her tail around and got what was coming to her—but my brother was the one hurting from it fifteen years later. He couldn't change jobs over and over, flitting like a bat to a new roost each night, in order to protect his little sister, and I felt both sorry for and thankful that he wanted to do just that despite knowing better.

"I've always tried to make the right choices in my work. It's not what you or our sister-in-law seem to think. Prosecuting people doesn't mean turning poor little petty thieves into ex-cons. I've talked a lot about justice in front of other people and, as a result, there've been many times when I've had to sentence someone and send them to jail even though it pained me to do so. But the reason I'm not ashamed is because someone has to be the bad guy. Because that is what has to happen in order for good people to receive legal protection. Because there is such a thing as justice. If you do something wrong, then it doesn't matter how much money or how many connections you have. That's why I've stuck with this job, so I can prove that."

I felt like I could hear my heart beating. It was like he was prying open a very old wound and peering inside.

"It's okay. Just hearing you say that means a lot to me. You don't have to do anything."

I meant it. I wasn't satisfied, but it did give me some consolation. Having suffered the insufferable, I had become a liar. That was because the people I thought were there to protect me, love me, and defeat anyone for me had laughed at and ridiculed me instead. The incident itself had been horrible, but their reactions to it afterward left a scar I could not wash off. It was worse because I had loved and trusted them. But now my oldest brother said he hadn't known. Maybe it *was* true, because there were things I hadn't known either.

For example, I used to make fun of my youngest sister-in-law. When my mother sneered at her, saying, "I don't care if she is married to a professor who makes barely any money, how can she go out dressed like that?" I used to agree with her. It had never occurred to me that my brothers might have their own struggles. And it would probably always be that way. Just like the shock I'd felt the first time I visited the detention center. I'd had no idea that some of the inmates were so poor that they didn't have even a thousand won to their names while incarcerated. I'd had no idea that a vicious criminal like Yunsu, who'd raped and killed, could smile so brightly or cry so bitterly. But I couldn't do anything about things I didn't know. When Jesus said, "they know not what they do," not only was he referring to us, but we were not even aware that we were the ones he was talking about.

My brother looked anguished. I patted his hand to calm him down and forced myself to smile.

"Don't make a decision right now," he said. He sounded genuinely distressed. "Give it some thought."

"Yusik, how do retrials work?" I changed the subject. He looked surprised. "Can people who've been sentenced to death live if they get a retrial?"

The anguish and compassion disappeared in an instant from my brother's face and was replaced with a kind of fatigue. It was the same look my mother gave whenever she told me I was just like my aunt.

"Retrials only happen when the real criminal is found, or if some conclusive evidence is found that could overturn the case. Why?"

I hesitated before responding.

"Yusik, this guy on death row I've been talking to, Jeong Yunsu, the one who was involved in the Imun-dong murder case, he hasn't said so himself, but I heard from other people that he took the blame for his accomplice's crime. That's not something he told me. The accomplice said so himself. The accomplice has been bragging about it, so it must be true. Right now, the accomplice is in Daejeon or Wonju. He only got fifteen years, and they say he could get out sooner if he's lucky."

My brother scoffed, as if to say, *Is that all?*

"Why are you laughing?" I asked him. "If there is a way, then I'll try to get him to tell the truth."

He stared at me, his gaze that of an older brother looking down at his childish, pathetic little sister.

"The truth? Yujeong, that case is over. And the courts in this country are not that naïve. They don't care about the lies those people tell."

He picked up his cigarette pack and tapped it, feigning indifference, as if to say he was done talking.

"This person I've been meeting, he doesn't lie. I found out about his accomplice from a prison guard. I've gotten to know him. He said when he was caught, he just wanted to die. When he first met Aunt Monica, he told her the same thing. He asked her to let him die. That must mean he took the blame because he was suicidal. I trust him. And you know I never trust anyone. But I know it's true because I've wanted to die, too. I would have done the same thing. He's not a liar. He may be bad, but he's not a liar!"

"That's enough."

He cut me off, firmly, angrily, as if he could not hold back his displeasure. I felt like I'd fallen flat on my back, like we had been playing and having fun but he suddenly turned serious and shoved me hard. Five minutes ago, he said he would resign and endure public censure for me, but that man had disappeared and Mun Yusik, public prosecutor for the Republic of Korea, had taken his place. Didn't the word *persona* originate from the Greek theatrical term for a mask or a role? In that case, which one was my brother's mask?

"What's so great about the courts? They're not God. How can they know everything?" I demanded.

My brother gave me a stern look. His face said that he could forgive a lot of things, but not that.

"What kind of era do you think we're living in?" He raised his voice. "Do you think we execute any criminal who asks for it? You think judges hear confessions and say,

'Well, all right then,' and hand down their verdicts?"

"But you never know. The only people who know the truth of the case are the people involved and God. They say that even countries like America have ten bad cases every year, and the real criminals are discovered only after the person has already been murdered. So how can you be so confident? Innocent people die unfairly. You can't say they don't!"

"It's not murder, it's execution!"

My brother sounded really angry.

"It *is* murder."

"Execution!"

"But that's murder!"

He sighed. I kept going.

"Execution still means killing a person. That guy who blew up the Hangang Bridge during the Korean War, Choi What's-his-name, was wrongfully executed for following orders. Then there was O Hwiung, who was tortured into confessing to a murder, and the People's Revolutionary Party incident, when those men were falsely accused of organizing a communist revolt and were tortured and executed. And there have been a lot of people who went all the way to the Supreme Court and were on the verge of being sentenced to death when the real criminal was found and they were released. Those real criminals were all caught by accident. The prosecutors and the courts aren't interested in finding the truth!"

My brother sighed again. I could tell he wanted to get up and leave. I tried pleading with him.

"Remember that cop who was arrested for murdering his girlfriend? You heard about it, didn't you? They spent the night in a motel, and he left for work the next morning at seven. After he left, she was found dead in the motel room. He knew he would be accused of her murder, so he changed his timecard to make it look like he'd gone to work earlier. He manipulated evidence in a murder case and would have surely been given the death penalty. But then he said he killed her. Why do you think he said that? Because he knew police work all too well. He knew he had no way of getting out of it, so he confessed in order to get a lighter sentence. But then, some local thug happened to be arrested for petty thievery and was found with a motel key belonging to the cop's dead girlfriend. That's how they found the real killer, and the cop was released. And you know what else? There was that guy who was arrested for murder in Gyeongju. He insisted that it wasn't him and that he hadn't killed anyone, but the police pulled some tricks to come up with evidence that he couldn't dispute and arrested him. That case was even added to the text-book for the Judicial Research and Training Institute as an example of an outstanding investigation, but later they caught the real killer and realized he was innocent. And that, too, was by chance!"

My brother looked appalled.

"When did you study all of that?" he asked.

I shook my head. I wanted to yell, *Why do you think so little of me?* It occurred to me that it was the same thing Aunt Monica used to say to me. I guess I really did take after her. Suddenly I wished I weren't this new me but the old me who used to smash up all her vinyl records. Which one was my *true* persona? When I look back on it now, I know I wasn't making any sense. Just five minutes earlier, I'd said I couldn't forgive my cousin, but now I was acting like I was Yunsu's mother.

"Yusik."

"Even if I were president, I couldn't do anything about it. And, to put it bluntly, did that asshole say he didn't do it? Those people have no qualms about lying. Listen, Yujeong.

I know what you're feeling, but you have to at least admit that I know more about those people than you do."

"But not all convicts are liars. Just like sometimes we feel like dying, and sometimes we go a little crazy. Even if convicts do lie sometimes, you and I lie, too. If someone were to say that all Korean prosecutors are bad people, then that would be a lie, too. There are prosecutors in this world who are worse than murderers, and there are convicts who are like angels. There's no such thing as homogeneity. Our lives are as different as our faces."

He glanced at his watch. He looked tired. I knew that he wanted to get out of there as fast as possible and that he couldn't understand why his own little sister was defending the scum of the earth.

"Can't you just save him?"

My brother laughed again. He rubbed his eyes. The tiredness in his face said that he was wondering how the conversation had taken this turn when he had only come to comfort his little sister.

"I'm only asking you to spare his life, not to release him."

My brother crossed his arms and slowly shook his head. He seemed to find the idea preposterous.

"He's going to die eventually," I yelled, "even if he is spared the death sentence! We'll all be dead within the next fifty years at most. Are you that fond of life? Does it make you that jealous to spare his?"

While I was talking, I thought, *Have I really been this sad about it?* I stopped talking—or rather, stopped yelling. I had to acknowledge the fact that I was grieving over his plight. My tears were on the verge of spilling forth. My brother's face hardened and turned pale. I looked at him again and spoke slowly.

"Yusik, I wanted to kill him!"

He stared at me. He looked shocked.

"That's right, I did. More than once. I wanted to take a knife and go to our cousin's house and kill him in front of his wife and children. His daughter must be about fifteen years old now, right? I wanted to kill that asshole in front of her. With a knife. Stab him to death in the most painful way possible. Because no matter how I think about it, that asshole, that prick, was not a person. And when that asshole's family portrait came out in a magazine with a story about him going to church and praying, when I saw that article, I wanted to go right to his house and stab him."

"Yujeong!"

My brother looked scared. I lowered my voice.

"Yes, I know. Murder is bad. That's why I couldn't do it. I lacked the courage and the opportunity. But what would have happened if I had? If I thought he deserved to die because he was scum, and I hanged him for it, would that have been murder? And if I was then arrested and hanged for murder, would that have been justice? In both cases, one human being is deciding that another human being deserves to die. It's one human being killing another human being. But according to you, one is murder and the other is execution. One person is branded a murderer and dies for their crime, while the other gets a promotion. Is that justice?"

My brother stared at me silently. His face was hard. He laughed and said, "So visiting a prison has turned our little Yujeong into a good girl."

Then he grabbed the check and left.

We sit in musty bomb cellars and cramped prisons and groan under the bursting and destructive blows of fate. We should finally stop giving everything a false glamour and unrealistic value and begin to bear it for what it is—unredeemed life.

– Alfred Delp, who died in a Nazi prison

BLUE NOTE 15

Is there really such a thing as fate? Maybe there is. That day, my friend's friend and I decided we would knock over a jewelry shop in Uijeongbu. We got on the subway to go check it out. We were supposed to transfer lines at Dongdaemun, but we were so absorbed in talking that we got off at Dongdaemun Stadium by mistake. And that's where I ran into that fateful woman. If I had remembered correctly where we were supposed to transfer, what would have become of me? Would I have been saved?

The woman was in her forties and ran a small bar that I used to go to back when I ran around with a bad crowd. She treated me well, like a younger brother, and sometimes even gave me spending money. Her behavior wasn't very nice (although, what is "nice behaviour" anyway?). She used to flirt with me all the time. I could never have done anything with her since she was practically an older sister to me, but for some reason I didn't like her. I don't know. Maybe I sensed some ill fate? She said it just so happened that she had the day off and invited us over to her house for drinks. I didn't want to go because I couldn't stand the way she was openly flirting with me, but the other guy gave me a look that said we should. It turned out that he knew she had a lot of money. But I interpreted the look to mean that he just wanted to have a drink. So even though I didn't want to, I went to that woman's apartment in Imun-dong.

As soon as we got into the house, the woman changed into a see-through skirt and brought out a bottle of alcohol. She asked if we could talk in private. I told the other guy to wait in the living room, and we went into the master bedroom. When I thought about how the woman I loved was hovering between life and death, pregnant with my doomed child, there was no time for small talk. I begged her to loan me three million won and promised to do whatever it took to pay her back. She listened to my whole story and then made me an offer: she would save the woman I loved but, in exchange, she wanted me to move in with her instead after the operation was finished. I looked at the woman who had invited us over just so she could proposition me, wasting my time in my moment of desperation, and I got angry. I lost my temper and told her there was no way I was going to do that. I stood up to leave. Just then, we heard a scream coming from across the living room.

CHAPTER 15

Summer was ending in wind and rain. I looked forward to every Thursday the way the fox looked forward to the little prince's arrival every afternoon at four. I avoided making any dates or appointments on a Thursday, and I spent my Wednesday nights wondering what Yunsu and I would talk about. When I thought about him waiting for me all week long in a place where no one ever came to visit him, I didn't dare to even get sick on Thursdays. Yunsu was reading through books at a tremendous pace. Sometimes he even mentioned poets I had never heard of. When I saw him like that, I felt happy and afraid at the same time. My heart sank whenever I saw a news article about another criminal, and when people said, *They should all be killed*, I pictured Yunsu's face. Several times, while talking to Aunt Monica on the phone, I started to say that I wanted to stop going, but then the thought would occur to me that the next Thursday could be our last, and I never said those words. I couldn't leave him. I thought maybe this was how Aunt Monica had wound up visiting the same place for thirty years.

One Thursday, I was walking back down the long corridor of the detention center after meeting with Yunsu.

There were a few roses blooming in the lawn in front of the center, but it was no golden wheat field where the fox waited for the little prince. Officer Yi was walking with me, carrying the lunch bag I had brought along. Across the street from the detention center, there were already several fallen leaves that had wilted early.

During our meeting, Yunsu had told me that even though everything was still green, he could tell from the rustling of the wind that autumn was on its way. Everything might look the same, he said, but the sounds change. The trees may all be the same green, but they sound different in spring and summer and autumn. There was more than met the eye, he said.

Yunsu had sounded especially calm that day. He spoke more slowly, too. He reminded me of a lake in autumn. Though it was always the same lake, in autumn the color of the water seemed to settle into a deeper place. Likewise, something in Yunsu seemed to have settled.

"Did you know that I've been looking forward to Thursdays, too?" Officer Yi said.

"You have?"

I tucked my hair behind my ears and smiled. I felt a little shy. At school, the other teachers had been telling me that I'd changed. *You look happy*, they said. *Something good must have happened to you. You used to look so stressed out.* Though I wished they wouldn't mention my looking stressed out, I liked the fact that they said I looked happy. Looking back on it now, Yunsu and I were mirroring each other. When he was at ease, I was also at ease, and when he was anxious, I matched his anxiety. Autumn would arrive, and then the end of the year, and we would have no choice but to think about death again. Considering how intense that anxiety was, for people on death row—as well as their friends and family—it must have been like being executed day after day. They must have felt as if they had received a threatening letter from a giant monster that read, "Wait right there. I'm coming to kill you." Every day, they were already in the monster's clutches.

"When I first started this job, I was only thinking about the civil service examination. But now I'm grateful. Working here has caused me to think about what it means to be a human being, as well as what it means to die."

It was the most that Officer Yi had ever said to me. This, too, seemed like a real conversation. He had worked here for ten years. He must have brought in dozens of death row convicts like Yunsu, and seen them go.

"Now that it's fall, I'm getting nervous and having trouble sleeping. There weren't any executions last year, which means there will probably be one this year. It must be even worse for the inmates. They tend to be on edge starting around this time and continuing until the end of the year, so we get more incidents. I'll hear someone scream in the middle of the night, and when I go to check it out, they're just having a bad dream. I guess they're executed in their dreams as well."

"How has Yunsu been?"

Officer Yi laughed.

"From what I hear, he's practically a monk. He reads all night and prays. As for the money you've been putting into his account, he takes it out and gives it to whoever needs the most help. When Sister Monica came for Mass last time, she said that there are monks and nuns in the Catholic Church who spend their lives behind steel bars, and that some monks even live in caves. Then she looked at Yunsu and praised him, saying that he's like a monk. Since I've been working here, we've had a former president, as well as one of the current presidential candidates, a national assemblyman, a government minister, a *chaebol* leader...

I don't know that much about politics, but this place is like a glass house where you can see everyone's lives stripped bare. It's made me think about a lot of things."

I didn't ask him what kinds of things he had thought about. I don't think I needed to ask. We passed through a door and then another door. When we were about to part ways at the entrance, I paused to ask him a question.

"About the executions, do they ever give you advance notice?"

Officer Yi hesitated before answering.

"We find out the night before. When that happens, all of the guards have to have a stiff drink to get through it. They may be criminals, but they grow on you after a while. When you see them in the newspaper, they're animals. But when you get to know them, they're people. And once you get to know a person, they're all the same, deep down. After an execution happens, it takes a month of drinking to get over it. There's a saying that people who witness a murder become pro-death penalty, while people who witness an execution become anti-death penalty. That's another way of saying they're both wrong. A moment ago, I said I was grateful for being a prison guard, but I always feel like quitting after an execution. A surprising number of people who work as prison guards wind up becoming missionaries and monks. It's probably all for the same reason."

"When we first met, didn't you say that Yunsu was the worst of them all?"

Officer Yi laughed.

"Even if he is the worst," he said, "he's still a human being. No one is bad every day. I have my bad moments. Hey, I guess we're having a real conversation, too."

We parted at the entrance. On the way to my car, I turned to look back. Officer Yi was still standing there. I waved. He waved back. Suddenly I wondered what would happen to him and me after Yunsu was dead. Would we be able to face each other without him? Then I realized that I had deluded myself into thinking that death only came to those on death row. The truth was that I would also die, and though we did not know when, Officer Yi would die, too. And even though her cancer had not in fact relapsed, my mother was lying in hospital, trying to stop a death that refused to come.

People dressed in suits and carrying briefcases were busily heading into a building where many black luxury sedans were parked. They looked like lawyers. They, too, would die. Even if there were no rush to die, not a single person here today would still be alive after a hundred years. And yet everyone was in a rush. *Hurry up and kill them*, they said. But my brother Yusik would get angry if he heard that. He would say, *It's execution.*

My cell phone rang. It was Aunt Monica. It had been a long time, and with autumn rolling in on a dry breeze, I felt like seeing her. She told me over the phone that someone in Seongnam had passed away and implied that I should meet her there. Another death. Of course, according to the Buddha, the most surprising thing in this world is that we forget that we can die at any time. I drove through Bundang to get to Seongnam. On a steep mountain slope on the side of the road, I saw a cemetery. I sometimes took that road on my way home from the detention center, but I had never noticed the cemetery before. Today, Yunsu had said, *I read in the newspaper that a Korean Air plane crashed in Guam. I couldn't stop thinking about the fact that two hundred people died, and I couldn't sleep. I don't know why God didn't take a sinner like me instead of those innocent people. It makes me sad. Those people, they must have had people who loved them. It's so heartbreaking.*

A cemetery and a plane crash—that autumn seemed to be getting off to an ominous start.

Several white awnings had been put up in a vacant lot in an alley behind the marketplace where houses were huddled closely together. I parked the car at the entrance to the market and went to find Aunt Monica. A woman showed me the way. Aunt Monica was sitting with some other people beneath one of the awnings. As I walked up, she pulled me over to her.

There was a long line leading into the room where the mourners were paying their respects to the deceased. I wondered who on earth could have died in this rundown neighborhood that so many people should have flocked here. Most of the people in line were crying. They looked genuinely sad.

Aunt Monica held my hand and looked up at my face. In the clear autumn sunlight, the hair behind her ears looked white. I thought, *What am I going to do when she dies?* Aunt Monica's hand was as small and rough as a weathered piece of wood. Before we knew it, we were at the front of the line.

Inside the room, a funeral portrait showed a smiling woman dressed in a traditional Korean gown. Her hair was parted down the middle and pulled back into a bun. The room—though I did not know if it was even big enough to merit being called a room—was five square meters. With the coffin, there was barely enough room for one person to sit down. Everyone else had to wait outside in line. I placed a flower before the funeral portrait and bowed. While I was doing that, Aunt Monica stood pressed up against the wall of that cramped room. In the corner where she stood, a stack of letters was piled up to the ceiling. There were other stacks all around the room.

There was an old saying about people who would cry

their eyes out at a funeral first and then ask who died—I wasn't much better, bowing to a complete stranger. Aunt Monica led me out of the room. The line of people waiting to burn a stick of incense in front of the funeral portrait had grown while we were inside.

"These people have come from all over the country. Everyone who's involved with the detention center knew her. She was widowed when she was still young, just over forty, I think. Her husband left her quite a lot of money, and they didn't have any children. She sold everything they owned, rented this tiny room, liquidated all of their assets, and stored the cash in that armoire you saw in there. She went all over the country to meet prisoners and deposit money in their commissary accounts. You saw all those letters in there? People from all over the country sent her those. I asked her once what she was going to do if she got sick after she ran out of money. She said there was nothing to worry about. She said if she had work left to do, God would either provide more money or take her. At the time, I thought she was being irresponsible. She passed away this morning. They said she visited Daegu Prison yesterday. She had dinner with some people, and afterward she went home and died in her sleep. When they opened her armoire in the morning, there was exactly enough money in there for her funeral."

I turned and looked back at the tiny room.

"Really?" I asked.

"Yes, really!"

"But why wasn't this in the papers?"

As soon as the question popped out, I felt foolish for asking it. But I honestly couldn't believe it. This wasn't some fairy tale that you tell to children or a story about a miracle that you doubt is true and assume to be in part a lie. I felt a chill run down my spine. It wasn't once upon a time, it wasn't the Middle Ages, and it wasn't the West. It was Korea. It gave me a chill to wonder whether there really were people like her in this day and age.

"She would have loathed the idea of being in the papers," Aunt Monica said without letting go of my hand. "Nevertheless, she was in the news once or twice. Just an article, no interview."

"But why didn't I hear about her?"

Aunt Monica didn't answer. When I thought about it, I realized that I used to be the kind of person who had no idea people like her existed, regardless of whether she was in the papers or not. I wouldn't have wanted to know. Because, as my uncle had told me in his sad voice, you had to hurt in order to be enlightened. And in order to hurt, you had to look and feel and understand. When I thought about it that way, a genuine life founded on enlightenment could not exist without compassion. There was no compassion without understanding, and no understanding without interest. Love meant taking an interest in other people's lives. So maybe when my brother Yusik said he'd had no idea I was raped, it meant he didn't really love me. He had carried me on his back, bought me ice cream, and said he worried about me all the time, but when he saw what was happening to me, his only thought was that he had no idea why. So perhaps the words *I didn't know* were not an exoneration of sin but rather the antonym of love. They were the antonym of justice, of compassion, of understanding, the antonym of the true solidarity that everyone was supposed to show for each other.

"By the way, I called you here because Yunsu knew her, too. Last winter, when I went to see Yunsu without you, he told me all about her and said he wanted to meet her. I told him I would see what I could do, but she wound up dying before him. Of course, death doesn't follow a particular order. Now that I'm old, my mind doesn't work as well as it used to, and I tend to forget things like that."

We went to the end of the awning and sat down. Women in aprons were serving food and alcohol. An older man who had been standing nearby waved at us. He came over to where we were sitting and said, "Sister Monica, long time no see." The man looked like he had greased not only his hair but his face as well. He looked fit and healthy.

"This is the former warden of the Seoul Detention Center," Aunt Monica said. "He's retired now." When I introduced myself, he looked excited to meet me.

"I heard you were registered as a clergy member. I wanted to meet you. When my children were younger, they really loved your song *Toward the Land of Hope*."

Something about him rubbed me the wrong way. It was an instinct that people like me who weren't so bright but had keen senses possessed. Particularly when it came to men, I had especially overdeveloped feelers. Whether right or wrong, I tended to judge men the moment I saw them. I'm sure it was because of my cousin. Whenever someone reminded me of him, my first reaction was repulsion. It was another of my scars. Aunt Monica was probably right when she said I needed to free myself of him. My cousin had been dominating my whole life through that one incident. All of the saints from every religion could have come up to me, and I would have judged them the same way. I felt a little bad for judging this man as well. He offered Aunt Monica a shot of *soju*. She hesitated before raising her cup.

"Sure, let's have a drink," she said finally. "The woman who passed away really liked *soju*, and she used to pester me to drink with her. Being a nun, I always refused on account of religious doctrine, but in the end, I missed out on a good opportunity."

Aunt Monica looked genuinely remorseful. She slowly raised her cup as she spoke.

"She told me once that she wanted to become a nun, too, but couldn't because of *soju*. She teased me about it. She said ordinary *soju* was closer to God than some sacred dress. She said the most egalitarian thing people had ever made was *soju*. *Chaebol* leaders and day laborers alike drink cheap six-hundred-won *soju*. Other countries rank their liquor, like whiskey and wine, but *soju* has no rank. She asked me how I could have grown old without knowing the taste of *soju*. And now that I've tasted it, it's really good."

She'd had less than half a shot, but she sounded like she was already drunk.

"She used to try to convince us to give a single shot of *soju* to our inmates on holidays," the warden said. "I can't tell you how much she made me sweat over that. Of course, I know she was only joking, but she said the same thing to me about *soju*. She said it was such a shame that our boys behind bars couldn't enjoy that egalitarian drink. I am just so thankful to have lived in the same day and age as a woman like her."

Aunt Monica didn't say anything. There was a lull in the conversation.

"So what did you think of death row?" he said to me. "Our goal is rehabilitation, but the truth is that we're short on manpower. Plus, if you do anything nowadays, people make a stink about human rights. Prison guards are having a really hard time because of it. You met Jeong Yunsu? Now there's a real headache. Has there been any progress?"

His question caught me off guard. I found myself thinking that maybe he had not worked in the actual detention center but in some government department. If

I hadn't been meeting him for the first time, I might have answered the way my old self would have: *If you're that curious, why don't you ask him yourself?*

"Yes, thanks to him, my rehabilitation is coming along nicely," I said.

He laughed out loud at my response. Then he changed the subject, as if it weren't really the answer he had wanted to hear.

"I heard that Father Kim has recovered. Now isn't that a miracle?"

"Medical science has come a long way," Aunt Monica said. "The medication is working, and he himself has the will to fight the disease."

It sounded as if she was the warden, and he was the nun. It was comical.

"Actually, the last time I visited Father Kim," he said, "I urged him to forget about everything else and recite Psalm 23 over and over to help him get through it. Then he would get better. A friend of mine had cancer, and I gave him the same advice. It really helped."

I thought I understood why Aunt Monica had brought up medical science. But I was curious about this incantatory passage from Scripture.

"What is Psalm 23? Is that a good remedy?" I asked.

The warden stared at me in surprise. The look on his face said he wondered how a member of the clergy could not know that. It probably didn't help either that I used a word like *remedy*. I got a little worried. I wasn't sure what to do if he were to ask whether I went to church. But I also wondered why he couldn't just tell me what Psalm 23 was. Why did he have to be such a show-off? He didn't respond and gave me an arrogant look that said if I really wanted to know I should go home and look it up myself.

Aunt Monica jumped in, as if to quell the tension.

"That's the one that reads, 'The Lord is my shepherd; I shall not want. He makes me lie down in green pastures. He leads me beside still waters... Though I walk through the valley of the shadow of death, I will fear no evil.' That one."

It was not a difficult passage. Even if you weren't a Christian, you would probably have heard that at least once.

"Oh, you mean the stuff written on those plaques that they put in all the restaurants!"

The warden's face fell. He looked like I had wounded his pride by belittling the psalm, and after he had greeted me so warmly.

"Anyway." Aunt Monica cut me off. She seemed alarmed by the way I was talking. Of course, since I was accustomed to causing trouble, I wasn't surprised that she was embarrassed by it. "Members of the Catholic, Buddhist, and Protestant communities are talking about working together to campaign for the abolishment of the death penalty. Would you be interested in joining us?"

"Abolish the death penalty? I don't know about that. Even if you do campaign, it would still have to pass through the National Assembly. The assembly members might be tempted to support it so they can be seen as progressive and gain some popularity, but I'm not so sure how I feel about it. First of all, Sister, it would create a budget problem for prisons. Each death row inmate has to have a guard posted to him around the clock, so they would have to increase the number of guards. Who could afford that? And this is a more extreme issue, but does it make sense for the victims to have to pay taxes to feed the animals who killed their loved ones?"

"I guess that's true," said Aunt Monica. "When you consider the victims' point of view, there doesn't seem to be any solution."

I butted in.

"So you're saying we should kill them because it'll save money?"

He stared at me as if to say it wasn't money, it was an *expense*. Then he just turned away.

Too late have I loved you,
O Beauty of ancient days, yet ever new!
Too late I have loved you!

– Saint Augustine

BLUE NOTE 16

We ran out to the living room. My accomplice was coming out of the bedroom where her daughter had been asleep. He had raped the girl and stabbed her. His shirt was soaked with blood. Later, he claimed that he thought the look we gave each other in the subway station meant that we should go to the woman's house, kill her, take her money, and leave. He assumed I went into the woman's room to kill her, and that he was supposed to go into the other room to kill her daughter. I was shocked, but there was nothing I could do. I was a five-time offender, so no matter what I said, there would be no way out for me. The woman turned white. She couldn't even scream. I only hesitated for a moment, but when I saw her backing away into her room, I got scared. My accomplice followed her and strangled her to death as she begged for her life. I thought about how she used to flirt with me and walk around with her nose in the air just because she had some money, and

I decided she deserved to die. I didn't feel even the slightest bit of sympathy for that lecherous insect. I went over to the dead woman calmly and stole the rings from her fingers. I was filled with a courage I had never felt before, as if the demon that had been growing inside of me for a long time was finally goading me on and telling me I did well. All I thought about was how much money she might have. I hoped it was a lot. That was the only thing on my mind. We took the credit cards, cash, and jewelry from her dresser and were about to make a run for it, but her daughter came crawling out into the living room. She was still alive. In the heat of the moment, we had just assumed she was dead after he stabbed her. Do you know how it feels to be toyed with by fate? Then, to make matters worse, we heard a key turning in the lock.

CHAPTER 16

"For the love of—you've got to start acting your age! You're a professor now! It's one thing to talk that way to me or to the rest of the family, but how can you be so outspoken in front of other people? Everyone's been saying that you've settled down and gotten better lately, but now... Do you have any idea how much those people have helped us, or what they let us get away with? It's technically against the rules for me to take pastries into the prison or for you to bring packed lunches. You're over thirty now. When are you going to grow up? Do you want to be an idiot your whole life?"

Along the streets near the convent in Cheongpa-dong, the trees were already dropping their leaves. Aunt Monica was still getting over a bad cold, so I had driven all the way there to pick her up. I was the one who had called myself an idiot in the first place, and I told Aunt Monica over the phone that the three of us—Yunsu, the guard, and I—had started calling ourselves The Idiot Bunch after I used it with Yunsu, but nevertheless I hated the fact that she was throwing that word back in my face a full month later just to criticize me. I had spoken to Aunt Monica over the phone since the last time I saw her, but rumors must have been going around in the meantime. The warden had started enforcing the rules more rigorously with the prison ministry.

"I don't care," I said. "I couldn't stand the fact that he said executions save money. Yusik would insist that it's not about money but about *expenses*. They're all the same. Government officials are all the same. Anyway, it made me mad. Didn't it make you mad? That was coming from a former prison warden!"

Aunt Monica sighed.

"Of course I was mad. Do you know why your mother says you take after me? If someone had said that in front of me when I was your age, I would have gone right up to them and smacked them over the head!"

I almost lost control of the steering wheel.

"Then why are you telling me not to say anything?"

Aunt Monica thought for a moment.

"Since I've spoken out before, I know that not only does it not remedy anything, it backfires on you. I almost got kicked out of the convent several times because of it. So that's why I'm telling you to be careful."

"Aunt Monica, are you sure you're a nun?"

She laughed.

"I don't know, Yujeong. I have no idea. Wearing a black dress doesn't make you a nun, and carrying a Bible doesn't make you a Christian. Now that it's autumn, I don't feel right. If I have to say goodbye to another of those boys this year, I don't know how I'll carry on. Last time, Father Kim attended the executions. The shock was so bad that he couldn't do anything for three months. Maybe that's where his cancer came from. We're not just campaigning against the death penalty for those boys, we're also doing it for our own sake."

She sighed. Lately, each time I met with Yunsu, I pictured a round noose dropping down over his eyes. I thought I could imagine how white his face would turn when that happened. But then again, Yunsu's face was always pretty pale. Each time I pictured it happening, my heart screamed, *No! Don't!* To be honest, I felt pathetic, wondering how on earth I had become involved with these people and been made to imagine things I shouldn't have had to. I wondered, too, who had come up with the expression, "turning into the gallows' dew" to refer to a hanging. Whenever I heard someone use it, I clenched my teeth and told them they shouldn't call it "gallows' dew" but rather "gallows' blood and sweat".

Officer Yi had told me that the noose they used in the execution room was stained black—most likely from the bodily fluids that were wrung out when the rope tightened around the prisoners' throats—and he had added that they sometimes talked about getting a new rope but no one had taken the initiative yet. When the subject of the death penalty came up in conversation, one of my friends would invariably say that she or he had heard that execution by hanging was the least painful method, and I would retort, *Did you ask them yourself? Did you ask the dead whether that was the best way to die?* I would get all worked up for nothing, but in countries like the United States, which, along with Japan, is one of the few advanced countries to still have a system of capital punishment, executions by hanging have long since fallen out of practice. When given the choice between the electric chair, lethal injection, and the noose, no one ever chose the noose.

"Yunsu is donating his eyes. After he dies, they'll go to someone else," Aunt Monica told me. "He said the thought of a blind person being able to see through his corneas makes him feel like he's atoning. He wrote me a letter asking me to sign the release form. He doesn't have any family members to do it for him. He tried to locate his mother, since she's the one who's supposed to sign the form. She's listed as missing for now, and the priests have been asking around. But no one has found her yet."

We walked back to the Catholic meeting room along a path swirling with fallen leaves. This time, when Yunsu saw Aunt Monica, he went up to her first and hugged her. The two of them stood there for a moment. Tiny Aunt Monica was crying in Yunsu's big arms. She apologized for crying and said that she was getting silly with age, but Yunsu's face darkened when he saw her tears.

We sipped coffee and talked.

"I saw an article in the paper about viewing the fall foliage," Yunsu told us. "It hit me that falling leaves are really a form of death for trees, and yet people travel a long way to look at it and remark on how beautiful it is. It got me thinking. When I die, I want to die as beautifully as a falling leaf. I want people to see it and exclaim over the beauty of it."

We sipped our coffee for a while in silence. Yunsu seemed excited, probably because he had not seen Aunt Monica in a while. Or maybe now that he had offered to donate his eyes, even his body had become lighter. He was more talkative than usual that day.

"After the incident, when they first brought me here, there was a seventeen-year-old kid who was doing time for petty larceny. They let him out on probation. He was really clever and nice, so I treated him like a little brother. When he left, I told him to never come back and that if he kept up his old ways, he would turn out just like me. But they brought him in again last week. Again, for petty larceny.

Seems he stole a cell phone. The prosecutor saw that he already had a strike on his record and went ahead and had him incarcerated. I asked him what happened, and he said when he left here the last time he stood alone outside for three hours."

Aunt Monica clucked her tongue.

"What could he do? He had nowhere to go. He met up with his old accomplices again and wound up back in jail. I decided it can't happen a third time, so I asked one of the CEOs in here to give the kid a job at his factory. It has a dormitory, so he'll also have a place to stay. I think he likes me, because he agreed to do so."

"You know a CEO?" I asked.

Yunsu smiled.

"We have a president, a government minister, and a *chaebol* leader in here as well. How could we not have at least one CEO?"

He smiled proudly. When he put it that way, it made sense.

"I was reading a book of poetry recently. This guard who bullies me every time he sees me said, 'Who are you kidding?' And he walked on by. Immediately, I thought, *I'm gonna get that asshole next time I'm outside.*"

He stared at us. Then he lowered his head.

"With my temper, I would have, too. But then I pictured your faces."

He dropped his head further. The conversation seemed to be getting too heavy for him, because he pulled several letters out of his pocket instead of continuing.

"Sister, I've been writing letters to these kids lately."

We spread open one letter and saw that it was from children living in Taebaek in Gangwon Province.

Yunsu had read a magazine article about children at a branch school in Taebaek who were struggling because they could not afford school supplies. He had been with-drawing some of the money we put in his commissary account and sending it to them every month. The children had sent him a thank-you letter. An inmate awaiting death had become a pen pal with lonely kids living in a distant mountain village. I didn't have to read the letters to know how ardent they were. Both the children and Yunsu were probably as lonely as caged deer.

While Aunt Monica and I were looking at the letters, Yunsu sheepishly said, "Sister Monica, I have a favor to ask. I'm in trouble."

We stopped perusing and looked up at him in surprise.

"I accidentally promised them something."

Aunt Monica smoothed the front of her dress and said, "Watch what you're saying. You gave me a start when you said you were in trouble."

"I asked them what they want to do more than anything else in this world, and they said they want to see the ocean. Where they live, it's nothing but mountains, mountains, and more mountains. The ocean is only an hour away by train. They said that's their wish. So I told them I would make their wish come true. They don't know who I am, and my return address is a PO box in the Gunpo post office. They must think I'm some rich CEO who lives in Gunpo City, because they wrote to me to say they came up with a plan and decided to go to Gangneung to watch the sun rise on January 1. Sister, what should I do?"

I could tell that Yunsu was thinking about his little brother, whom he sometimes mentioned. Since he had told me his brother was blind, I knew he was thinking about him when he decided to donate his corneas. I didn't ask him anything about it until he brought it up himself, but I'd had a feeling that was why he did it. Since all I knew about his little brother was that he had died in the streets, I wanted to help Yunsu make those kids' wish to see the ocean come true.

"I'll take care of it," I said. "I won't get anything in return this time, which means I'll be left empty-handed, but I'll cover the expenses."

He smiled brightly as if he knew I was going to say that.

"Since the balance is already tipped, I'll add just one more favor," he said. "Please take pictures so I can see it, too. The rising sun, the kids' faces—please take big, clear pictures of all of it. I would love to go to the beach myself and see those happy kids. But if I can at least see the photos, I'll be happy even if I can't be there myself."

I wrote the school's address down in my notebook. While I was writing, it hit me that Yunsu would never go to the beach again. I wondered if he would still be alive when the children went to the beach, the sun rose on 1998, and the photos were printed.

"But I can make this fair," Yunsu said.

He pulled something out from beneath the table and said, "Ta-da!" It was a cross. Two rough pieces of wood were criss-crossed, and hanging from them was a dark-gray, hand-molded Jesus. Aunt Monica and I looked at it in wonder, and Yunsu laughed.

"I'll give you this in exchange. I saved a few grains of cooked rice each time I ate and used them to make this."

We took a closer look. The gray color had come from the dirt that rubbed off of his hands onto the rice when he was molding it. To our surprise, the face looked like Yunsu's—curly hair and a longish face.

"I'd like you to give this one to that lady."

He meant the mother of the woman he had killed.

"She wrote me a letter recently. I don't think she's doing well. She said she slipped in the snow and hurt her back.

I'm making another one. I'll give that one to you, Sister Monica. And this is for you, Yujeong."

Yunsu pulled a necklace out of his pocket. It was a blue plastic cross hanging from a thin red cord. I reached my hand out, and he placed it in my palm and paused there for the briefest moment. His hand was very warm. I pulled my hand away shyly.

"I made two. I'm wearing the other one."

I put the necklace on as a way of saying thank you. He explained that he had whittled the pendant without a knife by grating it against the cement. He had ground the plastic with his hands cuffed together. He had probably whittled away at it all day long and again the next day, grating it against the cement and blowing away the plastic dust.

"Now you two have matching necklaces," said Officer Yi. We laughed.

Aunt Monica clutched the cross he had made for her to her heart without saying anything. She looked like she was praying. Yunsu and I looked at each other. I realized for the first time that the cross was also an execution tool. Crucifixion—the diabolical punishment devised by the Romans to control the people they had colonized. Since nailing a person to a cross was not enough to kill them, the person was usually tortured for several days first. The torture would last all night long. Beating the person nearly to death was standard, and sometimes their eyes were gouged out as well. The moment they were nailed to the cross, they were all but on the verge of death.

Nevertheless, the victims would survive for several more days, and since removing the body was forbidden on principle, they were picked apart by birds and wild animals. Jesus was a death row convict, too. Even if it had been put to a direct vote, he still would have been executed. After all, it was recorded that the angry crowds shouted,

"Crucify him!" But if Jesus had been hanged instead, then Christians would have spent the last two thousand years wearing nooses around their necks and hanging them from church roofs, and statues of Jesus would have dangled by their necks in every church. I suddenly felt thankful that Jesus was executed as a criminal. Otherwise, who would have dared try to comfort Yunsu?

That year, Yunsu was baptized during the Christmas Mass. It was a Thursday. I attended his baptism. His baptismal name was Augustine, after the young heathen who consorted with prostitutes and led a life of debauchery until, one day, he was drawn by the sound of a childlike voice to open up the Gospel and read, after which he converted and became one of Christianity's greatest saints. Augustine was also the son of Saint Monica, from whom Aunt Monica had taken her Christian name. During the Mass, I was seated in the choir with other women who volunteered at the detention center. Yunsu was sitting far away from me; he was wearing a set of white clothes given to him by the female volunteers. They made him look strange and new. Swaddled in fabric like a baby, Yunsu looked as excited as a little boy on his first day at kindergarten.

Before Mass began, I stepped forward to sing the national anthem. Aunt Monica had asked me to. Some of the people there recognized me; I could hear them whispering. In the past, the idea of singing in front of these people, in front of people who would be ex-convicts upon leaving this place, in front of fake believers who were only there to get free Choco Pies, would have been unimaginable to me, but I told Aunt Monica I was happy to do it. I was doing it for Yunsu. And when I thought about it, I was a bigger fake and hypocrite than any of those people. I had even gone so far as to join the prison ministry. Yunsu told me he couldn't sleep at night at the thought that he was so close to death and yet would be reborn through baptism. He said it was the first time in his life that he had been too happy to sleep. He said he could not believe that God would accept someone who was even lower than an animal. For Yunsu, I went to the front of the chapel and picked up a microphone for the first time in ten years. While the prelude rang out, I caught Yunsu's eye. He was sitting with other death row prisoners in the very front pew. I gave him a quick smile, but he looked stiff. He was probably thinking about his little brother. I began to sing. *Until the East Sea runs dry and Mt. Baekdu wears away, God save us and keep our nation...* When I finished and stepped down from the pulpit, Yunsu had his head down. I could tell he was crying.

The last time I saw him, he had told me, *When the judge sentenced me—no, when I killed those people, I was already dead. But now I've come back to life because people helped me, because they held my hand and told me it was okay if I couldn't run because I should start by walking.* I wanted to cry with Yunsu. My heart was cracking open like the soil in a dry rice paddy. Yunsu looked over at the choir through his tears. He seemed to be looking for me. Our eyes met. His white teeth flashed as he tried hard to smile. I was struck by the sight of the handcuffs that bound his wrists even as his white teeth and curly black hair were being reborn.

Mass ended, and the banquet began. Yunsu smiled broadly as his fellow prisoners congratulated him. While passing out Choco Pies, I asked him how it was. "Yujeong," he said, "trust me. You've got to try believing in Christ. I promise you. It's really good." I didn't say anything.

"I heard an ex-convict was elected president," he said while eating a Choco Pie with cuffed hands. "He said there would be no executions while he's in office. The other guys think that means none of us will be executed, since he's president now. That's what he promised. Yujeong, I've been thinking. For the first time, I want to live. I didn't used to. But for the first time, I thought, what if I could keep living here, writing letters to children even though my hands are cuffed, passing along the love that I've received from everyone even though my body is shackled, spending the rest of my life praying and atoning for the people I hurt? I could think of this place as a monastery. I know I don't deserve it. It's shameless of me to even think that way."

That was the last time I saw Yunsu.

It takes the whole of life to learn how to live, and—what will perhaps make you wonder more—it takes the whole of life to learn how to die.

– Seneca

BLUE NOTE 17

We split the money and ran our separate ways. In my typical fashion, I headed straight for a room salon where I blew my money on girls and had a good time. I didn't find out until later, but the other guy went straight home. There, his wife convinced him to turn himself in. He went to the police and told them everything. But he switched the stories around so that what I did became what he did and what he did became what I did. Of course, what's the point of explaining all of this now? I was put on the most-wanted list for raping and killing a teenager and killing two women. My photograph was shown all over the country, and I became a hunted man. I searched for the friend I had loaned money to in order to convince him to pay for my girlfriend's surgery. He told me not to worry and said he would make sure she was okay after she got out of hospital. Then, that night, he and I went to another bar and drank and caroused with women to our hearts' content. We fell asleep in a motel, and in the morning I awoke to the sound of someone banging on the door. My friend had reported me to the police and run away. Maybe he thought that was the only way he would get out of paying me back the money I'd loaned him.

I pried open the motel window, jumped out, and ran into the first house I saw. I grabbed a knife from the kitchen and forced the woman and her child into a room. Then I called my girlfriend for the last time.

The woman I loved was with my friend. He had gone to her the night before. She said that he paid her hospital bill and had her discharged. She said she owed him now, and since he had asked her to marry him... She said he told her he had loved her from the moment he first saw her at the beauty salon. She asked me why I did it. Didn't she tell me from the very beginning how much she hated bad guys? The police tried to break down the door and get inside. I held the knife to the throat of the woman whose house I had broken into and taken hostage. The woman's child cried, "Mommy, Mommy!" It reminded me of Eunsu when he was little. A bullet hit me in the leg, and I was arrested.

CHAPTER 17

With the end of the year approaching, there wasn't much time left. I reserved hotel rooms in Gangneung, rented a bus for the kids, and had to make several phone calls to the principal of the branch school in Taebaek. All of the preparations were complete, but there was still the problem of the camera. I didn't own one and couldn't even remember the last time I had taken a photograph. I called my youngest sister-in-law. She was in the last month of her pregnancy. She agreed to waddle out to meet me to loan me her camera. While waiting for her in the lobby of a department store in Gangnam, I spotted her in the distance. Just as my brother Yusik had described, she had no makeup on and was dressed plainly. Since she was pregnant on top of that, who would have recognized her as the glamorous actress she once was? It was true that she looked haggard and wasn't very pretty anymore. But instead her face radiated something like peace. She had the dignity and grace of a person who's become perfectly centered in their body. I took the camera from her and handed her a shopping bag.

"What is this?" she asked.

"Clothes... for the baby. Just something pretty that caught my eye."

She looked surprised. Despite all of the nieces and nephews that had been born, I had never once bought anything for them. If I ran into one of my brothers' wives, I would say, *Congratulations, I hear it's a boy*. But each time I did, it felt like asking someone who was clearly not in a good mood how he or she was doing. That day, I stared at my sister-in-law's enormous belly and wondered for the first time what it would feel like to become a mother. I started to ask myself, *What if?* The idea of my being a mother was absurd; nevertheless, I thought I could hear something tapping inside of me, the desire beginning to sprout like a wildflower poking its way through the mortar of a brick wall and blooming there.

"Miss, I heard you've been doing some important volunteer work. It shows in your face—you're glowing."

She had an unaffected way of speaking. I used to doubt every word that came out of her mouth. I thought that behind her words were machinations and scheming. Or that she was a fool. But she was not the fool: *I* was. And the only machinations and scheming were the ones going on in my own mind. I was always scheming to see other people as bad, one way or another. And in the end, that was a foolish thing to do. It made me uncomfortable to be alone with her, as if I were a bad student who had suddenly been caught doing a good deed for the first time in a long while. I turned to leave but she stopped me.

"Miss, you should go see your mother. I think she's waiting for you."

Not that again, I thought and started to walk away, but she added, "Your mother's lonely," although it was possible that I misheard her. I dragged my tired body through a few more errands and then went home.

It made me happy to think about how delighted Yunsu would be when I showed him the photos of the sun rising on the first day of the year and the children's faces like bright flowers. Aunt Monica had teased me about it. "Thanks to Yunsu, you're finally doing something for others." In the past, whenever I saw people who did things for others, I thought, *Hypocrites, you're all just doing it to make yourself feel better, aren't you?* But now I wanted to do things for Yunsu. If he was happy, I was happy. For the first time in my life, I realized that being a hypocrite could feel good, too.

I hummed as I took a quick shower. Then I made some tea and was grading my students' work when a strange feeling came over me. I can't explain exactly what it was, but it felt like a sudden restlessness. No matter what I did, the feeling would not go away, and my heart began to beat in a strange rhythm. The walls looked like they were bobbing up and down. I had never felt this way before. I went to the kitchen and poured myself a glass of wine. I glanced out the kitchen window out of habit: the teenagers were back in the park behind the apartment complex. This time as well, there was a swarm of them, and they were beating someone up again. I looked at the telephone and debated what to do but wound up taking the wine glass and returning to my chair.

The winter sun was already hanging low to the west. The phone rang. It was Aunt Monica. From the way she said my name, I could tell that she was shaking. Even before she said anything, I thought, *No!* Everything went white before my eyes.

"Aunt Monica—"

"Father Kim just called. He was told to go to the detention center early tomorrow morning. Yunsu…"

I could not bring myself to ask. How could I say those words out loud? But it wasn't the words. My mind went blank, and the space before my eyes seemed to lose its shape and wobble like tofu.

"I'm going to the detention center at dawn tomorrow," Aunt Monica said. "Yujeong, you need to pray. Pray."

It was the first time she had ever told me to pray.

After we hung up, I picked up my wine then set it down again. The color really did look like blood, and I couldn't drink it. I went back to the living room, sat down, and then stood up again. *No*, I thought. *No, no, no.* I wondered what Yunsu was doing at that moment. He would have no clue. In that place where I could not call and could not visit, he was probably spending his last night without any idea that it was his last. That seemed crueler than dying. I called Officer Yi.

When he answered his phone, his voice sounded very distressed, and I could tell that he didn't feel like talking.

"I'm heading over now. Please let me see him. Just five minutes—no, one minute."

"I can't do that. It's against the rules."

"You can. I'll take full responsibility. Even if I can't stop him from dying, he at least deserves to know he's going to die! He needs to be ready. We can't just let him spend the rest of the night not knowing what's going on!"

Officer Yi didn't say a word. Of course, Yunsu already knew he was dying. He had spent two and a half years knowing he would die. The only thing he didn't know was whether it would be today or the next day. We all know it: that we will die some day. But even though he was on death row, was it right not to notify him of his death and allow him to prepare for it? But what could Officer Yi do?

I hung up and paced back and forth in my room. No. It was too mean and inhumane. It was murder. And then it occurred to me. The only type of death that can be predicted, and stopped, is a death by execution. Yet we were helpless to do anything about it.

I tried getting on my knees, but I couldn't pray. It had

been too long. "Save him. Please save him," I mumbled. "I know he did a bad thing, but if you would save him, if you would only save him..." At that instant, the memory came back to me. Fifteen years ago, in that brute's room on the second floor of the head family's house, when I cried in his grasp, not knowing what else to do, I had prayed just like this. My prayer had gone unanswered. I felt like the wind was knocked out of me. I stood up. I could hear the clock tick. It was five in the afternoon. The execution was set for ten the next morning. In seventeen hours, he would be gone. The clock ticked on and on, oblivious. I pulled the batteries out. A breathless silence filled the room as time stood still.

All of the hours that I had spent with him began to flash before my eyes. Not the times when he clenched his teeth and lashed out at Aunt Monica or when he scoffed at her, but rather the times he laughed and the times his tears fell. The time he shook and said, "I'm sorry, I'm sorry" when he met the mother of the woman he killed. Would he shake like that when he entered the execution room and the noose was lowered? Just four days earlier, he had told me, *What if I could keep living here, writing letters to children even though my hands are cuffed, passing along the love that I've received from everyone even though my body is shackled, spending the rest of my life praying and atoning for the people I hurt? I could think of this place as a monastery. I know I don't deserve it. It's shameless of me to even think that way.*

How many minutes had gone by? Time had lost all rhythm. A sudden anxiety came over me: What if the whole night had already gone by and dawn was approaching? I grabbed my cell phone to check the time. It had only been three minutes. It scared me all over again to see how slowly this parched hour was passing. Then I realized that maybe it was better for Yunsu not to know. I realized it might be unbearable for him otherwise, and I started to feel a little better. I looked at my hands and stood up. Then I slowly walked over to the telephone.

I dialed information.

"I'm looking for someone named Mun Yuseong." My lips kept twitching as I spoke. It was the first time I had ever said his full name out loud. Before it happened, I used to call him Brother.

"Mr. Mun Yuseong? What is the address?" I told the operator I didn't know. I knew I was being stupid. But I couldn't call my brother Yusik and ask. "There are many people named Mun Yuseong all over the country," she said politely.

"He lives in Seoul," I told her. "In a rich neighborhood. I'm not sure where."

"I'm sorry," the operator continued, "but I will need more information to locate his phone number for you." She was friendly, but her voice was flat. I hung up and left the apartment. When I got in my car and turned the key, my hands were shaking. I clenched my teeth and put the car in gear.

My mother had her reading glasses on and was flipping through a magazine. She lifted her head as I came in. I stood in the doorway and stared at her.

"What are you doing here?" she asked.

When she said that, I wanted to turn around and leave. It would have been easier for me if she had at least looked a little more haggard, or just a little bit more pitiful. Or if she'd looked a bit lonelier, as my sister-in-law had said. But to my regret, my mother looked healthy and relaxed.

Mummy, it hurts, it hurts really bad. She may have been my mother, but it was still hard back then for me, a grown girl, to show her my private parts. She had looked at me down there for a moment and then pulled my underwear back up. Then she had said coldly, "You don't know what you're talking about."

I couldn't believe it at first. When I had left the head family's house, I had trouble walking because of the swelling in my crotch. I had walked down the street crying, a girl in a grown-up body. Each time I thought I could not go any further because of the pain that threatened to tear me in half with each step, I told myself that if I could just get to my mother, if I could just tell her what had happened, everything would be okay. I believed that I would be comforted and that he would be punished. But the moment I heard her words and saw the cold look on her face, a clear barricade seemed to drop like a guillotine blade and lodge itself between us.

"Cousin Yuseong called me into his room. He said he had something to tell me. So I went upstairs. He pulled off my underwear... Mommy, it hurts. I'm scared. It hurts so much."

I was crying and overwhelmed with pain and fear and could not keep talking.

My mother went downstairs and returned after a moment. She handed me a tube of generic ointment.

"Put this on it and go to sleep. And keep your mouth shut. You got what was coming to you, wagging your tail around like that, a grown girl..."

I collapsed on the floor, the ointment my mother had given me clutched in my hand.

"You have no shame. Keep quiet and don't go prancing around in front of your older brothers. Understand? You really do read too many storybooks!"

"No!"

I screamed as hard as I could. My mother covered my mouth. "No, no, no!" When I struggled, she slapped me on the cheek over and over. It was the first time she had ever hit me.

⟶══◦═⟵

I walked over to my mother. With a scowl on her face, she turned over the magazine that she had been looking at and sat up. To my surprise, she looked scared.

"What's wrong with you?" she yelled.

I couldn't open my mouth. My lips trembled. I wanted to turn around and go home.

"I didn't know what else to do. So I came here... to tell you... I forgive you."

My heart felt like it was being sliced into a million pieces. Tears sprang from my eyes, as if the blood that had congealed in a corner of my parched, cracked heart had started moving again. My eyes ached.

"I couldn't forgive you before. And even right now, at this very moment, I don't want to! What you did was even more unforgiveable than what he did. But I'm here today to try to forgive you."

My mother still had no idea what I was talking about, but she snorted like it was nothing.

"You sure find all sorts of ways to worry me. Your mother is dying and you don't even visit once. But now you show up—and for what? Who should be forgiving whom?"

"I should forgive you!"

My mother pushed her blanket away and sat up straight.

"Are you crazy? Do we need to call your uncle? What's wrong with you?"

I wept loudly like a child. The crying I could not do at

fifteen, and the crying I did not do even once after that day, was forcing its way up my throat. I felt I would suffocate to death if I did not let it out.

I tugged at the blue crucifix necklace Yunsu had given me. Even that seemed to be choking me. Is this what it would feel like to hang from the gallows? The face is covered in a white cloth hood, and the rope is looped around the neck. The order is given, and five bailiffs pull five levers. I read that only one of the five actually works, but the purpose is to lessen the sense of guilt for the bailiffs. When the real lever is pulled, the floor opens up beneath the kneeling prisoner, and he is hanged. Often, his feet are still shaking, even after he has been hanging for fifteen to twenty minutes. After the doctor presses a stethoscope to the prisoner's chest to verify that the heart has stopped, he is left hanging for another twenty minutes. Some people are still not dead even after all of that, and sometimes the rope breaks or is too long. Others just fall and wind up bruised and bloodied. If that happens, they start over from the beginning. Such is the ceremony they call an execution.

My tears would not stop. My throat ached from crying for the first time in fifteen years. It ached as if I were being throttled.

My mother tried to sneak around me toward the door. Though my mouth had spat out the word *forgive*, my eyes were probably brimming with murder, just as Yunsu's once did, and just as mine had for a long time. But I thought maybe it would be better if my uncle were there, as she had suggested. Then maybe he would say, *That's right, Yujeong, go ahead and cry. You should cry.* Then I would probably tell him, *I'm sorry, Uncle.* He would ask me what I was sorry about. And I would say, *I don't know, I don't know why I am sorry.*

"I don't want to forgive you," I said to my mother. "But I think I'm supposed to. I think maybe I'm supposed to make a sacrifice of my own. And it should be the hardest thing there is for me to do, the thing I'd rather die than do. That means forgiving you!"

My brother Yusik opened the door and came in. He must have been stopping by on his way home. My mother ran over to him.

"Yusik! Something's wrong with Yujeong. How am I supposed to die peacefully when she keeps acting like this? That poor thing. I don't know what's wrong with her."

She started crying, too. Was she afraid? I had no idea. Was she hurt because of me? I thought maybe so. She was probably thinking the same thing I was: *Why the hell does the world keep angering me and refusing me even the tiniest sliver of peace and happiness?* It was just a guess, but I figured she was crying out of anger.

Yusik sat her down in a chair and tried to calm her down. Then he came over to me. He grabbed my arm hard, and I staggered. "I need to forgive her," I muttered. He dragged a chair over and sat me down in it. "I came here to forgive her," I said stubbornly.

"The execution is tomorrow," I told him. "They're going to kill him! I thought if I did something I don't normally do... I know it's stupid, but there was nothing, not a single thing, that I could do. I thought that if there really is a God, then he would know how hard this is for me, he would know that this is something worse than death, and he would look kindly on me and maybe, just maybe, a miracle would happen. Can you understand?"

He let out a long sigh.

"Everyone expected Father Kim to die, but he got better. So I thought this was what I was supposed to do. We need to open our eyes... Yusik, what am I supposed to do? It's not fair. I tried to kill myself more than once, so God should take me instead. I'm just as much a sinner."

He grasped my shoulders, his face filled with patience.

"I... I was going to love him. Since I can never be with any man anyway, I thought it would be okay if Yunsu were alive, even if he had to stay in prison forever. I just want him to live."

My brother seemed to understand everything at once. He shouldn't have understood it, or accepted it, but he at least knew what I was trying to say. Yunsu wasn't gone yet, but since there was nothing I could do to stop the execution from happening, my brother probably felt reassured that there wasn't any real danger.

"Why didn't you tell me that in the first place?" he asked gently.

"Would you have tried to save him if I did?"

He didn't say anything.

"Yusik, I haven't told anyone else."

I lowered my head. I had failed again. I had done a foolish thing.

⋅→══◉═══→⋅

It was a long, long night. I still remember that night. Everything was so vivid and yet so numb at the same time. I kept flipping back and forth between both extremes. And then dawn came. I had fallen asleep. When I woke up and looked out, the sky was hazy. The air was cold. I felt ashamed for having fallen asleep at a time like that. I couldn't shake the thought that I was alive while he was about to die. I ran out and got into my car. When I look back on it now, I was like a shaman dancing on knives. I was neither tired nor hungry. Everything felt unreal, like the time I smoked hashish in France and time and space seemed to drift around. The only difference between now and then is that back then I was powered by drugs, whereas now I was powered by suffering. When people reach an extreme, they all feel the same thing: numbness.

Aunt Monica was already waiting outside the execution room. She looked like she had shrunk into a black ball. The execution was scheduled for 10:00 am. I checked my watch: 9:50 am. She held a cloth bundle in her hands. He was not dead yet, but we were already holding his mementos. Aunt Monica closed her eyes, her hands clasped around her rosary. I took the bundle from her hands. The simple bundle held everything he had owned in his twenty-seven years. I looked through it. A Bible, underwear, socks, a blanket, and some books. And a blue spiral notebook. I pulled it out. Written on the cover in black marker were the words: *Jeong Yunsu's Diary*. I clutched it to my heart as if it were Yunsu himself.

A Buddhist monk, a pastor, and a priest filed into the execution room, while the family members and volunteers stayed outside. One person had already fainted and had to be carried out. A woman dressed in the gray robes of a Buddhist hermitage approached Aunt Monica and took her hand.

"Sister, be strong."

Aunt Monica nodded weakly.

"Those boys are barely even human when they come in here," the woman said as she cried, "but they are angels when they leave. We kill them after they become angels. Sister, let's stop this. I can't take it anymore."

Aunt Monica patted her on the back.

The Buddhist woman hugged Aunt Monica and cried. I moved to a corner. A woman I had seen several times in the detention center came over to me and asked, "Are you okay? Your lips are white." I told her I was fine, and she said, "Don't be sad. They're going to heaven today." I wanted to snap, "I bet you wish you could send them there yourself," but I didn't have the energy. I walked away from her. She pressed her hands together, raised them up in the air, and mumbled something. Then she came over to me again with a bright look on her face. I would've preferred it if she weren't there.

"Don't cry," she said. "They're going to heaven today. Their suffering is over. You're the inmate's older sister, right? I think I've seen you here a few times."

"No, I am not his sister!"

I shouted at her and walked away. As I did so, I spotted someone in a uniform hovering on the other side of the room. It was Officer Yi, looking like he could not bring himself to come over and join me but could not quite leave either. The moment my eyes met his, he dropped his head and avoided my gaze. His eyes were very bloodshot. Suddenly, I thought about how I had said I was not Yunsu's sister. I stood next to the wall and wept. I wept like Peter when he denied knowing Jesus three times. It was 10 o'clock.

Have I any pleasure in the death of the wicked, declares the Lord GOD, and not rather that he should turn from his way and live?

– Ezekiel 18:23

BLUE NOTE 18

Before I started writing these notes, I wrote a letter to my accomplice at his prison in Wonju. I told him I forgave him. I forgave him for switching our stories and hiring a lawyer and making me the main culprit. And I forgave the police for not investigating the case properly and wrongfully accusing me of rape and murder, the public defender who only came to see me twice in eight months while my three trials were taking place, the prosecutor who treated me like an insect rather than a human being, and the judge who pretended to be cool, as objective as a god, even while enraged at me for committing murder. I wrote that I forgave them all. I forgave my father who ended his life like a helpless animal. And, before the merciful Lord, I forgave myself. I told Him I forgave myself for beating up my little brother Eunsu, for not singing the national anthem for him even though it was his final wish, and for cursing in his face and running out on him when he was sick. And, for participating in the murder of three innocent people. Only then was I finally able to get down on my knees and beg for forgiveness from the two women and the helpless girl who died because of me. I was able to kiss the earth and exclaim: I am not a human being. I am a murderer.

The reason I was able to do this is that, after coming to the detention center, I have been treated as a human being for the first time in my life. I understand for the first time what it means to be human and what it means to love. I know finally how people can speak to and treat each other with respect, and love each other with trembling hearts. Had I never murdered anyone and wound up here, I might have been able to extend my physical life, but my soul would have wandered forever through maggot-infested sewers. I would not have even known that they were maggots and that I was in the sewer. After coming here, I have experienced happiness for the first time. Waiting, getting excited about meeting someone, sharing a real conversation with another human being, praying for someone, meeting without pretense—I understand now what that all means.

Only someone who has been loved can love. Only someone who has been forgiven can forgive. I understand that.

Probably no one will find this notebook until after I am dead. If the president who used to be on death row puts a stay on further executions as he promised, then I will have to say all of this myself, even though the words have so far refused to come out of my mouth. Nevertheless, if I do die, then please, whoever is reading this, please pass it along to Sister Monica's niece, Mun Yujeong. I wanted to tell her everything and have more real conversations with her, but I couldn't bring myself to. I was afraid she would be disappointed in me. I was afraid she would be disappointed and leave, like everyone else in my life. If she refuses to take this notebook, then please tell her one thing for me: The times we spent together, the instant coffee we drank, the little pastries we shared—those few hours each week enabled me to bear any insult, withstand any pain, forgive any grudge, and truly repent for my sins. Tell her that, because of her, I have had so many warm and precious and happy times. And tell her that, if she were to allow me, I would do whatever it takes to comfort her wounded soul. Finally, if God permits me to before I die, I want to tell her the words that I have never once said to anyone else in my life: I love you.

CHAPTER 18

The Gwangtan-ri cemetery was cold. During the funeral Mass, I stood at the back and did not participate. I had prayed earnestly twice in my life. Both times were to ask for someone's life to be saved. God should have listened to at least one of those prayers. But he didn't. The woman who died at Yunsu's hands had probably prayed as well. What was the point of holding Mass after someone is hurt and killed? Wasn't it just so the living could comfort themselves? Yunsu had told me to trust him and to try to believe in Christ. Did I have to believe in a god who had probably never once listened to Yunsu's prayers? I stared at the spot where Yunsu was going to be buried.

Gwangtan-ri Catholic Cemetery Park. A liberal priest had donated a little bit of land that became a burial place for executed criminals. It was not a warm and sunny spot but the dark northern slope of the hill that even the sunlight skipped over. Yunsu had spent his life in the cold, and now that he was dead, he would be buried in the cold as well. Statues of the Virgin Mary and an angel stood close to where Yunsu would be buried. I asked Aunt Monica, "Why are the Mary and angel statues always so dirty where poor people are buried? Someone should clean them. Those

251

statues are filthy. That makes me so angry." But all Aunt Monica did was cry.

Father Kim, who was present during Yunsu's final moments, had come to see us right after the execution was over. His hair had fallen out from the chemotherapy, and he was wearing a black cap to cover up his baldness. He looked like he had not yet fully processed the fear and awe that come over someone who has witnessed a death. Aunt Monica went up to him and said, "Father." He lifted his head, but I couldn't exactly say that he was looking at her. Never before in my life have I seen such a troubled expression on a man's face.

"He died peacefully." Father Kim had struggled to get the words out for those of us who had been waiting. "When I went in, I was shaking. Yunsu said to me, 'If you shake like that, Sister Monica will get mad at you.' He told me to be a man."

Aunt Monica reeled backwards. I caught her.

"I prayed, gave him communion, and asked if he had any last words, and he said he first wanted to offer one final sincere apology to those who had lost their lives because of him. He apologized to their families, too. Then he apologized to the mother of the cleaning lady. He said he was thankful to her, and that her courage enabled him to be reborn. Then he said that he forgave his mother. But he changed his mind and asked me to tell her instead how much he missed her, how much he had always missed her, and that he only wanted to see her one last time before he died. He asked me to pass that message along."

The women who had been volunteering at the detention center for a long time began to cry even louder.

"Then Yunsu mumbled, 'Father, it was so simple, all I had to do was love.' He said he figured it out too late. I asked him if he felt like singing, as the prisoners from other denominations are allowed to do, and I asked if he knew any hymns. He said that since he was baptized recently, he did not yet know any. Then he said he would sing the national anthem instead."

I couldn't listen to any more of it. Aunt Monica squeezed my hand.

"So he sang it. The national anthem."

Father Kim paused, teary-eyed, as if it were difficult to keep going.

"When the bailiffs made him kneel, he..."

We were all staring at Father Kim.

"He started to struggle. The last look in his eyes was of fear. The bailiffs rushed to cover his face with the hood, and Yunsu screamed, 'Father, save me, I'm frightened. I'm still scared even though I sang the anthem.' I couldn't look at him anymore..."

Father Kim was as pale as if he had been the one hanging from the noose.

We went down to the basement to view the body. Yunsu's eye sockets were empty—an ambulance had been waiting to take his eyes immediately after the execution. In death, Yunsu had turned as blind as his younger brother. But we comforted each other by saying that his corneas would enable another blind child like Eunsu to see. Aunt Monica rushed over to Yunsu's body, which had not yet turned stiff, and embraced him. She stroked his neck. There was a black mark, like a skid mark on asphalt, around his throat. Aunt Monica patted his neck as if he were still alive, rubbed his cheek, and prayed quietly.

I stood beside her and held Yunsu's hand—a hand that was uncuffed only after he was dead. His skin was as cold as a candle. I remembered how his hand had hovered over mine, though only for a moment, when he gave me the cross necklace he had made. His skin was so warm then.

Why didn't I smile and take his hand? Why didn't I tell him I loved him? As Yunsu said, it was so simple. All we had to do was love each other. And now that warmth was gone. If the fading of warmth signifies death, then the moment we lose the warmth in our hearts—that must be another kind of death. There was a time when he and I were oblivious to that knowledge and just wanted to die. Maybe that, too, was already a type of death.

❖

After Mass, Aunt Monica and I rushed to leave for Gangneung. She slept while I drove. Though I had neither eaten nor slept in two days, I was not tired. A strange feeling came over me while I was driving. My back grew warm, so I turned to look. The back seat was empty. But something definitely felt different. Yunsu had never been in my car or even seen it. Yunsu? I said his name quietly. There was no answer.

We reached the ocean. Since it was the end of the year, the hotel was crowded. The principal of the branch school in Taebaek had arrived with eight students. The children chattered and ran around excitedly when they saw the beach for the first time. I realized that I had forgotten to bring the camera my sister-in-law lent me. Then I realized that I no longer needed it. Yunsu had said that he wanted to see the beach; maybe he was seeing it now. That's what I wanted to believe. The sky was overcast. The ocean looked gloomy. But there was no telling how the weather would be tomorrow. Nobody knew that.

A small, thin man headed over to where Aunt Monica and I were standing and introduced himself as the principal of Taebaek Branch School. He thanked us for arranging the trip and then scratched his head in bewilderment.

"I got a phone call from the Seoul Detention Center today," he said. "They said Jeong Yunsu was sending me money. I told them I heard he was executed yesterday, and they said he had asked the prison guard in advance to send any money left in his account to us if he was suddenly executed. I don't want to use this precious money unwisely, so I wanted to ask for your advice."

The principal took a bankbook out of the breast pocket of his coat and showed it to us. It was a very small amount.

"We're currently installing a permanent awning next to the schoolyard. If it's all right with you, we were thinking of putting the money toward that. The classrooms are spacious enough for us, but when the children are playing in the schoolyard, they have nowhere to go to get out of the rain, and in the summer, there's no shade where they can just read a book or relax. It has been difficult for them. So we wanted to ask what you thought of putting the money toward the awning."

Aunt Monica whispered, "Oh Lord." She and I were thinking of Yunsu's journal, which we had read together the night before when we couldn't sleep. We were both picturing little Eunsu crying in the rain like a motherless sparrow, waiting for his brother who was at school. Aunt Monica made the sign of the cross.

"I'm so sorry," the principal said. "If that's not a good idea, we could put the money to some other use."

He seemed confused by the looks on our faces. We were crying as if in shock, so he probably thought it meant we disagreed with him.

"Oh no, you have to use the money for that," said Aunt Monica. "Don't use it on anything else but that. Please put that awning up so they can keep dry when it's raining and stay out of the sun when it's hot. That way, if there's ever a young child waiting there for his big brother, he won't get wet in the rain, and his big brother won't feel sad to see—" Aunt Monica couldn't continue. She started crying again.

I walked Aunt Monica, who was weak from not eating or sleeping for several days, back to the hotel. The day was growing dark. Aunt Monica suggested we turn in early so we could get up at dawn with the children. I asked her, "Will the sun rise tomorrow?"

"It will rise," she said. I pointed out that the kids were having a good time, and she said that they certainly were. On the way into the building, I suddenly stopped and looked back. The first line of the song that Yunsu and Eunsu liked so much, the national anthem, started with that ocean. *Until the East Sea runs dry and Mt. Baekdu wears away, God save us and keep our nation...* I knew it was just the sound of the waves, but from somewhere out there, way out past the water, I thought I could hear, very faintly, two young brothers singing beside a garbage can in an alleyway. *It's a great country, isn't it? Whenever I sing this song, I feel like we're good people.* Blind Eunsu's whispered voice seemed to follow the waves in, just barely reaching my ears. Out past the scampering children, the gray sea shimmered over the earth like brimming tears.

I would always like to say just this one thing (it is almost the only thing I know for certain up to now)—that we must always hold to the difficult; that is our part.

– Rainer Maria Rilke, Letters to a Young Poet

BLUE NOTE 19

P.S. Please deliver this message to Sister Monica and Father Kim: Thank you, I am sorry, and I love you. They remind me of that poem about someone making griddlecakes with their tears. They always knew exactly when to turn the cakes to keep them from burning, they shared those warm cakes with us, and in the end they taught us all grace.

CHAPTER 19

Several people were already in the hospital room. Father Kim greeted me when I walked in. He had put on a lot of weight since I last saw him, and his hair had grown back. "You got bigger," I said. He laughed, patted his belly, and said, "Indeed, I keep getting fatter." Things change when you're alive. Sometimes they get worse, and sometimes they get better. In the seven years that had passed since Yunsu's death, I had met many other Yunsus. I don't think I was just imagining it. It didn't matter whether you were a judge riding around in a fancy black sedan or a diabolical murderer, we were all equally pitiful and equal debtors in life from the point of view of a greater judge. No human being was fundamentally good or fundamentally bad. We all struggled to make it through each day. If there were a fundamental truth, it was that everyone fights death. This was our common thread, pathetic and as old as time, and it could not be severed.

Aunt Monica was wearing a white cap instead of her usual veil. It was a round sleeping cap edged with lace, like something you would see in a movie. I wasn't sure if it was because of the cap, but Aunt Monica's body was so tiny that she looked like a baby in a cradle. If her face were not so old, it might have looked as if everyone was surrounding the bed to celebrate a new birth. She had been talking to Father Kim just before I walked in. She gestured to me to sit down and turned back to him.

"So like I was saying, he asked for a Bible. That means he agreed to meet with you, right? How was he when you saw him?"

I thought back to that snowy day when I had rushed to the detention center because Aunt Monica slipped and hurt herself, only to find her sitting there with a pink floral handkerchief wrapped around her head. Back then, I had looked at her and thought, *You win*. I felt the same way again today.

It sounded like Aunt Monica and Father Kim were talking about a serial killer who had just been sentenced to the death penalty.

"Well, he didn't have much to say," Father Kim said. "He must have had some experience with Christianity when he was young. He said he killed his victims in front of a window where a church cross was easily visible. Also, he said that he sees himself as evil and that he's afraid to stop thinking of himself that way. But when I met him, he was just an ordinary person."

Father Kim laughed bitterly. Aunt Monica closed her eyes, as if overwhelmed.

In 2004, there wasn't a soul in Korea who didn't know about that murderer. Because of him, voices calling for the reinstatement of the death penalty—which had been abolished after December 1997 in keeping with the president's campaign promise—were gaining strength, and people's legal sympathies toward death row convicts were growing cold. Even the other people on death row that I had been meeting with after Yunsu's death said that they had read about him in the newspaper and caught themselves thinking,

He must be killed. And they laughed, despite themselves.

Aunt Monica was in the middle of talking to Father Kim about the murderer when I came into the room.

"We don't have the right to give up on someone," Aunt Monica said, "no matter how horrible his crimes are, even if he is the devil incarnate. None of us are entirely good. No one is completely innocent. Some are just a little more good and some are a little more evil. Life gives us the opportunity to decide whether to atone for our sins or continue committing them; therefore, we do not have the right to stop that from happening. You have a difficult task ahead of you, Father Kim. I wish I could help you, but I think my time here is nearly up."

Aunt Monica sounded calm. When she brought up dying, Father Kim looked like he was about to offer some clichéd words of comfort, but he stopped himself. Aunt Monica turned to me, the same expression in her eyes as ever. That playful look still glimmered there every now and then, but for a long time it had become harder for her to make jokes. After Father Kim left, I sat beside her.

"Dr. Noh called you?"

I nodded and gently stroked her face, just as she had done for me one winter long ago. She must have been thinking about that winter, too, because she smiled.

"So," she asked, "now that you've made it this far without dying, how do you feel about it?"

"I guess I feel like I have more living to do."

I wanted to cry. Aunt Monica looked like a candlewick about to go out. Once again, I thought, *What am I going to do without her?* I had been wondering that for a long time. But now I was sure of one thing: I would go on living, even if I felt like I was dying. I knew that saying such things as *I felt like I was dying* or *This isn't really living* were actually statements about life. It was the same with *I'm so hot I could die* and *I'm so hungry I could die* and *I want to die*. You could only feel like you were dying if you were alive and were therefore a part of life. So instead of saying I wanted to die, I had no choice but to change it to *I want to live well*.

"How is your mother?" asked Aunt Monica. I told her she was in good health, and we both smiled.

"I found Yunsu's mother," she said.

The moment I heard Yunsu's name, my throat locked up, and I could not respond.

"I found out she's living nearby," Aunt Monica continued. "One of the sisters from our convent was helping with the elderly who don't have anyone to take care of them, and there she was. Who knows what has happened to her over the years? The sister thinks she might have Alzheimer's. She contacted me after she checked her records."

I took Aunt Monica's hand without saying a word. She took out a cross that she had placed near her bedside, her hand trembling, and handed it to me. It was the cross that Yunsu had molded for her from rice paste before he died.

"Please take this there and give it to her. They said that whenever it's not too cold out, she spends the whole day sitting outside waiting for someone. The nun asked her who she was waiting for, and she said her son. She asked what his name was, and the woman said 'Unsu.'"

I tried repeating the name 'Unsu' after her and got a lump in my throat. It sounded like it was halfway between Eunsu and Yunsu. I took the cross. Aunt Monica was so weak that she closed her eyes again.

"Will you pray for me to die soon? I'm in a little bit of pain... Actually, I'm in a lot of pain. Even the morphine isn't helping."

I said I would.

"It's strange. Before you got here, I dreamt that all of those boys I've seen executed were here in the room with me. Yunsu was here, too. They were all dressed in white. They were smiling so brightly, but they had black rope marks around their necks. I guess even in death, the marks don't go away. It was just a dream, but it was heartbreaking."

I couldn't hold back anymore and burst into tears.

"Don't cry, my beautiful Yujeong. When you survived, when you went with me to the detention center for the first time, when you struggled to understand Yunsu, when I heard you went to see your brother to try to save him... I was so proud. The truth is that I was always secretly keeping an eye on you, always with my heart in my mouth. You have so much passion in you, and passionate people always hurt more. But that's never anything to be ashamed of."

I cradled Aunt Monica's face in my hands. Her face was very small and covered in wrinkles. I wanted to tell her how sorry I was. I wanted to tell her how frightened I was and that I didn't know how I should live. Just like Yunsu, I had figured it out too late. For the first time in my life, I wanted to say those words that I had never been able to say before, the words could not be replaced with any others.

"I'm sorry, Aunt Monica. I'm so sorry I hurt you."

She smiled lightly and stroked my hands.

"It makes me so happy to see our Yujeong all grown up," she said.

Aunt Monica smiled, but the pain must have been bad because it turned into a grimace.

"Pray. Please pray. Not just for those on death row, not just for criminals. Pray for those who think they are without sin, those who think they are right, those who think they know everything and who think everything is fine. Pray for those people."

Gong Ji-young

I wiped the sweat from Aunt Monica's brow and nodded—even though God had never once listened to my prayers, and this time would probably be no different. Since Yunsu had told me to trust him, and Aunt Monica was once more telling me to pray, I wanted to say that I would, but I couldn't get my mouth to open. I felt that if I opened my mouth, I would fall to pieces. If that happened, Aunt Monica would be hurt, so I was trying to bear it. I had learned from Yunsu that love meant gladly enduring for another person, and that it sometimes meant having the courage to change yourself.

Aunt Monica smiled and took my hand. Her hand felt as rough as a broomstick that had spent a lifetime sweeping a courtyard. She smiled once more and then closed her eyes. She looked like she was asleep. I pulled her blanket up around her so she would not get cold, and her tiny feet poked out. Covered in white socks, they were as small as a child's. She must have traveled to so many places on those feet. Over her lifetime of nearly eighty years, she must have seen so many dark alleys and abandoned woods that the rest of us simply turned our backs on, valleys of fear and deserts of truth, proud and merciless rivers. She must have realized how all of those rivers begin as tiny streams, each with its own name, and flow on until they reach the sea that has but one name, and that no one can stop those waters from reaching their destination. I straightened Aunt Monica's blanket and kissed her pained forehead. I thought about the desire that had flashed through me when I took the camera from my sister-in-law, the day before Yunsu died. The desire to have a child. But Aunt Monica had cast away all of her desires to become a mother to those who had lost their own. Quietly, I whispered, *Rest now. I love you, my dear mother...*

© Dahuim Paik

Gong Ji-young is one of Korea's most acclaimed novelists. She has sold over 10 million books in South Korea alone. Her awards include the 2011 Yisang Literary Award, the 21st Century Literary Award, the Korean Novel Prize, the Oh Young-soo Literature Award, and the 9th Special Media Award from Amnesty International for *Our Happy Time*.

A Marble Arch Press Readers Club Guide

This readers club guide for Our Happy Time includes an introduction, discussion questions, and ideas for enhancing your book club. The suggested questions are intended to help your book group find new and interesting angles and topics for your discussion. We hope that these ideas will enrich your conversation and increase your enjoyment of the book.

Introduction

After her third failed suicide attempt, beautiful and privileged Korean pop star Yujeong agrees to accompany her aunt, an elderly nun, on her weekly visits to death row inmates. There Yujeong meets Yunsu, a convicted murderer awaiting death. Though she is repulsed by his crimes, Yujeong relates to Yunsu's suffering, and feels compelled to continue visiting him week after week.

During their visits Yujeong and Yunsu slowly reveal the tragic circumstances that have shaped their lives and discover, through their compassion for one another, a way to forgive.

Questions and Topics for Discussion

1. Yujeong's mother constantly tells her that she is just like her aunt Monica, but Yujeong claims that she is more like her mother. Do you agree with either of their claims?

2. Yujeong and Yunsu had very different upbringings, but when they first meet they both long for death. Why do Yujeong and Yunsu feel this way? Do their reasons overlap at all?

3. Describe Yunsu's relationship with his brother, Eunsu. How does this relationship contribute to Yunsu's downfall?

4. Yujeong refers to the painting of the prodigal son hanging in the prison. What are her initial feelings about the prodigal son? Do you think her feelings changed as she grew closer to Yunsu?

5. The author, Gong Ji-young, often writes about strong women. Which of the female characters in Our Happy Time would you define as strong? What do you consider to be their weaknesses?

6. Why is forgiveness so important to the mother of Yunsu's victim? What role does forgiveness play for each of the main characters in Our Happy Time?

7. Why does Yujeong want to have a "real conversation" with Yunsu? How does Yunsu feel about having "real conversations" with Yujeong?

8. What do you think Yunsu means when he writes, "I also can't help thinking that this is the very first spring of my life"? (p. 156)

9. At what points in the story do you think Yujeong and Yunsu begin to truly value their lives? What do the characters realize about themselves that inspires these changes?

10. What value does Yunsu get from becoming a Christian?

11. Yunsu is exposed to injustice at a very early age. What role does the concept of justice play in shaping the course of his life? Do you think justice prevails in the end?

12. According to Yujeong, "If there were a fundamental truth, it was that everyone fights death." (p. 258) What are

some of the ways that the characters in Our Happy Time fight death?

13. What do you think happens next for Yujeong?

Enhance Your Book Club

1. Letter writing plays a large role in Our Happy Time. Contact your local prison or search online to get involved in a letter-writing program, and have each person in the book club write a letter to a prisoner. You may choose to share your letters with the book club before sending it on.

2. The books Aunt Monica gives Yunsu in prison help him in a variety of ways. Organize a book drive with your book club and donate the books to your local prison's library.

3. Research more about the author Gong Ji-young and her involvement in the Korean student and labor movements, and watch the film adaptation of her book *The Crucible*. Discuss how you think the author's personal experiences inspire her work.